D1276321

MORE ROMAN TALES

Other books by
ALBERTO MORAVIA

The Woman of Rome
The Conformist
Two Adolescents
(*Agostino* and *Disobedience*)
The Fancy Dress Party
The Time of Indifference
Conjugal Love
Roman Tales
A Ghost at Noon
Bitter Honeymoon
Two Women
The Wayward Wife
The Empty Canvas

MORE ROMAN TALES

BY

Alberto Moravia

Selected and Translated by

ANGUS DAVIDSON

New York: FARRAR, STRAUS AND COMPANY

Library of Congress catalog card number 64-10561
Manufactured in the United States of America
First Printing, 1964

Acknowledgment is made to the editors
of *Cavalier, Cosmopolitan, Playboy* and the *Saturday Evening Post,*
in which five of these stories have appeared.

CONTENTS

MORE ROMAN TALES

THE CHIMPANZEE

WINTER in Rome. I was going down the avenue in the Borghese Gardens leading to the Museum, and all the time it was pouring with rain. But you could see each drop, as it came down, streaking the black sky with white, because the sun was shining brightly beyond the groves of trees, amongst luminous clouds that streamed away on every side. It was raining and the sun was shining; if I had not known it was January I should have thought it was March, so mild was the air, so tall and thick and green the grass in the plantations. It was raining in torrents and the sunshine was brilliant as gold, and the grass under the trees was drinking in both rain and sunshine alike. All at once I felt happy, and I felt a great strength in my legs as though I were a gigantic grasshopper, able to leap at one bound on to the roof of the Museum, whose fine yellow façade could be seen at the far end of the avenue; and I did actually leap into the air, opening my mouth towards the sky, and a drop of rain fell right into my mouth and seemed to intoxicate me as though I had taken a gulp of liquor, and I thought: "I am twenty years old . . . and I still have another forty or fifty years of this glorious life ahead of me. . . . Three cheers for life! " To the right of the avenue, on the top of a little hill, I saw two or three large, well-fed horses with well-dressed young men in the saddle sheltering under the holm-oaks as they waited for the rain to stop, and I don't know why these horses looked so beautiful to me, and again I thought: "I feel really happy." In the meantime, almost without realizing it, I had started humming a popular song of the time; and I suddenly remembered the title of a film I had seen some time before: "Singing in the Rain".

Perhaps the reason why I was happy was that I was on my way to my first appointment with Gloria, the cashier at a bar in the neighbourhood of the Piazza della Regina, where I worked as mechanic in a garage. I had made my first advances to Gloria in the dark, while watching television in the bar: first I had rubbed my arm lightly against hers, then, becoming bolder, I had placed my hand on her hand; and in this way, when the television came to an end, I had fixed an appointment with her for Thursday, which was the day when the proprietress of the bar relieved her at the cash-desk. And now this was Thursday, and I was on my way to keep the appointment and I felt happy.

My only worry was that I had very little money. This is the sort of thing that happens when you are twenty and a mechanic in a garage. I had so little that all I was able to offer Gloria was a visit to the Zoo, and afterwards, at most, a cup of coffee standing in a bar. No question of a cinema, because the cinemas in the neighbourhood of Via Veneto are expensive; and for the same reason it was still less possible to take her to a dance-hall, even the Quadraro. But I have a passion for animals and I fooled myself into thinking that Gloria shared this passion with me. Besides, I was counting on feeling: if there is true feeling, what does money matter? With these thoughts in my mind I reached the Museum, which was to be our meeting-place. I found shelter from the rain under a projecting cornice, and waited.

At last Gloria arrived, coming along one of the deserted avenues in the rain, huddling under an umbrella. I don't know how it was, but I saw at once, from the way in which she was got up, that I had made a mistake: this was not the girl for me. She was all decked out, with a brand-new, red coat and a bottle-green silk dress; her hair was done in a new way, so that I very nearly didn't recognize her. She usually wore it smooth and unconfined at the two sides of her face. Now, on the other hand, it was all gathered up in a lot of little curls on the top of her head, and her features, which were large and slightly coarse, seemed to stick out in an uncompromising, naked-looking fashion. I was struck by her nose which, without being ugly, was by no means beautiful, being rather shapeless and lumpy. Her mouth was like a negro's; and it was supercilious in expression and so smothered in lipstick that it glistened. As soon as we had greeted each other she said: "Ugh, this rain is the last straw. Well, where shall we go? Why not go to the cinema, just near here in Via Veneto?"

"That's a nice kind of amusement," I answered. "Sitting together in the dark in a cinema and then, when the film's over, good-night and good-bye." "Let's go and dance then." "I can't dance." "You can't dance? Well, it's high time you learnt. . . . Dear me, I seem to be out of luck to-day! Where *shall* we go, then? To sit on a seat in the gardens?"

"There's always the Zoo . . ." I began. But immediately, curling her lip, she replied: "Like a servant-girl and a soldier on leave. Thank you very much, I think I'll go home." And she made as if to go away. So then, almost hoping, secretly, that she really would go: "All right," I said, "good-bye." But now she was afraid I would leave her. "Very well then," she said, "let's go there. There's nothing else for it."

So we went down towards the Zoo, by a deserted avenue, in the rain. Gloria came unwillingly, as could be seen even from the scornful way she walked, dragging herself along. When we reached the gates of the Zoo, there was not a soul to be seen—or rather, the only person to be seen was the man who sells coloured balloons, sheltering under a tree. I bought two tickets, and I also bought two little bags of nuts and gave one to Gloria. "What's this for?" she asked. "For the monkeys." "Well, you can give them to them. I can't bear monkeys."

We went in and she started off towards the elephants' enclosure. There was an enormous one, its grey skin falling in folds as though it were too big for it, standing with its forehead pressed against the bars. Feeling pleased already, I said: "I say, look at the elephant." She answered rudely: "Yes, I see it; what is there special about an elephant?"

The elephant, friendly creature, was looking fixedly at us with its little intelligent eyes; so I stooped down, picked a handful of grass and handed it to Gloria, saying: "Try giving it this." She did not want to do so, but then agreed unwillingly. The elephant put out its trunk, took the grass from Gloria's hand, curled back its trunk very slowly and put the grass into its mouth. Gloria was unable to restrain a cry of pleasure: "Look, it's eating, it's eating!"; and for a moment I hoped that she was beginning to enjoy herself. But she immediately regretted what she had said. "Just look!" she cried: "I've dirtied my hands with mud . . . look at that!" And she wiped her hand, with a look of disgust, on my waterproof. We went on from the elephant to the rhinoceros, a truly ugly animal with that single horn between its eyes, standing as still as a monument, all gleaming with rain. I said to Gloria: "He's ugly but it's not his fault. Under all that armour-plating he has a nice character: he only eats grass." But Gloria answered contemptuously: "What ever can you find interesting about the creature? It looks as if it was all stitched together like a football." And she walked away and went into the hippopotamus house.

It was dark inside the house, and in one corner were a number of bales of hay, and behind the bars you could just see a big tank of dark, still water; the hippopotamus was not to be seen. "It's not there, let's go," said Gloria, still contemptuous; and she ran out again. I stayed behind and, just at that moment, there emerged from the water two things like little shining horns, the eyes of the hippopotamus, followed by part of its rump, like a piece of black bark, and then its whole head. Poor beast, it was slow because it was so big, and it had taken some time to come up out of the water; but now it was anxious to show itself off, in a good-natured kind of way, and in fact it opened its mouth wide, its huge flesh-lined mouth, with short yellow teeth planted crosswise and a tongue that looked like a cushion made of pink flesh. Filled with joy, I called out: " Gloria, Gloria, it's come up out of the water! " But it was a wasted effort, for she was already a long way away, over near the brown bears.

The bears were lying down behind the bars, flat on the ground with their cheeks resting on their furry forefeet full of big claws, peacefully sleeping; and Gloria refused even to look at them because, she said, bears reminded her of a bearskin bedside rug belonging to an old aunt of hers. In fact she was thoroughly ill-mannered, and it was clear that she was behaving like this deliberately. She was even more disagreeable when we came to the gazelles, those highly attractive creatures, with their slim legs and beautiful black eyes and their curly horns. " Goats? " she said; " have I come here to look at goats? "

I was counting on the felines, that is to say the tigers, lions, panthers and so on. In one cage there were two truly magnificent tigers walking up and down ceaselessly in opposite directions, and every now and then they looked at us, their great, angry, yellow eyes glowering from their black-and-yellow-striped heads. Gloria admitted half-heartedly that they were beautiful to look at, and we were standing there admiring them when there was a general rush, on the part of such few visitors as there were, towards another cage: it was the lions' feeding-time. I said to Gloria: " Quick, let's run and see "; and this time she allowed me to drag her away, but unluckily she stumbled and all of a sudden cried out in a plaintive tone of voice: " O dear me, I've broken the heel of my shoe! " It was true; as she ran she had tripped up and the heel of one shoe was snapped off. " These shoes—I know how much they cost me; and who's going to pay for another pair? " she began whining as she fingered the broken heel; and meanwhile I was standing beside her fuming, and from the lions' cage came a tremendous sound of roaring, and then there was nothing more to be heard: the best part of their dinner was over. When we arrived there, in fact, with Gloria limping along hanging on to my arm and I supporting her, there was nothing much left to see: the lions were crouching in the darkest corners of the cage, their big tawny heads lowered as they gnawed at some horse's rib-bones already stripped of flesh. "They stink, anyhow," Gloria remarked; and that was all she found to say about those three lions, which were so beautiful that one could stand and look at them breathlessly for an hour on end.

I was in a bad temper too, by this time. I could have killed her, I swear. We came to the terraces where the polar bears and sea lions are kept. The polar bears were sitting about foolishly, here and there, in their thick white fur coats; one was lying with his paws in the air and rubbing his back, as if he had the itch; another was nodding his head up and down with such a stupid air that it made me laugh. Gloria's comment, however, was: "More bedside rugs." I myself liked the sea lions too: they swam about happily, two by two, as though they were dancing, then jumped up, legless and armless as they were, on to the slabs of imitation ice, wriggling their black, gleaming bodies, and then dived again into the water. But Gloria dragged me away, saying: "I'm only interested in seals when they're made into shoes or handbags."

In fact there was no pleasing her. I decided, at this point, to let her see that I was fed up, and so, after the seals, I turned straight into an avenue leading towards the gates. She understood and, hanging on to my arm, asked: "Where are we going?" "We're going out." "And what about the monkeys—aren't we going to see the monkeys?" "No, we'll see them another time." "But what's the matter, are you angry with me?" "Yes, I'm fed up with you." So then, in her most charming way, she said: "Come on, don't be offended. D'you know, I was thinking about you yesterday?" "What were you thinking?" "Nothing, I was just thinking about you, that's all. Well now, come along, let's go and have a look at the monkeys."

So we went to the big cages where the monkeys live. There were a number of small monkeys, with long tails which they held in their hands while they quickly and neatly picked out fleas, gazing at us, as they did so, with little sad faces; and there were other larger ones, with backsides that looked like bunches of purple fruit and heads like dogs. Gloria was now anxious to prove to me that she liked monkeys; but she set about it with such an obvious effort that I should almost have preferred her to go on being as ill-mannered as before. So much so, that I said to her: "Now, shut up! Anyone can see from a mile off that you haven't the slightest interest in animals." "That's just like you," she replied, "always discontented. I do like them, yes, I like them very much, but I can't exactly dance with joy. Now give me those nuts." It had begun to rain again, very finely, against the light of the sun which was shining brightly behind the palm-trees inside the Zoo.

We were now standing in front of the chimpanzee cage. One of the chimpanzees, as tall as a boy, with all its brown fur ruffled up, was in a little corner eating a banana just like a human being, that is to say, holding it in its hands and taking small bites, after pulling away the skin in a dainty and well-mannered way; another had climbed up on the swing and was going up and down, standing upright, and you wondered why it was doing so, it looked so serious. Standing beside us were two young men, one tall and thin and one small and fat, who were laughing as they commented upon the gestures and grimaces of the monkeys.

The chimpanzee on the swing came down and stood upright against the bars. He stretched out his mouth, which was black outside and pink inside, as if he were going to speak, and made a queer, yelping sound; and all the time he was scratching his paunch at the point where the hair was thinnest. Gloria held out a nut towards him but the chimpanzee did not even notice it. "I wonder what's the matter with him?" said Gloria: "doesn't he like nuts?" The chimpanzee gave a kind of whistle and walked off, bent and tired-looking, towards the back of the cage, then turned round all of a sudden, picked up a handful of some sort of filth from the floor and rushed back and hurled it in our faces.

The only one of us to be hit was Gloria: I myself was standing behind her, and the two young men jumped nimbly to one side. It all happened in a second: Gloria looked at her beautiful red coat splashed from top to bottom; the two young men burst out laughing; Gloria cried: "Curse the Zoo and curse these filthy animals," and ran away sobbing. I started to follow her but she warned me off. "Don't come near me! Go away! Leave me alone!" And so I gradually slackened my pace and finally stopped altogether. Gloria slipped through the gate and vanished.

In the meantime a great, full-coloured rainbow had appeared against the black sky, although it was still raining. I too went on my way, leaving the Zoo and going back up the avenue until I found myself again in the same place where, a couple of hours before, I had felt so happy. But now I felt crushed and depressed and the Borghese Gardens seemed the ordinary Borghese Gardens of every day and the same rain which had given me such pleasure before, so that I had wanted to drink it, now irritated me. Ah, why is it that women have the power to make us happy, yet they don't know it, and they spoil everything with their abominable characters?

THE SPELL

THE gipsies who live in the huts at Mandrione, near the Porta Furba, are different from us Romans. Romans live in huts only if they have to, only if they cannot possibly help it; but my impression is that gipsies would live in them just the same, even if they had the houses in the Parioli quarter at their disposal. And inside the huts, whereas with really poor people you can see that they are poor, with the gipsies you can see that they are gipsies, that is, people different from ourselves: often all they need is a carpet on the floor, and that's all the furnishing there is. And then, the women. Roman women dress as best they can, according to their condition, but they always dress like normal women; but the gipsies, no: they wear long, trailing skirts, brightly coloured but dirty, shawls of the same kind, long hair thrown back over their shoulders, and great quantities of gold, silver and coral ornaments on their necks and wrists and in their ears. The men dress like dandies, for, as I have said, the gipsies are not poor; but always with a touch of gaudy colour that leaps to the eye, a flame-red tie, parrot-green socks, a yellow and blue handkerchief. And they too, like the women, often wear ear-rings. The gipsies, moreover, have dark skins, darker than the darkest sunburn. And they speak a strange language, which anyone would be clever to understand. This language they call Romany; I thought this alluded to Rome, but Geremia later explained to me that Rome had nothing to do with it.

Geremia, to be precise, was a gipsy of about seventeen, like me, and for some time he was my friend. Geremia was a blond gipsy, with a head thickly covered with small curls, a hard, bumpy forehead, blue eyes and a hooked nose with wide nostrils. We had made friends one day at the cinema, when he was sitting next to me and had placed his hand, with a curious ring on his finger, on the back of the seat in front. This ring appeared to be made of tin and had in it a pink stone that reminded me of the eye of a white rabbit. I asked him what the stone was, and he replied that it was the stone of his own month, which was May. Now I was born in May too, on the twentieth, so I asked him if he would swap the ring for something or other. At first he did not want to, but then he agreed to give it to me in exchange for cigarettes, for a carton containing ten packets of American cigarettes, which I procured from my brother who sells them in the daytime in Via del Gambero. With this ring on my finger I felt a bit of a gipsy myself. And I felt this all the more afterwards, as I saw Geremia nearly every day, either wandering round the quarter in which I lived or going for a walk in the country, on one side or other of the Via Appia Nuova.

Geremia's character was a strange one: he felt himself a gipsy, boasted of it and wanted all the time to prove to me that he was a gipsy, by surprising me and even—yes, even by frightening me. In my opinion, he told a pack of lies; but he told them in such a way that I, although I knew they were lies, was in fact compelled to believe them. He said, for example, that if one made a charcoal circle on the ground with a scorched stick, in such-and-such a place, at full moon, at midnight on Tuesday the seventeenth, uttering a certain gipsy word, there was a possibility that the air, which for everyone else is merely air, for us who had cast the spell would show itself to be crowded with spirits as thick as if they were in a jelly. I asked him what would happen once we had seen the air crammed full, like a bus at the rush hour, of spirits tightly jammed together; and he answered that, by uttering another little gipsy word, I could make one of these spirits detach itself from its brothers and transform itself into a handsome yellow dog, which would follow me everywhere, as good as gold. He himself, he added, had had one of these yellow dogs for some time; but the dog had died because, in order to keep it, you had every evening to pronounce that same gipsy word, and on one occasion he had forgotten and then the spirit had flown away and the dog had fallen down stone dead on the spot. Deeply impressed, I then said to him that I felt a great desire to cast that spell myself, so as to get one of those yellow dogs. At first he wouldn't hear of it; in the end, however, he agreed, but named a price—five thousand lire. This was the whole, or almost the whole, of my savings, but I accepted at once because by now I was set on it and I wanted at all costs to cast the spell.

In the evening Geremia arrived punctually for our appointment outside the Porta Furba, with a motor-scooter that he had borrowed from his brother. As I was about to get on to the pillion behind him, he showed me a long, narrow package: this contained a dry branch dipped in tar. At the right moment I was to set a light to this branch and wait until it had burned a little; then, in the dark, I was to make a circle on the ground, pronouncing the word "mulo" which in gipsy language means death. Then the charcoal circle would light up all round with a number of little blue flames, rather like gas-jets when you put a match to them; and by this light I would see that the air is not air but a jellied confection of spirits. Having uttered another gipsy word which I do not now remember, I should immediately have at my feet, wagging its tail, a handsome yellow dog which would follow me everywhere.

Geremia gave me these explanations, with unchanging professional gipsy seriousness, while the motor-scooter flew along between two rows of big modern buildings on the Via Tuscolana. Then, once we were out of the town, he turned into a secondary road; and we started going along between round, black hills, with the sky brilliantly clear above the hills and the full moon hanging in the sky, exactly like a copper saucepan lid turned to show its tin lining. It was cool, and I looked at the moon and reflected that between me and the moon there were millions of spirits coiled up one against another and that all that was needed was one little word to make me see the whole lot of them, just as you can see pickles inside a glass jar. However, I asked Geremia: "I say, isn't there a danger that these spirits might play some ugly trick on us?" "Don't worry," he said; "it's a potent spell. . . . Of course they'd like to, but they can't."

After going round and round among these hills, on a road that seemed like a snake, we came out on to a straight road running between two cliffs of tufa. This road was dark as the inside of an oven, and there were cars parked here and there with lovers inside who hastily composed themselves as we passed and looked at us sideways, waiting impatiently until we had gone away. Finally the cliffs fell away and we were among fields again. At a bend in the road a dark, rounded mass was outlined against the clear sky; Geremia put on the brake and said: "Here it is."

It was a Roman ruin, brick-built, in the shape of a loaf of bread, surrounded with brambles; and I could distinguish, amongst the brambles, a black, crooked opening. The moonlight fell on it sideways and you could see every brick and, behind the ruin, the brown fields in which the corn had been cut, with the sheaves, paler in colour, piled up at regular intervals. Geremia told me it was there, inside the ruin, that I must cast the spell: but it was still early, and it was therefore better for us to wait. I was feeling a little frightened, especially as there was not a living soul to be seen; and I was now looking at Geremia with some suspicion, for fear he might suddenly be transformed—who knows?—into a he-goat; he already had so much of the he-goat in his face. So I was almost relieved when I heard a tapping of heels and a woman appeared on the road. She was a woman of a certain type, such as are always to be found on the country roads round Rome, not far from the villages in which they usually live. She saw us standing to one side, leaning against the scooter, and came towards us. I remember her well. She was wearing a dark skirt and white blouse, and as she came up, I saw that she was young but not pretty: a pyramid of black hair, in big curls, an over-painted, expressionless face, with small eyes and a big mouth, and, in particular, below the waist, legs so crooked that she seemed to be walking with her knees bent. "Good evening," she said; and Geremia answered: "Good evening." "Will you give me a cigarette?" she said; and Geremia gave her one without a word. She lit it, puffed the smoke from her nostrils and then uttered the usual words: "Well, darling, d'you want to come with me?"

Geremia pretended to be stupid. "Why, what for?" he asked.

"If you come with me," she replied with an encouraging look, "I'll tell you a nice story."

I was struck by these words, and I must tell you why. When I was a child, I never wanted to go to bed; and my mother used to take me by the arm and say these same words to me. Then she didn't even tell me the story; however, for a moment I had hoped and had been almost happy. Now, Geremia answered: "Hey, who d'you think we are? We're not here to listen to stories."

"Ah, so you don't want to hear my nice story," she said, disappointed; and without another word she went off slowly and stood farther along, on the other side of the road. At that moment a car arrived and stopped in front of her. Geremia said to me that, as it was still early, we had better drive round for a little. No sooner said than done; we mounted the scooter and off we went.

We went straight on for a quarter of an hour and then stopped near a farm and Geremia gave me a few more explanations. He said that I must go alone into the ruin, because otherwise the spirits would not show themselves. They knew Geremia by now and were angry with him, so that he would have to cast a stronger spell and I should see nothing. He, therefore, would go off and leave me there, and would come back after half an hour. "And the dog," I objected, "how shall we manage to take the dog with us on the scooter?" Geremia replied that he would go slowly, so that the dog could keep up with us. "In the meantime, give me that five thousand lire," he concluded.

So I paid him, and then we got on to the scooter again and went back to the ruin, and this time there was nobody there at all. Geremia handed me the tar-soaked branch and a box of matches and went away.

From the road to the ruin there was a kind of path of trampled earth through the grass, showing that many people had been there before me. I was trembling all over; even the wind that whispered lightly in my ears terrified me. With some difficulty I pushed aside the brambles in front of the opening, scratching my hands, and went in. It was completely dark inside and there was a nasty sort of smell, and I was now more frightened than I can say. With a trembling hand I struck a match and held it to the branch, which at once caught fire.

It made a clear red flame; and a number of flickering tongues of shadow leapt up all round me on the brick walls. In this light I lowered my eyes and then I saw, lying on the ground in a corner, the woman who shortly before had wanted to tell me her pretty story. I recognized her by her clothes and also by her face which was turned towards me, although she was lying on her side with her back to the opening. I was so taken up with the spell that, at the moment, I thought possibly a spirit had assumed the aspect of this woman: one trick is as good as another. But then, as I looked closer, I saw that she had a big dark stain on her blouse, below her shoulder. And, as I looked again at her face, I noticed that her eyes were open and shining but sightless, like two pieces of glass. Then I realized that the stain was a bloodstain, and, at the same moment, I threw the branch down on the ground and ran away.

I don't know how I managed to walk all the way back along that road which seemed to go on for ever; but suddenly I came out on to the Via Appia Antica. I was terrified out of my wits; not so much, now, of the spirits as of being implicated in the murder. But at the same time, I don't know how, the idea of the spirits was mixed up with the crime, as though the spirits, offended, had wanted to play this trick on me, of putting a dead woman in the place where I had hoped to find a yellow dog. In short, I was certain that the woman had been murdered; but I was not so certain that the murder had not been brought about by the spirits.

That night I did not sleep; early in the morning I told my parents I was going to Genezzano, where I have an uncle who is a farmer. In the train I opened the newspaper and read about the crime: at such-and-such a kilometre on such-and-such a road, inside such-and-such a ruin, had been found the corpse of a prostitute. I reflected that she, poor thing, had tried to tell her pretty story to some other man. And he, instead, had told her his own story, by putting a knife into her.

I stayed a couple of weeks at Genezzano, frightened as I was; then I came back to Rome. But I did not go to Porta Furba, to my parents; I moved, instead, to Prima Porta, on the other side of the town, where I found a job as a waiter in a country restaurant. I had no wish to see Geremia again, partly because of the five thousand lire and partly because of the memory of that night. So I lost sight of him. But on my finger I still wear the white-metal ring with the pink stone.

THE UNCLE

TAKE note, in the first place, of my age: until I was thirty-five I had lived with my sister Elvira who was thirty-eight, her husband, and their daughter Agatina who was eighteen. This had been my home and my family, up to that time, more especially because we all lived with my mother; she then died; but, as long as she was there, family feeling, so to speak, came before our own personal feelings, so much so that, when I got engaged to be married, not long before my mother's death, I seriously thought of bringing my wife to the house and continuing to live with them as before. We were a truly united family and I was very fond of my sister, a good friend of my brother-in-law, and I looked upon Agatina positively as my own daughter. Agatina was a dark-haired girl, with a pale face and dark, serious eyes; at sixteen she was still a child, and then, after a couple of years, she had become a grown woman. I had a great affection for her, partly because I had watched her grow up and partly on account of her character, which was prudent, calm, gentle and full of charm. Possibly, even, she confided more in me than in her parents; and I, on my side, saw no harm in having a talk with her from time to time, as uncle to niece, especially as she was intelligent and often surprised me with statements and observations much in advance of her age.

But my mother died and I became engaged; and, in short, when I married—a year after my mother's death—I realized that my old family life was finished, or rather that the time had come for me to create a family life of my own. So I left; they lived in Via Tuscolana; I moved to the other side of the town, near the Tomb of Nero. I was sorry to leave them, but I saw that it had to be done now; besides, the garage that I had taken over in partnership with my brother-in-law was in Via Cassia, only a short distance from my new home. Agatina and my sister, however, helped my wife to set up house; and after that we went on seeing each other often, for the most part on Sundays.

It was, in fact, on a Sunday morning, three months after I had moved into my new house, that my sister rang me up on the telephone and asked me to come and see them at once: she said she must speak to me. I asked her what had happened and she began: "Agatina . . ." and then stopped. I said, anxiously: "Agatina? What's wrong with Agatina?" Then she answered hurriedly: "Nothing, nothing. I can't say more on the telephone; come here and I'll tell you."

So I told my wife I had to go and see Elvira; then I jumped on my motor-bicycle and, by way of Via Cassia and Via Flaminia, the Corso, the Colosseum and San Giovanni, I reached Via Tuscolana. My brother-in-law lived in one of those big, yellow blocks of flats outside the city gates which have courtyards as large as public squares and staircases numbered from A to F; I left my motor-cycle with the porter, who knew me, and went up to the fourth floor of staircase B. Elvira let me in at once, as though she had been waiting for me behind the door. She's a tall, strongly-built woman, my sister, with a dark, healthy-looking, aquiline face. But I saw at the first glance that she was washed-out and pale and tired round the eyes; she looked ten years older. She led me into the dining-room which they also use as a sitting-room and said abruptly, without sitting down: "Agatina has tried to kill herself."

"D'you mean that—seriously?"

"With sleeping tablets. Nothing of great importance, however. The people at the hospital told me she could come back home at once. She's in bed now."

"But why did she do it?"

"Goodness knows. She won't tell us anything. She doesn't speak, she won't say anything, her father has implored her and even got angry with her, but it's no use. I asked you to come because you're so much in her confidence and it may be that she'll tell you."

I was so astonished that I said, as if I were thinking out loud: "Agatina, of all people—I can't believe it."

"Yet that's how it is," said Elvira with a sigh. "It's she, of all people, who is now giving me so much to worry about that I can't sleep. But come along, you go and have a talk with her and see if you can find out what's the matter." She left the room and I followed her down the passage.

I watched her as she went to the door of Agatina's room, opened it, put her head in and announced: "Here's Uncle Alessandro who'd like to see you." I did not hear what Agatina answered; but my sister pulled back her head and nodded to me in agreement, as much as to say: "It's all right, you can go in; please do all you can to help us." I had to summon up all my courage then, because I suddenly felt highly embarrassed, as though this matter did not concern Agatina but some complete stranger. Then I went in.

The room was small, hardly more than a continuation of the passage, with the bed lengthwise along the wall and a window at the further end, in front of which were a desk and a chair. Agatina was sitting up in bed with two or three pillows at her back, her arms lying limply at her sides and her hair falling untidily round her face. It was hot, and she was wearing a sleeveless nightdress, with nothing but a sheet over her recumbent body. I was struck by the pallor of her face—a profound, exhausted pallor, indeed, but not that of a person who is physically ill; it had in it a suggestion of languor, of maturity that again gave me the feeling that I was in the presence of a stranger. Then I reminded myself that I was, after all, her uncle Alessandro, and that she was my little niece Agatina; and entering, with an effort, into the part I had to play, I sat down beside her on the bed and exclaimed: "Now, Agatina, I should like to know what this is all about. Really, Agatina, this time I'm seriously angry with you. Agatina, d'you know I don't even recognize you?" I was at once conscious that my playful, fatherly tone was a false one, for some reason that I could not explain; in order to recover myself I put out my hand and gently caressed her poor pale cheek; but I withdrew it quickly as though I had been scalded: I realized that my gesture too, for some reason, was out of place. In the meantime she was looking at me, motionless and serious. Then she asked me, almost severely: "Uncle, who told you?"

"Your mother told me. But what I should like to know is why you did it."

She answered immediately, in a tone of vexation: "And yet I particularly asked her not to speak of it to you."

I paid no attention to these words, but went on: "You know you're eighteen years old? And d'you know what it means to be eighteen? It means that you still have your whole life to live. And so, the thing that you did—it's just as if somebody, at a meal, after eating, so to speak, the *hors d'œuvre*, got up and went away, thinking he'd had the whole dinner. What do *you* know of life? Just a few little artichokes with oil, a small slice of ham. You have still to taste the better and the greater part of it. And you wanted to leave it so soon?"

I should have liked to continue further with this comparison of life to a table that she wished to leave almost before she had started eating—the first figure of speech which, in my embarrassment, had come into my mind; but all of a sudden, beneath the serious, intelligent look with which, with strange attentiveness, she was studying and examining me, I grew confused and almost ashamed and concluded abruptly: "Well, what I should like to know is why you did it."

As I said this, I took her hand as it lay on the bed, and she allowed me to take it; in fact, unless I was mistaken, I was conscious of a very slight pressure of her fingers against mine. Meanwhile she was looking at me, and I noticed that her eyes were shining with tears. I thought she was now really on the point of telling me what I wanted to know; and I persisted, saying: "Now, I'm your uncle and you know I'm very fond of you and you can talk freely to me; come on, tell me, why did you do it? Your mother is worried and distressed, your father is anxious; you can't leave them in uncertainty like this. If it's a question of something they can do for you, they'll do it. But if you don't speak, how can they possibly do anything? Come on—why did you do it?"

Finally she answered, in a very low voice: "They can't do anything for me."

"Well then, I, if you'll only tell me—I'll see if *I* can help you."

"You can't do anything, either."

I recalled the possible motive I had thought of in the first place: love. I said to myself that parents are always the last people to find out that their children are in love; that a girl can carry on a love affair even if she stays at home all day long—out of the window; that people who kill themselves for love always think that others cannot do anything for them—and fundamentally they are right. I asked, cautiously: "Was there, by any chance, what might be called a sentimental reason? Have you, in fact, by any chance, fallen in love?"

I was expecting—I don't know why—a curt denial. However she answered, in a languid sort of way and at unnecessary length: "No, no, really I haven't, I couldn't say I've fallen in love. And anyhow, who should I have fallen in love with? You know me. . . ." She broke off, and gave me a faint smile.

Suddenly I understood why it was that I felt so embarrassed: in reality, although I was trying to find out, I did not, in my inmost heart, wish to know. Nevertheless I asked her, though unwillingly: "Are you sure you're telling me the truth?"

"Why shouldn't I be telling you the truth?"

"I don't know; you wouldn't tell your parents."

"You—you're another thing. I'd tell *you* the truth."

Silence followed. I should have liked to ask her, now, why I was "another thing" and what sort of a "thing" I was; but this time, decidedly, I did not feel inclined to speak. Agitated and ill at ease, I rose to my feet, went over to the window and looked out into the courtyard; then I turned round and, almost without realizing what I was doing, lit a cigarette. I remembered at once, however, that she was unwell and promptly enquired: "But perhaps you dislike my smoking?"

I noticed that she contemplated me for some time, with eyes that were no longer tearful but gentle and caressing; then, in a strange, faltering, breathless voice almost like a sigh, she said: "No, please do smoke; I don't mind at all." And now I understood.

I did not stop to think about it, however. Instinctively I decided that, if I had tried so far to make her tell me the truth, I must now, on the other hand, do everything I possibly could to prevent her from letting me know it. And so, still standing near the window, and gazing at the door so as not to look her in the face, I slowly pronounced these words: "Agatina, I do not know why you acted as you did; however, since you don't want to tell me, I do not wish to force you to do so. But you must realize that, at your age, there can be no reasons for killing oneself. Do you understand?"

"Yes, Uncle."

After a moment's silence, I went on: "Did you not think, when you did it, of your parents, who love you and who certainly did not deserve that you should bring this sorrow upon them? Did you not reflect that if, God help us, you had succeeded, you would have ruined their lives? Because, as you know, Agatina, they live for you and have nobody else but you."

"Yes, Uncle."

"That's enough of this 'Yes, Uncle'," I said to myself. With a grimace I threw my cigarette on the floor and stamped it out. Then I added: "I'm no good at preaching. But I ask you just one thing: that you promise me not to do it again."

"I promise you, Uncle."

"And whatever the thing may be that made you do it, you must promise me further that you won't ever think about that thing again. Never again. Is that agreed?"

This time she said nothing; but I did not, for that reason, look at her; I felt her eyes upon me and I did not wish to see them. Finally I concluded: "Well, I think I'll go now. I ought to get home. I was willing to come because it was you. But, to tell the truth, I would far rather all this had never happened. Good-bye then, Agatina."

I had moved away from the window; now I was standing near the bed again; and we looked at each other. It seemed to me that, somehow or other, the colour had returned to her face; that she was less languid and exhausted; and, in fact, that she was once again my niece Agatina, of whom I had hitherto been so fond. So I added, a little more affectionately: "Get up now, because you're all right; as long as you stay in bed your mother worries. Find something to do, try and distract your mind. And, I tell you what"—I went on with a smile—"find yourself a young man to get engaged to, if you haven't one already."

We gave each other a last smile, then I waved good-bye to her and left the room. My sister was waiting for me in the passage; and she at once rushed to meet me, anxiously. "Well, did she tell you?"

"She wouldn't tell me anything," I replied. "But don't worry. I don't believe it's anything of importance. What is one to say about it?—it's just a question of age."

"Yes, of course, it's her age," she said eagerly; "but she did give us such a fright . . . and who would ever have thought it—such a quiet girl, so gentle. . . ?"

I stayed a little longer with my sister; and in the end it seemed to me I had convinced her that it was nothing: a mere childish extravagance. Then I left her, went down into the courtyard and mounted my motor-bicycle again. Since that day, however, my sister and I see much less of one another. I am sure she did not understand; but I feel she is afraid of understanding; and that, for this reason, she prefers to see me less often than in the past.

THE VOW

WHEN the fine weather came, I began to long for the sea again, and for trips to the seaside. I had been ill all the winter and part of the spring, first with Asian influenza and double pneumonia, which nearly resulted in my going to the other world, and then again with the after effects of the flu. Finally, somehow or other, I had another attack of Asian flu—more lightly than before, however. Meanwhile the months were going by, and I, shut up in my little car-accessories shop, kept thinking of the sea, the lovely sea with its clean, fine sand and ever-moving, ever-living blue waters and blazing sunshine that scorches and burns but does not make you sweat. I had such a longing for the sea that I even dreamt about it at night; and as the bathing season drew near I used to go out every morning on the balcony to see what the sky looked like behind St. Peter's. We were now at the end of May; and one Saturday I suggested to Ginetta, my *fiancée*, that we should go next day to Castelfusano for our first bathe of the year.

We were at an eating-house, with our two families, mine and hers, and the children were asleep in their mothers' arms, and one or two friends of mine were there too. Ginetta's face at once took on a disconcerted expression. "I can't go to the sea," she said. "You must go with some other girl."

"But why?"

"Go with Tilde, whom you like so much. I'm not coming."

I began to get angry. "What's Tilde got to do with it? Why don't you want to come?"

She bent her head and said nothing. Then, in an authoritative way, her mother broke in: "When you were ill, Ginetta made a vow. She swore that, if you got well, she would give up sea bathing for this year. Now you know why she refuses to come."

This made me feel uncomfortable. On the one hand, I felt I ought to be moved by this vow which proved her affection for me; on the other, however, her vow would ruin my enjoyment of the trip. "Thank you," I said. "But what necessity was there for this vow? Wasn't penicillin enough for you?"

Immediately there was a chorus of protests from all the women present. "Don't say that. . . . Perhaps it was just because of Ginetta's vow that you got better. . . . You never know. . . ." I waited until they had calmed down, and then said: "Very well then; but I want to go to the sea and I'm going. You must come too, and break your vow."

"I'm not coming. And I'm not going to break my vow; why, for all you know, you might get ill again."

"I give you permission to break it."

"You needn't even think of such a thing," she said obstinately. "I've told you: go with Tilde."

The thing that irritated me most was her ungraciousness. It almost seemed that she was angry with me because, by falling ill, I had, so to speak, forced her to make this vow. So, after a little more bickering, I jumped up abruptly from the table, calling out that I would go with Tilde, since that was what she wanted; and that was that.

I went straight off to the bar where Tilde worked as cashier. This girl Tilde was exactly the opposite of Ginetta. Whereas Ginetta was touchy, nervous, complicated, full of humours and subtleties, Tilde, on the contrary, was simple, unshakable and serene. And, as in character, so also in physical appearance. Ginetta was thin, dark, eager, Tilde fair, plump and placid. "Hullo, Tilde," I said to her, "would you like to come to Castelfusano to-morrow?" I knew that men meant nothing to her, but that she was a glutton for amusement. And indeed she answered, with a smile: "What time d'you want to start?"

Next morning I made a little bundle of my bathing-costume and tied it on to the handlebars of my motor-bicycle, then went to fetch Tilde at her home. Yet I was conscious of a certain kind of remorse: after all, Ginetta had made that vow out of love for me; besides, between Ginetta and Tilde there was the same difference as exists, let us say, between a doll that opens its eyes and says "Papa" and "Mamma" and a living person. When I gave our agreed signal of a whistle, Tilde appeared at the window of her home in Vicolo del Cinque; she was bare-armed, her hair was arranged so that big yellow ringlets fell on her shoulders, and her bosom was well displayed in her low-necked blouse; and she cried out gaily to me: "Now we must wait for Ginetta."

I was completely taken aback. "Ginetta?" I asked.

"Yes, of course. She came round to the bar yesterday evening and said we were to wait for her and we'd all three go to the sea together."

Before I had time to recover from my surprise there indeed was Ginetta, a venomous smile on her lips, all dressed up, in spite of the heat, in grey wool up to her neck. "Well," she said, "shall we go?"

"Haven't you brought your bathing-costume? Surely you could undress, at least?"

"I vowed not only that I wouldn't bathe but that I wouldn't even put on my costume."

"While you were about it, you might as well have put on your fur coat."

"There's nothing wrong with this dress."

Well, in the end we all three got on to the motor-bicycle, Ginetta behind me and Tilde behind Ginetta. We started off, going by the Passeggiata Archeologica and into Via Cristoforo Colombo. Ginetta had put her chin on my shoulder and was pouring the poison of her discontent into my ear. "I did wrong to come," she said: "I'm dying of heat."

"And why *did* you come?"

"You wanted it so much, I did it for your sake."

"What I want is that you shouldn't spoil my outing. But what I should like to know is, why you made this vow?"

"And what *I* should like to know is, why *you* got ill?"

And so on. All of a sudden I couldn't bear that little whispering voice any longer; and at a certain point I stopped abruptly and said: "Now let's change round. Let Tilde come behind me and you go behind Tilde."

"But why?"

"Because you talk to me and I get distracted and we might finish up in a ditch."

So we changed round and I had peace: Tilde, for her part, did not talk because, as usual, she had nothing to say. Then, suddenly, at the Naples crossroads, someone gave me a violent pinch in the arm, so that we very nearly did finish up in the ditch. I stopped and asked Tilde angrily: "What on earth is the matter with you?"

She laughed and said: "Ginetta told me to pinch you, so I did."

"Are you crazy?" I asked Ginetta; "what's the matter?"

"I just felt like it," she said. "I'm sick of you. And d'you know why I'm sick of you? I made that vow for your sake. And in return you wouldn't even make the sacrifice of giving up this trip to the seaside."

"But, after all, I've been thinking about the sea for months. It's your own fault: you should never have made that vow."

At last we saw the sea. The road was like a strip of bright light going down into the far distance, cutting through the countryside and the pinewoods, losing itself in the even brighter light of the sea, ablaze with sunshine. As we went down the hill I started singing from sheer joy; Tilde joined in and Ginetta was silent. We went along the main street of Castelfusano, and then, passing the bathing-huts, came to the thicket and the beach and the sea. Here I stopped and left the machine; and then ran down through the scrub, holding the laughing Tilde with one hand and, with the other, Ginetta, who sulkily let herself be dragged along. The beach was almost deserted, with only a few groups of bathers here and there; there was an old jetty with rotten planks which stuck out some way into the calm sea. Drunk with delight, I went behind one of the bushes and was undressed in a moment. "Hi, Tilde, are you undressing?" I shouted. And, from behind another bush, she answered: "I'm already in my bathing-costume."

I had undressed in such a mad hurry that I failed to notice I had no costume. Ginetta had taken it at the moment when we left the motor-bicycle. "Ginetta," I called out, "give me my costume!"

"I'm here," she replied promptly, "on your left; come and get it."

I stole out cautiously but could see nothing. At the same time I heard, from my right, Ginetta's voice calling out in a spiteful tone: "Yah! I've caught you now!" I turned and saw that my clothes, which I had left on the ground, had vanished.

Disconcerted, I called out: "Ginetta, give me back my clothes, and my costume too!"

The same spiteful voice answered, from some hidden spot: "I'm not giving you back anything. It's not fair for me to be roasting in the sun while you wallow in the sea and enjoy yourself."

"But what fault of mine is it that you made that vow?"

"Of course it was your fault: you shouldn't have got ill."

In the meantime Tilde, stupid as usual, was shouting: "Come along, Attilio, let's go and have a bathe!"

"I can't," I replied, "I've nothing on."

A long argument followed. I was shouting to Ginetta to give me my costume; she kept on refusing; and Tilde kept repeating that she wanted to go and bathe. Finally I lost patience and said to Tilde: "Now look, surely you can manage it; go and get my costume from Ginetta."

With joy in her voice, she answered: "D'you give me leave to do that?"

"Certainly I do."

If you could have seen Tilde! She took a great leap and made as if to seize hold of Ginetta. But Ginetta was quick to avoid her, and ran off with my clothes under her arm. From the bush in which I was standing immersed up to my chest, I watched Tilde, in her bathing-costume, and Ginetta, fully dressed, the one chasing the other in a long race, first across the beach and then along the edge of the sea. Tilde was laughing good-humouredly; but Ginetta appeared to be quite serious. They went on running like this for some time, and then Tilde caught up with Ginetta and seized hold of the clothes, which fell on the ground. Ginetta turned round; Tilde, who was laughing all the time, stooped down to pick up the clothes. Then I heard a shrill scream and saw that Ginetta had seized Tilde by her long curls and was dragging her along the sand; and then suddenly she threw her back against one of the sand-dunes, leapt upon her like a wild beast and slapped her face again and again, right and left; I was able to follow the movement of her arm and hand rising and falling upon Tilde's pretty cheeks. To tell the truth, I was astonished at her violence; it was violence of a spiteful, bloodthirsty kind. Now Tilde had risen to her feet again and was walking away along the edge of the sea, her arm across her face, her shoulders shaken by sobs. "Tilde!" I shouted. She certainly heard me, but she shrugged her shoulders and walked on. As for Ginetta, she had vanished, together with my clothes and my bathing-costume, behind the dunes.

I was now alone. The bush concealed me, it is true, up to the chest, but I couldn't stay there for ever; on the other hand, the idea of issuing forth, naked as I was, was not to be thought of, at any rate until the few bathers who were to be seen here and there on the beach had gone away. Furiously angry, I stayed there for I don't know how long, standing upright and still in the scorching sun and looking into the thicket which surrounded me and which appeared to be deserted as far as the eye could reach. All of a sudden Ginetta's voice, quite close to me, made me jump. "How are you getting on?" it said.

"Very badly," I replied angrily; "come on, give me that costume."

There was silence. Then the voice went on: "If I give it to you, what will you give me in exchange?"

I could not make out where she was hiding, amongst all those round bushes that were so exactly alike. But from the soft, playful tone of her voice I seemed able to see her, and to see that she was calm again after the slaps she had given Tilde, in which she had vented her ill-humour, and was now smiling, affectionate, gentle. However I said harshly: "I won't give you anything. And in fact, if you don't give me that costume, it will be *my* turn to make a vow."

"What vow will you make?"

"I shall swear that everything's finished between us. That'll be *my* vow."

I heard her laughing. "Well, why don't you swear it, then?"

I felt troubled, now, because I realized that I was incapable of making this vow: I loved her too much. After a little her voice went on again: "Well then, in exchange for the costume, what will you give me?"

I moved in order to see where she was and the bush pricked my bare skin in front and behind. "A kiss," I said with a sigh.

"Here's your costume."

The costume flew through the air and landed at my feet. I slipped it on, and then I asked: "Where are you?"

"Go and have your bathe. You can give me the kiss afterwards."

So I went and had a bathe. The water, so delicious in the month of May, rose very slowly right up to my neck as I walked along the sandy sea-bottom. Finally I came out again and walked back up the beach into the thicket, circling round among the bushes. All of a sudden something fell violently on top of me. It was Ginetta, in her petticoat, and she had thrown her arms round my neck and was laughing. I gave her the kiss I had promised; and then she said: " It's an ill wind that blows no one any good. Now we can be together for a little, by ourselves, without Tilde."

" But what if Tilde doesn't come back? "

" Oh, she'll come back. She's left her clothes here. Besides, she'll want something to eat."

And so it was. After about an hour Tilde called to us from the beach, in a frightened, despairing voice. Ginetta ran to meet her and embraced her. Then she called me: " Come on, go and have another bathe with Tilde. I'll wait for you here and get the lunch ready."

I walked down beside Tilde, who appeared humiliated. " Well," I said to her, " Ginetta gave you some good hard slaps! "

" D'you know, I swore I'd never speak to her again? "

" And so. . . ?

" And so . . . instead of that, I came back here. Ginetta knows how to keep a vow. I don't."

HE AND I

I STARTED talking to myself a short time after my wife had left me because, so she said, she was tired of my silence. It is true, I was silent with her, as indeed with everyone else; but I was silent because I loved her. When you love someone there is no need of words, is there? All you want is to be near the person you love, to look at her, to feel that she's there. Having been silent with her, perhaps even too much so, I became talkative with myself, as I have said, as soon as she deserted me. I am a shoemaker, and a shoemaker's job, as we all know, demands concentration, if only because working in leather is fine work and it doesn't do to make mistakes: the human foot doesn't allow for mistakes. So, when I went home in the evening, my eyes dazzled, my head ringing with the sound of hammering, my lips hurting from all the nails I shove into my mouth to damp them before driving them into the leather soles, I should have liked to find—what shall I say?—a smile, a kind word, a kiss on the forehead, a bowl of hot soup. Instead of which—nothing at all. Merely, in the darkness, the dripping sound of the drinking-water tap in the kitchen. Now silence is a lovely thing when you are in the company of a person you love and when you know that you can speak to her if you want to; but it is a torment if it is imposed upon you. And so, after my wife went back to her mother, while I got my supper ready, all alone, in the kitchen, and then, still alone, ate it very slowly, almost without knowing what I was doing, sitting at a corner of the table, I began thinking out loud.

At first the things I used to say were impersonal and were not really addressed either to myself or to anyone else. For instance,

I would say: "How cold it is in this house, my goodness, how cold it is!"; or: "If it wasn't for the mice frolicking about between the ceiling and the roof, there wouldn't be a sound in this place except the tap dripping"; or again: "The bed's still unmade since this morning. Never mind, it's too late now, I'll make it to-morrow." I said these things aloud, sometimes very loudly, insignificant as they were; but it pleased me to hear my voice echoing round those three deserted rooms. Then, one day, when I was sitting as usual in the kitchen, I said: "Wine is good stuff, wine is comforting, you only need to drink a litre of wine and your troubles disappear"; and all of a sudden—how it happened, I don't know—I heard myself answering, still in a loud voice: "Guglielmo, you're a miserable wretch and you know it. Yes, of course, wine is good stuff, but it isn't comforting. You might drink a whole demijohn but still you wouldn't forget your wife nor the fact that she's left you. Yes, wine is good, but the company of a woman who loves you is very much better." I was struck by the truth of these words, and I answered—that is, my first voice answered: "You're right. But, when all's said and done, what is there left for me now? I'm fifty, and my wife, who is twenty-five, has deserted me. Where can I find another woman who would adapt herself to living with me? There's nothing left to me now except wine—isn't that so?" Then the other voice said: "Now listen, and don't act the philosopher. You know perfectly well that you haven't given up all hope of your wife." "Who told you that?" I replied; "I *have* given up hope, I have indeed." "No, you haven't," he said; "if you had, you wouldn't burst into sobs at the sole thought of her, wherever you may happen to be, even in the lavatory or on the stairs." Well then, I now had two voices, one of which, so to speak, spoke for me, and another which spoke for someone else who was also me but at the same time wasn't. Thus it was that, without realizing it, I changed over from monologue to dialogue—that is, from talking to myself to having arguments with myself.

These arguments, moreover, were not always arguments. Sometimes we were in complete agreement, he and I. For example, in the evening, after I had drunk my litre and a half or even two litres, I would go into the bedroom and there, in front of the wardrobe mirror, would make faces, just to amuse myself. Then he would say: "Here we are again, you've been drinking. A good thing you're at home and not in the street. You've been drinking and you can't stand up straight. But aren't you ashamed, at your age? "; he would say this, however, not without a hint of complacency in his voice. We went on like this for perhaps a couple of months, more or less in agreement; until one night, when I had drunk more than usual, a whole big flask of wine, lo and behold, when I took up my position in front of the mirror and put out my tongue, I was dumbfounded to see that *he*, in the mirror, remained serious and composed, with his tongue not out and his mouth not open. Then, after looking at me lingeringly and with compassion, he said: "Guglielmo, I'm fed up with you." "Why? " I asked. "Because," he said, "instead of fighting and struggling, you're letting yourself go. You've resigned yourself to the loss of your wife, you've become a drunkard, you've even lost your love of your work." "Who says so, I should like to know? " "*I* say so. Everyone in the neighbourhood knows you drink. And people take their shoes to be re-soled elsewhere. D'you know what you are, now? Just a rag of humanity."

This made me uneasy, and I scratched my head; then I asked: "Well then, what ought I to do, according to you? " "You ought to fight and struggle and make a firm stand." "But what for? " "To get your wife home again. Seeing that, without her, your life has come to an end, try to get her back again. Aren't you the husband? Haven't you the right to have her with you? Well then, bestir yourself, go ahead and take action." "But what ought I to do? " " What ought you to do, indeed! You know perfectly well what you ought to do." " No, honestly, I don't know." Then he stared straight at me and said: " You must contrive, by fair means or foul, to make her come home." He spoke these words in a particular tone of voice which, I confess, frightened me. " By fair means I've tried," I answered, " and it was no use. By foul means I don't want even to attempt it. I don't want to do anything bad." It seemed to me I had spoken rightly, in a way that ought to convince him; but he shook his head and said threateningly: " Very well. We'll speak of this again." At the same time he vanished from the looking-glass and I was left alone.

I went to bed much worried. No sooner had I put out the light than, suddenly, his voice began speaking again in the darkness: " Now that you're calmer and no longer tipsy, I'll tell you what you must do to get your wife back again. But don't interrupt me, listen till I've finished what I have to say." I told him to continue, that I was listening; and he went on to tell me, in a joking sort of way, that I must go next morning to the shop, fetch my shoemaker's knife, then go and find my wife, hold the knife under her nose and give her this warning: " Either you come home at once or else—you see this? . . ." I replied immediately, in the darkness: " You're crazy, it's no use even talking about such a thing. I want to get my wife back, that's understood. But there's a great difference between that and threatening her with a knife. I don't in the least want to end up in prison." " No," he said, " of course you don't want to go to prison. And yet, just possibly, you might be better off in prison than you are here." " Whatever do you mean? " " I mean that in prison at least you wouldn't be alone. In fact, you have nothing to lose: either your wife comes away with you, in which case, so much the better; or else she doesn't come, you give her a touch of the knife and end up in prison, and then at any rate you'd have the company of the other prisoners." " You're mad." " I'm not mad, and you know it. You're so lonely, Guglielmo, that even the idea of prison makes your mouth water." At this point I couldn't bear it any longer and, sitting up in bed, I said with energy: "It's no use even talking about it. And now be quiet, shut that wicked mouth of yours and let me go to sleep." "I warn you that, if you don't do this, *I* shall do it." "I told you to let me sleep." "I shall do it no later than to-morrow morning." "Shut up!" "Then we're agreed." I hung out of the bed, snatched up a shoe from the floor and hurled it at him, just like that, in the dark. He must have dodged it, cunning devil that he was. I heard a crash of breaking china and realized I had hit the water-jug on the chest of drawers. Then I fell asleep.

Next morning, however, when I woke up, I was at once conscious that there was no time to lose. Of him there was no sign, in any of the three rooms. It was quite possible that, while I was lingering at home warming up some coffee, he would run off to the shop (unfortunately he had the key, I had given it to him myself), would snatch up the knife, and then—the fat would be in the fire. It made my flesh creep, on my word of honour it did, to think of what might happen. And so, without waiting for any coffee, without washing or shaving, unkempt and with hair unbrushed, I rushed out, slipping into my coat as I went downstairs. It was very early in the morning, with a heavy dew and the streets full of mist, and just a few people on their way to work, their breath hanging in little clouds in front of their mouths. My shop was in the Vicolo del Fiume, and I almost ran all the way along Via Ripetta; as I turned the corner, I saw him in the distance coming out of the shop, very stealthily, and then running off in the direction of the Tiber. "Now we're for it," I said to myself. "He's a man of his word, no doubt about it; he said he'd do it and he's doing it. And now I've got to stop him." I too hurried into the shop, I too snatched up a knife in case he should turn his fury against me, then I went into a bar close by where there was a telephone kiosk. "There's no coffee, the machine isn't working yet," called out the barman, who knew me. I shrugged my shoulders; "Never mind about the coffee," I said. To tell the truth, I was so agitated that my hands were fluttering as I turned the pages of the directory, looking for the number of the police-station. At last I found it, dialled the number, a voice asked what I wanted, I explained what had happened: "You must go there at once. He's armed with a shoemaker's knife. It's a matter of life and death." The voice at the other end of the line enquired: "What's the name of this man?" I thought for a moment and then replied: "Palombini; Guglielmo Palombini," which is my own name too—one of those odd coincidences. I was assured on the telephone that they would attend to the matter as quickly as possible; and then I flew off to Piazza del Popolo, to the taxi rank: it was always possible that the police might arrive too late, and the best plan was for me to go there too. I called out the address as I jumped into the taxi, adding: "And quickly, for God's sake; it's a matter of life and death." The driver, an old man with white hair, asked what was the matter, and I told him: "A chap called Palombini, a shoemaker, has armed himself with a knife and is on his way now, in a taxi, to his wife who has left him, and he intends to kill her. . . . He's got to be stopped." "Have you informed the Police?" "Of course I have." "But how did *you* come to know about it?" "Well, Palombini and I are friends, in a way. He told me himself." The taxi-driver reflected a moment and then said: "There are plenty of people who pretend to be tough and then, when the moment comes, they go soft." "You're wrong, this man's really serious; I know him." All this time we were moving quickly through the deserted streets towards Via Giulia, where my wife was living.

The taxi stopped, I got out and paid and the driver went off; then I turned to look down the street, empty as far as the eye could reach, and saw him, the murderous ruffian, entering, at that very moment, the door of my wife's house. I recollected that my mother-in-law, a pious old bigot, always went off to church at that hour of the day; so that my wife would be alone in the flat, and in bed, into the bargain, for she was lazy and liked to sleep late into the morning. "He's chosen the right moment," I thought; "there's no denying it, he thinks of everything. . . . Now quickly, let's hurry; otherwise there's going to be bloodshed here." So I rushed in at the front door, ran upstairs four steps at a time and reached the landing just in time to see him knocking loudly at the closed door and shouting: "Gas meter, please!"—which is as good a way as any of getting a door opened to you. I drew back and, a moment later, was aware of the sound of shuffling slippers inside the flat; then the door was opened and I heard the sleepy, sing-song voice of my wife: "The meter's in the kitchen." He, as a matter of form, waited a moment, then slipped into the flat; I followed.

The corridor was in darkness; I recognized the warm, youthful smell of her body refreshed with sleep, and it made me feel faint for a moment. Walking on tiptoe, I went straight to the far end of the passage, where I knew her room to be, pushed open the door which she had left ajar when she went back to bed, and entered. The room was in darkness too, but not so much so that I was unable to distinguish the double bed and, white and full beneath the black hair spread loose over the pillow, the bare shoulders of my wife as she lay on one side, having gone back to sleep again. In truth, when I saw those shoulders, I was stricken with such a painful longing for the time when I used to see them in my own home, as I left stealthily in the morning to go to work, that I immediately forgot him and his knife, threw myself down on my knees and, seizing her hand as it lay on the coverlet, said: "My love, my darling, come back with me. Without you I can't go on living." I am sure that my wife, in such circumstances, would on this occasion have let herself be persuaded, if that vile wretch had not suddenly risen up on the other side of the bed, his hand raised holding the knife, and, shaking her by the shoulder, commanded her in a voice of terror: "You're coming back with me now; otherwise—do you see this?"

I do not intend to describe what happened after that: how I struggled with him, trying to disarm him; how my wife, screaming and upsetting things right and left, rushed half-naked across the room; and how a number of policemen suddenly burst in and jumped on me. I was careful to shout out: "Arrest him! He's dangerous. And look out for his knife!" But the policemen, possibly because I myself also had a knife in my hand, did not make such distinctions; they seized hold of me as well and hauled me bodily out of the flat and then down the stairs, while I struggled and kept repeating, with all the voice I had left: "It's *him* you must arrest, not me . . . you're making a mistake." In the street there was a great crowd. They forced me into the police van, and when I looked up, there he was, sitting handcuffed between two policemen, right opposite me, the sarcastic smile on his face seeming to say: "You see what I've done." I pointed at him and cried: "He's ruined me, that scoundrel over there . . . he's ruined me"; and then I fainted.

Now I'm in a padded cell, and they say they are keeping me under observation because they're afraid my mind has been affected by grief. I do not complain; but I feel so very alone. As for him, they took him off to the Regina Coeli prison, and thus we have been separated, he in gaol and I in an asylum. And so the only company I had has been taken away from me, and I have no one now, and I shall have to stay silent for ever.

ALL FOR THE FAMILY

AFTER what happened that night, I kept out of the way of Federico's family. To tell the truth, it left me feeling very uneasy. Could it really be true?—that a fine skilled workman, father of two little girls, a man like him, tall, strong, quiet, serene, the very sight of whom inspired confidence—that he should have been leading a double life? And what a double life! By day a mechanic, by night a thief. By day, in the workshop with me and the other chaps, or at home with his wife and children; by night, going round in a stolen car, in company with a band of crooks, breaking into shops—some said five, some said eight, in two years. Honest, hard-working, respectable by day; by night, with a black handkerchief over his face, a jemmy in his pocket and a gun in his belt. To tell the truth, if I hadn't seen his photograph in the papers—one of those photographs they take in prison, without a collar or tie, chin up and eyes wide open—I should never have believed it. Indeed, I couldn't make it out. And so, partly owing to my astonishment which made me almost hope it wasn't true, partly because I felt so uneasy, in fact almost hurt, I did not go and visit the family as I should certainly have done on the occasion of any other misfortune.

It was my wife who, in the end, persuaded me. At first I stood firm and said: "Federico ought not to have done a thing like this to me—to have kept it hidden from me, for two years, that he was leading a double life." "Very well," said my wife, "but if he had told you, what would you have done?" "How d'you mean?" "What would you have done? Would you have reported him?" "What? Me—act as a spy?" "Well, you see," said my wife triumphantly, "if he'd told you, you wouldn't have felt you wanted to report him. But now that he's in prison, you condemn him. Don't you see that you're contradicting yourself?" I felt undecided, and she went on: "You'd better go. After all, you'll be doing a good deed." This last reason seemed to me the best one, so I made up my mind to go.

It so happened that the following day was the Feast of San Giuseppe and Federico's wife was, in fact, called Giuseppina. In the bar underneath our flat I bought twenty or so little cream cakes and then went to catch the "circular" tram: I myself live in Via Giulia, while Federico lives in a new block in the San Paolo neighbourhood. In the tram I sat with the packet of cakes on my knee and once again started thinking about Federico. To tell the truth, I couldn't make head or tail of it. Above all, I was quite unable to reconcile the fact that Federico was such a good father and such an affectionate husband with the other fact of his going round at night and ransacking shop windows. Goodness me, I thought, either you're one thing or the other; and a man who is a good father of a family ought logically to be also an honest man. If he's not, it means that he believes in nothing; but then how does he manage to be a good father of a family? All this time the tram was moving along above the river. At the Ostia station I got out and took the San Paolo bus.

The building in which Federico lived was not far from the Tiber, after you pass the San Paolo basilica, in a group of brand-new blocks, all exactly the same, which, owing to the balconies that stick out on their façades, look like so many tall chests-of-drawers with all the drawers open. It was a fine day for San Giuseppe: a blue, luminous sky full of sunshine; numbers of children running about and playing football on the green lawns between the buildings; and a spring wind that made the washing, hung out to dry from all those balconies, flutter like countless flags. As I went up the stairs, I could not help thinking of poor

Federico who, on such a day, instead of sitting in blessed peace in the bosom of his family, was in the Regina Coeli prison, his face against the grating. When I reached the landing I rang the bell, and Lucetta, the bigger of the two little girls, came and opened the door, looking very clean, as usual, in a little newly-ironed dress, white stockings and shiny black shoes. I asked her: "Is your Mummy there?" Immediately an aggressive, drawling voice answered me: "Yes, yes, here she is, here she is."

I looked up in surprise, and almost failed to recognize Giuseppina, so much had she changed. Her face, which formerly had been so plump that it was almost round, was now flattened out, as it were, and elongated; her eyes shone with a strange sort of light, in the depths of their shadowy sockets, like wicks at the end of a candle on the point of giving their last flicker before being drowned in wax. Her hair was hanging down loose over her cheeks; and her dress, too, like her hair, seemed to be hanging lifelessly on her. And, from the way she leant against the doorpost of the kitchen, her shoulders thrown back and her belly pushed forward, it looked to me as if she was pregnant, into the bargain. Embarrassed, I said: "Giuseppina, it's San Giuseppe's Day to-day; my best wishes, and I thought I would bring you a few little cakes."

"Thank you, thank you. But there are no more feasts or saints for me. Come this way. And you—go into the kitchen and pick over the endive." Ungraciously she pushed the child into the kitchen; then she led me into the dining-room, which also served them as sitting-room. There was a strong light in there because the window had no curtains and looked straight at the sky, above the Tiber. Dazzled by it, I sat down opposite her and placed the packet of cakes on the table. For a moment we said nothing; I looked at her and she looked at the window. Finally I said: "Well, have you been to see him?" She turned quickly, like a viper: "Yes, I've been, yes." "And how was he?" "He was all right—for anyone who would like to see him dead; oh yes, he was all right."

I looked at her again; she seemed a bit over-excited. Now she was drumming on the table with her fingers. I persevered: "And when will he be brought to trial?" She answered, in a loud, indignant voice: "Goodness only knows . . . but they needn't fear, those people who hate him. He'll be condemned, sure enough, he'll be condemned to several years in prison; they needn't fear."

"But he," I asked, "what does he say?"

She shrugged her shoulders. "What can he say? He's in prison, he's awaiting trial, that's all there is to it."

I realized that she had not understood. "No," I said; "what I mean is—how does he explain what has happened?"

She looked at me sideways. "What is there to explain? He says it was a piece of sheer bad luck: if their car hadn't skidded because of the dampness in the early morning and run up against a tree, they would have got away."

For the first time it occurred to me that Giuseppina had been in her husband's confidence and had known all the time that Federico, by night, played the part of a gangster. I asked, cautiously: "But you . . . did you know that he . . . well, that he went round at night doing these things?"

Her eyes were wide open as she looked at me. "No," she said, "I didn't know. But I'm telling you now: if I had known, I should have said to him: 'You're doing well, go on doing it, do it more and more.' That's what I should have said to him."

I felt uneasy. "Well," I mumbled, "really it doesn't seem to me there would have been any point in encouraging him . . ."

She did not allow me to finish. "Ah, Alfredo," she exclaimed all of a sudden, in a tearful voice, "you can't have any idea of what I've been through. . . . There isn't a woman in the whole world more unfortunate and more unhappy than I am."

Embarrassed, I said: "Well, of course, it's understandable . . ." But she suddenly flew into a rage. "It damn well isn't understandable," she said; "it isn't understandable at all. I was so happy, so happy; and now from happiness I'm plunged into the blackest misery. Why, I say, why?"

This time I remained silent: I knew why, but judged it better not to say. She went on: "I loved Federico and Federico loved me. And we both loved the children. And he let us lack for nothing, he thought only of us, he lived, you might say, for his family."

I felt embarrassed, and murmured: "Oh yes, of course, a family's a very fine thing."

"Yes," she cried, "but our family wasn't like other families, Alfredo. It was a special family. There's never been a family like ours, and there never will be again. Ah, Alfredo, I can proclaim it out loud, a family like ours, where everyone loved each other so much, doesn't exist in the world."

She was silent for a moment, looking at the sky-filled window; then, seeing that I said nothing, she continued: "No one has any idea of how good that man is. Sometimes in the evenings, here, at this table, after I'd put the children to bed, he used to make plans for the future. Never once did he speak about himself, his whole thought was for his family. He would say, for instance"—and almost without being aware of it, she assumed a sugary tone of voice and pursed up her lips in order to quote Federico's words—"he would say: 'Now we have a motor-scooter; but if things continue to go well, what d'you say to our getting a small car? You know how much better it would be for you and the children: you could go to Ostia and Fregene and get the good sea air, every day if you like.' Ah, a husband like

Federico—where can you find him, Alfredo, where can you find him?"

I don't know why, but suddenly I lost patience; perhaps because I thought of where he would find the money to buy the car. I said dryly: "Well, Giuseppina, it's understandable that you should love your husband. . . . However, you must recognize the fact . . ."

"What fact?"

"That he's a thief."

I should never have said it. Suddenly she rushed at me, her eyes starting out of her head, her hair on end. "You're not even to speak of Federico. Woe betide you if you do!"

"But I . . ."

"You're not to speak of him, you're not worthy of him, you're not even worthy to kiss the ground under his feet."

I was left speechless and open-mouthed. She went on without looking at me, addressing the air. "Federico is a man like no other man in the world, that's what he is. No, no, no, nobody's to speak of Federico. . . . Only *I* can say what he is: a saint."

I exclaimed in astonishment: "Really, Giuseppina! But d'you know what a saint is?"

And she, getting more and more excited: "Of course I know, I've lived for twelve years with a saint. Federico is a saint."

"A saint," I reflected, "with a machine-gun on his arm and a jemmy in his hand"; but I said nothing, so as not to provoke her further. She was crying now, gulping down her tears with her head lowered, staring at the table. All of a sudden she cried out, in a shrill voice that made me jump: "And now they've taken him away from me . . . they've put him in prison . . . they've torn him from me . . . they've torn him away from his children . . . they've destroyed a family. . . . And why all this? Why, I ask?"

"Well, Giuseppina," I said, "you know why . . ."

"Yes," she said, "I know: simply to do evil . . . to destroy everything that's fine and good . . . to prevent our being happy."

"Perhaps there may be some other reason too."

"No, there are no other reasons. Envy, that's the reason, envy. Ah, I know I shall never be so happy again as I've been in these last years with Federico."

After she had said this, she started crying again; and I, not knowing what to say to her, suggested: "Giuseppina, do at least eat one of those little cakes; it'll sweeten your mouth."

She shook her head. "It's no use," she said, "my mouth will always be bitter now. Thank you, all the same, Alfredo. . . . You're kind-hearted. . . . You have something of Federico about you. Perhaps you're the only one that can understand Federico because you're like him."

I could not help protesting, in a grudging way: "Yes; however I'm not a saint." But she did not hear me; she was opening the packet of cakes. She took one and began eating it, her head bent, looking at the floor with an expression full of sadness and bewilderment. A little curl of yellow cream was left at the corner of her mouth, but she did not notice it. Then she blew her nose, and when she took the handkerchief from her face the cream was no longer there. I rose to my feet, saying: "Well, Giuseppina, I must go. We must meet again. . . ."

She rose too, and followed me into the passage, without speaking. But as we were about to say good-bye, she started forward, anxiously: "What d'you think, will they find him guilty?"

"Well, I don't see how they can help it."

"There's justice for you," she cried, as I started off down the stairs, "a fine sort of justice. . . . Plenty of men who actually let their families die of hunger are still walking about. And he, who took such care of his family, goes to prison. Does that mean, then, that people oughtn't to look after their families?"

This time I did not answer her. I hurried away down the stairs.

DANCING IS LIFE

IN March I reached the age of eighteen and obtained permission from my father to give up my studies. He gave me this permission out of despair, because by now I was four years behind and was the only one in the class who wore long trousers. My father, who is a man of the old-fashioned type, gave me the permission to leave off studying after a scene I can't describe: he shouted that I was breaking his heart and that he didn't know what to do with me. He finished up by suggesting that I should work in his shop, a big, old, respectable stationery business in the Piazza Minerva neighbourhood. I answered simply: "I'd rather die"; and then he took me by the arm and pushed me out of the room. And so, out of sheer despair, I was left free, at eighteen, to do what I liked.

The first thing I did was to buy a magnificent red sweater, a pair of blue American jeans with white seams, six pockets, turn-ups halfway up the shins and a label on the seat, a yellow handkerchief to go round my neck, and a pair of moccasins with brass buckles. My mother, who is very fond of me and always gives in to me in everything, gave me a little portable radio for a birthday present and persuaded my father to let me have a motor-bicycle. That same day I went to the hairdresser's and told him to give me a Marlon Brando hair-cut. While this was being done the manicurist, a rather common little girl, came up and asked me if I wanted her to do my nails. I looked up at her from below and, although she was by no means pretty, rather plain, in fact, I privately decided that this was the woman for me. I was not mistaken, Giacomina *was* the right girl; and while she was doing my nails, talking, as they do, about this, that and the other, I discovered that she, like me, had a passion for rock 'n roll. I suggested a meeting and she accepted at once. And so, when I left the shop, I was all complete: eighteen years old, a red sweater, blue jeans, a Brando hair-cut, a radio, a motor-bicycle and Giacomina. Life was beginning at last.

Life, for me, meant rocking 'n rolling, nothing more than that but also nothing less. I had the devil in me and, thin as a rake as I was, I felt, that April, that the spring wind carried me along the streets and that this wind, laden with the smell of flowers and dust, seemed to repeat the beautiful rhythms of rock an' roll. With my pockets full of fifty-lire pieces and Giacomina on my arm—she had in the meantime given up her job as a manicurist—I spent the whole day going round the bars that had American juke-boxes. I would go in, put a counter for a rock 'n roll record into the machine, and then, without more ado, between the coffee machine and the cash desk, improvise a number with Giacomina. I would begin moving my shoulders and hips, my hands held out in front with fingers spread and my mouth wide open, in one corner of the bar; in the opposite corner Giacomina would do the same; then we would meet, dancing, in the midst of a circle of people, customers of the bar or friends of ours who followed us round everywhere as a kind of retinue. These friends, most of them boys of my own age, teased me a bit for having chosen Giacomina out of all the many girls available, all of them superior to her. It was quite true that Giacomina, as I have already said, could not be called pretty, with her pony-tail hair, her small, sharp face, pale if not positively livid and with red blotches here and there, and her uninteresting eyes, of no particular colour. But underneath her skirt she had a pair of frenzied legs which never tired of dancing and which worked in perfect harmony with my own. It must be understood that between us there was not the faintest shadow of what is called love; nothing but rock 'n roll. Anyhow, what is love in comparison with the pleasure of dancing? Just a bit of fondling and foolery and affectation: nothing, less than nothing. Besides, love makes you heavy and stupid; whereas dancing makes you fly through life like a bird in the sky. No, no question of love; the one thing necessary was to dance.

Giacomina and I were in perfect agreement. Early in the morning I would go and fetch her on my motor-bike, with my portable radio tied on to the handlebars; and then, off we would fly wherever we felt inclined, into the country, to the seaside, into the suburbs. As soon as we arrived I would turn on the radio to some dance music and we would start dancing. Where, indeed, have I not danced?—on the sand of the seashore, on the asphalt of the streets, on the grass of the open fields, in public squares and in narrow lanes. If we did not go out, she would come to my home and we would take up the carpet in the sitting-room and dance there. Or sometimes we would go to *her* home, and, since they were poor people and had no sitting-room, we would dance on the landing. In the daytime, as I have said, we went round from one bar to another, followed by our friends, dancing all the time; in the evening we went to a dance hall and very soon created an empty space round us as we danced, while everybody else in the room made a circle round about us and beat time with their hands. Sometimes at night I actually woke up with a jump and felt my feet moving of their own accord, under the sheet, still mad to be dancing. Oh, how happy I was! Never in all my life had I been happy in this way.

But unluckily it could not last. I had already noticed, during our expeditions, that Giacomina clung a little too tightly to me as we went along on the motor-bicycle. And when we stopped she did, indeed, dance, but it appeared to be more in order to please me than because she wanted to do so herself. From time to time she would sigh, and take my hand, and gaze at me with languid eyes. Until finally one day, as we were walking through the pine-wood at Castelfusano—I don't quite know how it happened—we found ourselves embracing behind a bush, in a long kiss, a kiss of love. Annoyed, I said quickly, as soon as we drew apart: "There's no need for this sort of thing." "Why not," she asked, "seeing that we love one another?" "Loving doesn't come into the question," I said, still annoyed; "we got on very much better without love." Then, to my astonishment, she clasped me tightly to her, throwing her arms round my waist and placing my arm so that it lay round her shoulders; and she cried out in a shrill voice: "I love you, I love you, I love you. And I want everybody to know that we love each other, yes, everybody's got to know it, yes, yes, everybody." I pushed her away, saying: "Yes, yes, very well, but don't hang on to me like that." "Why not, if we love each other?" "Yes, but keep a proper distance." "Ugh, how perverse you are! If we love each other, it's quite right for us to embrace, isn't it?" "No," I said harshly, "it isn't right. What I wanted with you was to dance, not to embrace." Languishingly, she answered: "Darling little Alfredo, we'll do *both*."

Well, well, from that day onwards she became more and more clinging and less and less willing to fly with me through the intoxicating rhythms of rock 'n roll. She went on dancing, of course; but without the enthusiasm which is the first condition of dancing well. And, at the slightest opportunity, she clung on to me. Several times I pushed her off violently enough to take her breath away; but it was like talking to a deaf person: the more I pushed her away, the more she clung to me. Sometimes I said to her: "To-day we dance, and that's all. D'you see?" "Darling Alfredo," she would say, "how can I get through to-day without giving you even one kiss?" "Keep the kiss for to-morrow," I replied; "to-day we dance." She appeared to accept this with resignation; but then, treacherously, she would jump on me and harass me with kisses. I felt almost suffocated, just as with a playful dog that hurls itself on you and licks your face. In the end I would free myself with a great effort, remove from my mouth the two or three hairs which she, in her impetuosity, had almost made me swallow, and say: "This wasn't what we agreed to. Good-bye. See you to-morrow." I would go home, put on a gramophone record, then another, then a third; finally, feeling calmer, I would telephone to her. She would come hurrying round; and for that evening we would go back to the good old times, spinning like a couple of tops until late at night. But such returns into the past grew more and more rare. Something was finished between us; I felt this while I was dancing with her. So much so that one day I said to her: "You're not the same as you used to be, my dear." Obstinately she answered: "It's because I love you."

The thing that irritated me most of all was her mania for doing things in public. It is true that we had always danced the rock 'n roll in public; but dancing is one thing and kissing is another. I pointed this out to Giacomina: "Those same people who applaud you when you dance with me, will whistle at you if you kiss me. There's a time and place for everything." "That may be so," she replied, "but I want everyone to know that we love each other—yes, yes, everyone." To put it briefly, we were at cross purposes.

One day we took the bus in order to go to a friend's house where we used to gather from time to time to hold rock 'n roll competitions. I was in a bad temper, because at lunch my father had made one of his customary scenes; in the end, to calm him down, I had promised him that I would go to the shop and lend a hand there that same afternoon. Of course, I had privately decided that I wouldn't go to the shop at all; but I felt a touch of remorse, and also a certain degree of fear at the thought of the further scene my father would make as soon as he came to know of it. Sullenly I got on to the bus with Giacomina and then remained standing on the rear platform. She, as usual, was clinging to me and gazing at me with those shining eyes that annoyed me so much. "Do stop looking at me in that way," I said to her. "I look at you," she answered, "because you're beautiful. Give me a kiss." "You're crazy." "Yes, yes, give me a kiss, quickly; I want everyone to know that we love each other." "Stop it, I tell you! It's not the weather for it to-day." For answer, she took a jump, twined her two arms round my neck and kissed me. You should have heard the people in the bus! An elderly gentleman remarked: "Aren't you ashamed of yourselves? It's not decent; you should go to your own home if you want to do such things." Giacomina, still hanging on to me, replied: "And why? We love each other, and we do what we want to do, wherever we please." "Young lady," said the gentleman, "I am sorry for your parents." The other passengers, however, were not so polite. Somebody shouted: "You ought to go behind those big bushes in the Borghese Gardens; that's the place"; someone else remarked: "Just look at that poor little fish! Who does she think she is?"; and someone else said: "The more skinny they are, the more brazen they are." Naturally I was forced, though unwillingly, to come to Giacomina's rescue; but as always happens when you do something against your will, I hit upon an unlucky retort. "Be quiet," I said, "you only talk like that because you're envious." I should never have said it. A chorus of protest greeted my words; then the conductor thought it his duty to rebuke us; and finally, when I told him he ought to be thinking about selling tickets, he stopped the bus and made us get out.

It so happened that we were in the neighbourhood of Piazza Minerva, where my father's stationery shop was. I felt perfectly calm; it was just as if the incident in the bus had happened a month ago. I said: "Good-bye, Giacomina."

"But I . . ."

"I'm going to the shop now, I promised my father I would. But I'm afraid there's a misunderstanding between us."

"A misunderstanding?"

"For you, the most important thing in life is love. For me—you know what it is. Well, you'd better go home now: I'll telephone you."

"You'll telephone me?"

"Yes, of course."

We were standing in Piazza Minerva, in front of the little marble elephant. I knew I should never telephone her again; and, as I walked away, this thought suddenly brought me a feeling of immense relief. I turned partly round so as to take a last look at her; and it gave me acute pleasure to see that she was alone: it was true, then, I had really left her, I had broken away from her, I was going away for good. I almost danced into the shop, which at that hot time of early afternoon was deserted, and greeted Bice, the elderly assistant, with a gay: "Hallo, Bice!" I had my portable radio under my arm, and I walked straight through to put it on the table in the back room, adding: "I've come to give you a hand. In the meantime, if you don't mind, we'll have a little music."

The white blinds in the windows of the shop were lowered on account of the sun; inside the shop, amongst all the shelves full of different kinds of stationery, there was a soft half-light, a good smell of paper, a soothing silence. I turned the radio down low and stretched myself out on the old sofa in the back room, which was hard and cool, so that my head was down and my feet propped high up on the curly wooden arm. I was nearly dozing off, to the muffled rhythm of a dance tune, when I heard a little voice saying: "Four large sheets of drawing-paper. . . ."

I gave a jump, because I had recognized the voice as that of Ginevra, a young girl from the Art School, who was also a fanatical lover of dancing, and also had a pony-tail, like Giacomina; but Ginevra was fair-haired, with an almost albino face, a hypocritical expression, and china-blue eyes. I rushed out and took the sheets of paper from Bice's hands. "I'll serve this customer," I said. "How are you, Ginevra?"

"Oh, Alfredo!"

"You can fetch the paper later. Come along in here now; I want you to hear something."

So she followed me into the back room of the shop and I closed the glass door in the face of the astonished old Bice and immediately turned the radio full on. Then, without uttering a word—for she had understood already—I took her round the waist and embarked upon a frenzied dance which, I cannot help thinking, gave expression to the twofold joy of having got rid of Giacomina and of having already found someone to take her place. Finally we fell together, breathless, on to the sofa, and I said to her: "We'll meet again this evening, then; I'll come and fetch you at home."

"How about Giacomina?"

"Don't bother about Giacomina. I'll come and fetch you at nine. But let's be clear about it: it's in order to dance that you're coming with me."

"What should I be coming for, otherwise?"

OVERTAKING

YOU can't have two passions at the same time. My passion for the car which I had at last succeeded in buying distracted me, at that moment, from my passion for Ines, the girl to whom I was thinking of getting engaged. So much so that Tullio, my great friend, insinuated himself between Ines and me and tried to entice her away from me. Friends, friends—well, it's better not to say anything on that subject. And if it's absolutely necessary to say something, then we're forced to admit that friendship is a fine and splendid thing as long as there's no woman concerned. You've only to look at a hen-coop; two cocks will peck at their food together, will crow together, will sleep together; but as soon as you introduce a hen, a hen in the prime of life, one of those white ones with a little red crest—there's the end of all peace; the two cocks will go for each other and peck each other's eyes out.

What a strange thing is a thought: whatever you're doing, whether you're going for a walk or whether you're working, whether you're alone or in company, this thought comes popping up like something you can't understand and, just because you can't understand, it goes round and round in all directions and never stops going round and round. You can't understand why you love someone. This happened to me with Ines until I bought the car; once I had bought the car, it started happening to me with *that*. Certain things, of course, go without saying: Ines was made of flesh and bone, the car of pig-iron; Ines had a pretty, round face, with soft black eyes and a smiling mouth, the car a snout with bumpers looking like the teeth of a mastiff; Ines, although small, had a well-trimmed figure from top to toe, while the car was like all other cars, just a big packing-case; and yet, little by little, the thought of the car ousted the thought of Ines. If at least I had been satisfied with thinking about it! The trouble was that I talked about it: and other people noticed this more than I imagined. Tullio said to me one day, in the presence of Ines: "Why, Gigi, all you think about now is the car. If I were in your place, Ines, I should be jealous." Then Ines said, smiling: "Shut your eyes, Gigi, and tell me what you see: two legs or four wheels?" Of course I answered: "Two legs"; but to tell the truth I was lying; I had seen four wheels, four lovely wheels with new tyres which, as I knew, were awaiting me at the corner of the street to carry me wherever I wished.

Well, one morning—it was a Sunday—I telephoned to tell Ines I would come and fetch her to go to the seaside; and I hinted that I wanted to be alone with her: I wanted to talk to her about our engagement. Feeling gay and contented, I went down to the garage underneath where I live, took out my beautiful grey-and-blue car and went, in the first place, to the big garage at the corner of Via Candia, where I got them to give me a complete servicing: petrol, water, oil, tyres, even distilled water for the battery, as well as cleaning the windscreen. Then I got in again, went into bottom speed, then into second, then third, and finally went up the whole of Viale Giulio Cesare in top: it was wonderful. The car didn't merely move, it positively drank up the street; and the engine made an amorous sort of humming sound like bees in a flowery meadow in springtime. But, when I turned into Piazza della Libertà, I saw from afar that Ines was not alone.

This upset me, especially because I had warned her that I wanted to be alone with her; and I was all the more upset when I saw that the other person was Tullio. I already knew that Tullio, my friend and partner in my car-accessories business, had his eye on Ines; and his presence that morning was a confirmation of this. I must add that, of the two of us, Tullio was the strong, handsome one: he was tall, with broad shoulders and a small head well set on a neck like a bull's. I myself, on the other hand, being short and pinched-looking, had only my eyes, my intense, intelligent eyes, to remind people that strength, after all, isn't the only thing in the world. I noticed with distaste that Tullio was wearing a red-and-blue striped sweater and bright blue sailor trousers; he was looking more of a tough than usual. When I came abreast of them, I stopped the car, opened the door and said dryly: "Hello, Tullio." Ines explained gaily: "Tullio telephoned me and so I told him to come along too." Tullio said impudently: "It doesn't matter to you, does it? The only thing you mind about is driving the car, isn't it?" Imprudent words, which at once turned to poison inside me. Feigning stupidity, I replied: "Why, of course. The thing I mind about is the car, nothing else counts. Come on, jump in." So they got in, Ines into the back seat, Tullio beside me. This arrangement, at first, pleased me; but very soon afterwards I realized I had nothing to be happy about. Tullio, in fact, immediately turned round towards Ines, and she leant forward towards Tullio; and in this way, while I was taken up with driving, they embarked upon an intimate conversation, just like a pair of lovers, or two people who are on the way to becoming lovers. What did they say? Oh well, a bit of everything—jokes, allusions, compliments, hints, half-sentences, phrases left in the air. What disgusted me most, however, was the tone—excited, insinuating, sly, like that of two people who have an understanding between them and, because of this secret understanding, little does it matter what they say.

By this time we were out of Rome and driving along the Via Aurelia. Our idea was to go to Santa Marinella, and as it was already getting late I quickened speed. To say I quickened speed, however, is merely a manner of speaking. Along the whole length of the road one car followed another: big cars and little cars,

Italian cars and foreign cars, luxurious cars and utility cars. Every now and then there was a milk van, or a big lorry from one of the settlements along the sea driven by a madman who overtook other cars as though he were riding a motor-bicycle. So I settled down to a slow, steady pace, and I might perhaps have gone on like that if those other two, close beside me, had not got on my nerves with their chattering. Somehow or other, I don't know why, the nervousness of jealousy infected my driving and I started to accelerate, with the idea, perhaps, of getting as quickly as possible to Santa Marinella and so interrupting their altogether too confidential conversation. I therefore began overtaking other cars, one after another, like threading pearls on a string. At the insistent sounding of my horn there were some that immediately drew in to the side, well-behaved cars that observed the rules of the road; but there were also cars that wouldn't allow themselves to be overtaken at any price. One thing I noticed: the best-mannered cars were the most powerful ones, the big, luxurious cars driven by people who didn't care a damn about being overtaken, knowing perfectly well that, if they wanted to, they could go faster than anybody; the meanest ones were the small, cheap cars, full of women and children, with the father of the family at the wheel. These unfortunates, having spent the whole week sitting in an armchair, were anxious to prove to their wives and children that they were vigorous, dashing sportsmen; and so, just at the moment when they were being overtaken, instead of slowing down and drawing in to the side, they would accelerate. I could have killed them; all the more so because, while with solemn, set, imperturbable faces they urged on their little hire-purchase cars to the maximum speed, their whole families would be peering at me through the windows with mocking, triumphant expressions, as much as to say: "We've got the better of you. Papa's a cleverer driver than you are." I looked back at them and wondered why it was that faces which, if I had seen them in a shop or in the street, would have appeared uninteresting or even, possibly, attractive, seemed to me so completely odious when seen through the windows of a car. Meanwhile we had passed the turning to Fregene and were going towards Ladispoli.

Apart from Ines' and Tullio's chattering and the objectionable faces of the families on their Sunday outing, there was another thing that got on my nerves—the way in which Tullio from time to time interrupted his flirtation with Ines in order to urge me, out of the kindness of his heart, to overtake a car in front. "Now, Gigi," he would say, "do please pass that little car"; or: "Come on, give it him! Get past him—what are you waiting for?" or again: "Get on, what are you afraid of? Go into third and overtake him." Had we been alone, well and good: it's fun, sometimes, to have a race. But Ines was there; and nothing could get it out of my head that Tullio was pressing me to do all this overtaking in order to keep me occupied and distract my attention so that he could have it all his own way with her. And with a touch of ridicule, perhaps, into the bargain. Rather like a pair of lovers in a public garden saying to an importunate child: "Now come on, be a good boy and go and play ball." I lost my temper; and instead of slowing down and driving quietly as I should have, I felt myself so carried away by anger that I followed his promptings and overtook one car after another; and the more I did so, the more infuriated I became at the thought that I was thus playing into the hands of Tullio, who looked upon me as a mere trifler who had only to get the wheel of a car between his hands to allow his girl to be pinched from him.

But I kept my eye on them. Tullio was twisted right round in his seat, with one leg bent back on the cushion and his two hands gripping the back of the seat; Ines was bending forward towards him, and she too kept her hand on the back of the seat, although there was no need for it. At a certain moment, without drawing attention to what I was doing, I adjusted the driving-mirror in such a way that I no longer saw the road behind me but could see that part of the seat on which their hands were resting. After a short time I thus saw Tullio's hand sliding very slowly along until it was close to Ines' hand, which soon, at a bend in the road, it covered. At the same moment Tullio said to me: "Come on, Gigi, do please pass that little car; what are you waiting for?" I looked at the road: the car Tullio was talking about was close in front of me and going fast. It was an old rattletrap with a baby's pram tied on to its roof. Inside it could be seen the usual swarm of women and children; and in the driver's seat the usual *paterfamilias*, fat and square, his big head sunk into his neck, his black, hairy hands gripping the wheel: he looked like a puppet. But when I took my eyes off Tullio's and Ines' hands and looked at the rattletrap in front, the first thing I saw was not the driver, but, at the rear window, the face of a little boy of about six, ugly, pale, with fanlike ears, making rude faces and putting out his tongue at me. The child was making faces at me because he thought I had lost my temper at being outdistanced by his father; but I, for some reason, thought he was making faces in order to mock me about Tullio and Ines. I looked at him and frowned; and he, his mother's arm round his chest and his nose flattened against the glass of the window, looked back at me and again put out his tongue. I raised my eyes again to the driving-mirror and saw that Tullio's hand was now moving from Ines' hand to her wrist and then from her wrist to her arm. Tullio said to me, hypocritically: "What's the matter, are you dreaming? Why don't you accelerate?" Ines, her voice softened by sensual excitement, supported him. "We're going too slowly," she said. "We shall never get to Santa Marinella at this rate."

"Oh really?" I replied; "I'm not going fast enough? Well, now you shall see. . . ." We were on a straight stretch of road which ended, in the distance, in a hill. On the right there was a hedge along the top of a bank, on the left a row of plane-trees leaning towards the road, their trunks circled with bands of white. I changed into third, pressed hard down on the accelerator, sounded my horn and dashed forward, still hooting, with a powerful roar from the engine. But would you believe it? Instead of moving over to the right, as he should have done, *paterfamilias*, at the sound of my horn, planted himself in the middle of the road and accelerated too. I was thus forced to follow close behind him; and Tullio said: "What on earth are you doing? Aren't you ashamed?"; then I looked up and saw the little boy putting out his tongue at me. So I threw myself over to the left of the road again and, still sounding my horn, started moving along side by side with the other car. We were almost at the end of the straight stretch where the road started climbing the hill; *paterfamilias* was accelerating, I couldn't get the better of him and I was bursting with rage; then, all of a sudden, I began to gain ground. But lo and behold, just at that very moment there appeared, at a bend in the road, another car coming towards me at a moderate speed but still fast enough to prevent me from finally overtaking the first car. I ought to have given up the attempt and fallen back again; but some devil or other whispered to me to go on. *Paterfamilias* accelerated at the same time, and I had only just time to hurl myself right over to the left, into the ditch, to avoid a collision; I saw the trunk of a plane-tree rushing to meet me. I thought I heard Tullio's voice shouting: "Brake! brake!"; then I was conscious of nothing more.

Useless to relate what happened afterwards: if you get hold of that Monday's paper you'll find all the details. All I want to say is that I myself was the only one to come off lightly: ten days, apart from complications, which luckily there weren't. But Tullio broke a leg and was two months in hospital, where I went to see him almost every day. As for Ines, she had a fractured arm—that same arm that she had so submissively surrendered to Tullio's caresses—and she carried it in a sling for over a month. And the car—well, it's better not to talk about it; one of these days I shall sell it as scrap-iron. But d'you know what Dr. Frontini, a bright young man who was looking after Tullio, said to me when I told him the exact story of how the accident had happened? "In your subconscious," he said, "you wanted to destroy the car that prevented you from loving Ines, you wanted to kill your friend out of jealousy, to kill yourself from despair at being no longer loved, and to punish your girl friend for being unfaithful to you. In part, you succeeded." "But I should like to know," I asked, "what this subconscious is?" "It's what we don't know about ourselves," he replied. "That's as may be," I said; "but I wanted to overtake a car and I didn't succeed, that's all." However, since the accident I've given up driving and I've got engaged to Ines. And Tullio? Tullio and I are friends again as we were before.

GOLDEN HAIR

IN Rome, if they want to tell someone that he is countrified, ignorant, a peasant, they say: "D'you come from Sgurgola? Go back to Sgurgola. Why didn't you stay at Sgurgola?" That's just Roman arrogance; and the answer might be that rudeness gets you nowhere and that Rome, before it was Rome, was certainly no better than Sgurgola and was very likely something even more countrified. Anyhow, I come from Sgurgola, and it was the fact of my coming from Sgurgola that drove me to become a manservant, all for love of Consolina who came from Sgurgola too. We had become engaged in our village; then she went into service in Rome and so arranged things that she succeeded in getting me a place as manservant in the house where she was cook. She told them I belonged to her village, she did not say we were engaged. And so I found myself, in company with my betrothed, in the house of Signor Palombini, a rich tradesman whose shop was in Prati.

Consolina was a type of girl of whom there are a great many in our district, attractive, if you like—attractive to me, at any rate—but extremely countrified. She had red cheeks like two red apples and where they weren't red they were dark and also rather downy. Her little eyes were black and lively, as if they had been made with a gimlet, beneath a hard brow which seemed to be saying no even before you had spoken; and above her brow was a great mass of black, frizzy hair. Her figure was robust but slim: women like Consolina broaden out only after marriage. I, on my side, am short and sturdy, and I too am dark, very dark, in fact, with big, flashing black eyes, a pointed nose and a swarthy face.

Now take note of this fact that we were both of us dark, for it has an importance of its own.

Some people might think that Consolina and I, living as we did in the same house, sleeping in two adjoining rooms, having our meals together in the kitchen, would have become intimate, not to say lovers. But it was not so. After we had been together at the Palombinis' for barely a month, she began visibly cooling off. Finally, one evening when we had gone out together, she to do some shopping and I to exercise the dog, a black Alsatian with its own fixed habits, she said to me quite bluntly: "I don't care for you any more; here's your ring back again; I advise you to stop thinking about me." I was much upset, as you can imagine, all the more because by now I looked upon her as my wife and had made my plans. I insisted on knowing the reason, at least. She answered: "I don't care for you any more: that's the reason." And without another word off she went, furious, leaving me there holding the dog's lead; the poor beast pulling at it to try and follow Consolina, to whom he had by this time grown accustomed.

That's what women are like. And Consolina, after that evening, not merely ceased to consider herself engaged to me, but also wanted me as quickly as possible to leave the house into which she had forcibly (you may say) introduced me. She was rude to me in every kind of way; she did not answer when I spoke to her; she whisked round like a viper if I happened so much as to touch her arm. And she kept repeating, like a refrain: "When are you leaving?" Finally I said to her: "I shall leave only when I have discovered why you don't want me." She shrugged her shoulders and, for that day, that was the end of the matter.

One Sunday when Consolina was having a day off, I went into her room as soon as she had gone out, determined to find out the reason for the change in her. Consolina was poor like me, Consolina came from my village, Consolina, like me, was in service: I knew where to put my hands. Inside the high, dark room looking on to the courtyard there was the smell of Consolina, just as though it had been the lair of a wild animal, a smell so marked that for a moment I sat down, stunned, on the bed, remembering what that smell had meant to me when Consolina and I were still engaged. Then I got up again and started my search. I passed over the cupboard, a huge one, in which Consolina's small wardrobe was dispersed here and there; I passed over the chest of drawers where she kept the pieces of her bridal trousseau that she had been collecting for some years out of her savings; and without more ado I fell upon the fibre suitcase in which, as I knew, Consolina kept the things she was most fond of, the things to which she had taken a special fancy. Luckily it was not locked; the lock had long ceased to work. I opened it and indeed, as I had foreseen, found a whole collection of rubbish. Women are like magpies, they collect anything that glitters. What was there *not* in that fibre suitcase! Tin boxes that had contained tea or dry biscuits, pins of yellow metal worth a few halfpence, a sheep made of sugar from last Easter, a blue velvet pincushion, two or three necklaces of coloured glass, a few empty scent-bottles, boxes that had held wedding sweetmeats, a small bunch of ribbons of every colour, most of them short pieces snipped off and dropped on the floor, a broken fountain-pen, a glass ball with a view of St. Peter's, a mother-of-pearl rosary, a quantity of little images of saints and I don't know how many other objects. The thing I was looking for, however—a packet of letters, a photograph—was not there. I went on groping further and, all of a sudden, in an inside pocket, I put my hand on an envelope which had a sort of swelling in it and which was fastened with a pin. I opened it and realized I had made a discovery: it contained a little bunch of golden hair; but this was not hair cut from the head of the beloved to be put into a locket, it was hair that had been left in a brush after a vigorous hair-brushing.

It was this last detail that opened my eyes. Now, you must know that we in Ciociaria do not consider a person beautiful merely because he or she is beautiful; beauty, for us, consists in fair hair, a white skin and blue eyes. It is a question of rarity; and I am sure that in those countries where fair people are in the majority, the dark person is attractive, just because he is unusual. And, as to who the fair man might be who had taken Consolina's fancy—why, the very quality of the hair told me that. It could only be Alfredo, the young Palombini; I had removed similar hair, together with dandruff, from his hairbrush no longer ago than the day before. This young Alfredo was a student, and as refined as his father was coarse and unceremonious; not very studious, however, but a great lover of gramophone records, of English cigarettes and American drinks; and he was one of those fair men who begin to lose their hair in handfuls at twenty and are bald by the time they are thirty. His hair, now, was curly, and he had a big, bare forehead already bald at the temples, prominent pale blue eyes, a nose that drooped down to his mouth and a mouth that curved down over his chin: he looked like a sheep. Furthermore—even if the hair had not sufficed—I now recalled other facts which provided me with proofs of Consolina's passion: for instance, whenever he rang the bell, she would jump up and say: "It's the young master, *I'll* go." Now in that house *I* was the manservant and it was *I* who ought to have gone to the young master. Hitherto I had paid no particular attention to this, but now I understood.

That same evening, in the kitchen, I said to Consolina: "You've taken a fancy to the young master. . . . You silly fool . . . can't you see he looks exactly like a sheep?" Stung to the quick, she turned round on me: "Better a sheep like him than a he-goat like you." This answer gave me all I needed; and that evening I said nothing more; but during the following days I had opportunities of observing that Consolina got little comfort out of the blond young man. Alfredo was a stay-at-home kind of person, and when his father was at the shop and his mother and younger sister had gone out, he would remain in his own room at the far end of the big, gloomy flat; but, however stay-at-home he might be, he neither saw nor took any notice of Consolina. My own opinion, in fact, was that he must have become aware of something, for he insisted on being waited upon by me, and said so more than once, to Consolina's disappointment. He would ask for coffee, or for whisky, or for orange squash, and I would go and find him in his study, a large room which he had done up in the modern manner, with metal and glass furniture. He would be stretched out in an armchair with his feet on the table, on one side; on the other, stretched out in another armchair, would be his girl friend, a tall, thin, dark American with a very white face and a wide red mouth that looked like a wound. This American girl, it so happened, was called Consuelo, which has much the same meaning as Consolina. She was always dressed in tight-fitting trousers, her hair was cut as short as a man's, and indeed she looked like a boy. And would you believe it? They were in each other's company for hours and hours, but I would be willing to swear that they had never exchanged a kiss that you could really call a kiss. The air would be full of cigarette-smoke, and I would go in and put down the tray on the table and they wouldn't give me so much as a glance: they never ceased listening to the gramophone. I said to Consolina: "You're simply wasting your time. . . . That man neither sees you nor hears you. You come from Sgurgola, my dear, and *she* comes from New York. . . . There's a difference, and it's quite obvious."

Consolina was furious, and as she was hardly ever able, one may say, even to set eyes upon her blond young man—since she was doing the cooking and he had expressed the desire that *I* should answer his bell—she laid herself out, first in one way and then in another, to make him understand that she loved him. One day, for instance, she bought a bunch of flowers and coolly walked into his study while he was listening to music, as usual, with his girl friend. "I was given these flowers," she said, "and I thought they would go better in here than in my own room." The American girl immediately exclaimed: "Oh, what lovely flowers!" "D'you like them?" he asked indifferently, without moving; "you take them, then. . . . Consolina, will you wrap them up, and then the Signorina will take them away with her?" Consolina came back, bursting with ill temper, into the kitchen, and wanted to throw the flowers into the dustbin. I had to snatch them from her; then I wrapped them in paper and took them back again to the study.

One day, early in the afternoon, when the house was empty and no one was at home except the young master, suddenly the bell rang—but several times, in a special sort of way. I went along, and even before I had knocked at the door he came out, his hand pressed against his stomach. He was feeling ill and moaning loudly, and Consolina, who was always on the alert, rushed out of the kitchen and took him by the arm and he allowed her to do so and went with her into the bathroom where he vomited for a good five minutes. Consolina supported his head and kept repeating: "You must go to bed"; and he went on moaning and let her do as she liked. In the twinkling of an eye she had got his bed ready, helped him to undress and tucked him up; then she ran into the kitchen to heat water for a hot water-bottle. I watched her and saw the cheerful, relaxed, contented expression on her face: for her this illness was a piece of good luck, at last she could be near him. And I said to myself: that's what women are like, they take advantage even of an illness. So pleased was she that, while waiting for the water to boil, and while, through the open door of his room, the sick man's voice could be heard repeating over and over: "Oh God. . . . Oh my God. . . . Oh God," she started quietly humming a tune. At that moment there was a ring at the front door.

She went to open it, telling me to watch the water. What happened then I have never exactly discovered. It seems that when Consolina went to open the front door she found herself face to face with the American girl. Consolina jubilantly told her that the young master was ill and could not see her, and the other woman replied that, on the contrary, she had every intention of seeing him. Consolina, unwilling to allow the young man's illness to slip through her fingers, so to speak, told her to go away, but she insisted on coming in. Consolina then pushed her out, and the other one, in turn, pushed Consolina in. In short, one thing led to another, and finally they seized hold of each other by the hair. The next thing was that I heard loud, quarrelling voices, and then screams and then one or two thuds and then sounds of chairs falling over and furniture being pushed out of place. I rushed into the hall; Consolina and Consuelo, tightly clasped together, their hands gripping each other's hair, were rolling on the floor, struggling and screaming. "Miserable, worthless woman!" shouted Consolina; and the American girl answered: "Let me go, you crazy idiot, let me go!" Standing upright, one of them may have come from Sgurgola and the other from New York, I don't deny that: but on the floor they were nothing but a couple of women, a couple of fishwives, in fact, pitching into each other for love of a man. In the meantime the sick man had appeared in his pyjamas in the doorway of his room and kept on repeating in a feeble voice: "What on earth is happening? . . . Oh God, oh God . . . what on earth is happening? . . . Do separate them, for goodness' sake!"—all the time pressing his two hands to his stomach.

Well, well, the American girl ended up minus a handful of hair which got left behind in Consolina's fist; and Consolina's face was covered all over with scratches from the American girl's beautiful red nails. That same afternoon Consolina packed up her few belongings and departed. I left the place too: I belonged to the same village as Consolina and her behaviour cast a shadow of unpopularity over me as well. But I did not leave until a few days later and for some time did not see Consolina. Recently I met her by chance in the gardens near the station. She had had her hair cut short like a man's, in the same style as Consuelo's, with the result that her cheeks looked plumper and redder than ever; otherwise she was still the same. She was with an undersized youth, who was treating her to a coconut ice at one of the refreshment stalls. I noticed that he had a fair complexion and blue eyes. But he was wearing a shaggy peaked cap, so that his head could not be seen. I would be ready to swear, however, that underneath his cap he had golden hair.

A DOUBLE GAME

"UMBERTO does this; Umberto does that; Umberto's top of his class at school; Umberto's mother says they're giving him a medal; Umberto is working; Umberto brings his money home; Umberto, out of his own money, has bought a motor-scooter; Umberto is buying a car." At all ages, from the baby's high chair and bib onwards, I have always found Umberto getting in my way. It was natural: we lived in the same building in Via Candia, and the two small flats, the one belonging to Umberto's father, who kept the poulterer's shop on the ground floor, and our own, gave on to the same landing, and our mothers were friends and we two grew up together. It was natural, I say, that, when I grew up into a shirker and an idler and a loafer, my mother should point to Umberto as a model. I could have said, it is true, that my little finger was worth more than the whole of Umberto, with his sly, priggish, mean character; but what would have been the use? As everyone knows, mothers are all the same, and if the world was made as mothers would like it to be, it would be entirely made up of nonentities, in fact of sly, priggish, mean characters like Umberto.

I had a grudge against Umberto, but our relations were quite polite: when we met, we greeted each other and exchanged news. The relations, in fact, of a cold war, between people who await the first opportunity to pick a quarrel. This opportunity came on the very same day that I got the sack, for inefficiency, from the vulcanite works in Via Dandolo. As I was going downstairs with my mother's words still in my ears: "My son, you'll break my heart. . . . Now look at Umberto—there's a good son for you. . . . Model yourself on Umberto, my son . . .", I came across Umberto, who was also going out. I at once stopped him and said: "I say, do tell me, I suppose you always do everything well?" "What d'you mean?" "I mean, it never happens to you that you make a mistake, that you do what you oughtn't to do, that—let us say—you gamble away your week's money?" Would you believe it? Anyone else in Umberto's place would have taken offence. But he, his sly face assuming an expression of indulgence, placed his hand on my shoulder and said: "Peppe, do as I do and you'll see you'll be all right." I answered furiously: "Take that hand off my shoulder. . . . Anyhow, I didn't stop you in order to ask your advice. It's I who want to give *you* some advice: keep off Clara; she's practically engaged to *me*." "*Practically* engaged?" "Anyhow, she's my girl and you've got to leave her alone—see?" "What fault is it of mine if . . . ?" "That's enough: forewarned is forearmed."

In order to understand these words of mine you must know that at that time I was running after Clara, a girl who also lived in Via Candia, in a building identical with the one in which I lived, that is to say, old and ugly, with the same huge courtyard as big as a *piazza* and the same staircases numbered from A to F. On one of these staircases was the little flat belonging to Clara's mother, who was called, or called herself, Dolores, and who practised the odd profession of palmistry. She was a woman of about fifty, fragile, sickly, white as a ghost, with a face that looked as if it was covered with flour and two black eyes that made this face look like a plaster mask. Poor thing: she had been rich, or so she said, and now she was making shift with fortune-telling by cards and hand-reading. People say she was good at it, too; and besides the women of Via Candia, ladies, both married and unmarried, used to come to her from the fashionable neighbourhoods. As for Clara, she was the exact opposite of her mother. She was healthy, well-groomed, beautiful, with a bright expression, clear, smiling; eyes like two quiet stars, and a lovely pale pink mouth showing, when she smiled, teeth as white as peeled almonds—the mouth of a little girl who has not yet learned to smile coquettishly. Clara worked in an office as a typist and stenographer, and it appears that she was very good at her job. When she was at home and her mother was receiving clients she sat at the table in the kitchen, tapping at her typewriter or studying English grammar. Clara, as I say, was quiet. I can say now, she was so quiet that, much as I loved her, I could not help comparing her secretly to still waters. Not so much the proverbial still waters that run deep; rather, a beautiful calm sea, in August, at night, with the moon and stars reflected in it and making you long to make love in the old-fashioned way, hands clasped together, your arm round her waist, your head on her shoulder. Oh yes, still waters she certainly was—and in both senses.

That same day I told Clara I had confronted Umberto. She started laughing gently: "Is it possible you're jealous of a type like Umberto?" "Well, he's a man, after all." "Yes, but what a man!" Feeling slightly comforted already, I asked her to explain what she meant; and, still laughing in her charming, quiet, child-like way, she went on: "Oh, I don't know. . . . In the first place, physically: he looks like Fagiolino in the puppet-theatre, the one who always takes the knocks: with that long face and hair like a pin-cushion. And if you knew what a bore he is! He thinks the world of himself: *he* does everything well, *he*'s intelligent, he's this and he's that. . . . He's always talking about himself . . . and besides, he has certain ideas: according to him, a wife must stay at home, do the cooking and look after the children—and woe betide her if she so much as speaks to another man, even if it's her brother. I'd die rather than marry him." In short, she gave such a bad account of Umberto that, in the end, I was completely reassured; and I gave her leave to see him as much as she liked.

From then on, I felt I was avenging myself day by day for all the occasions on which my mother had held up Umberto as a model to me. My mother had placed him upon a pedestal; Clara, on the contrary, threw him off it. "I really don't like that man," she said to me. "I went with him to the yard where he's foreman: he spoke to the workmen as if they were dirt. The engineer arrived, and all at once he became a different person—humble, attentive, fawning." Or: "Let me tell you the latest: he gave a hundred lire to a beggar, and why d'you think it was? Because it was a forged note." Or again: "He has certain habits that I simply can't bear: when he thinks I'm not looking, he starts picking his nose." Clara abused him so much that sometimes I almost reached the point of defending Umberto, if only for the pleasure of hearing her rub it in. "But he's a good son," I would say. And she: "But he treats his mother like a slave." "But," I said, "he takes his money home." "Takes his money home?" she said; "he never does, now; he puts it in the bank." "He works hard," I said. "Works hard?" said she; "he's a shirker. He likes to make other people work and then take advantage of them."

By now I was so sure of Clara that I said to her, one day, that it was fitting that we two should now regularize our position and become officially engaged. She said at once: "I was thinking of that too but I didn't dare say so to you. But these things have to be done properly: you must go and tell Mother; you know her already." So we agreed that I should go and see her mother that same evening; in the meantime she would see Umberto, but for the last time. "I really can't bear to be with him," she said; "he wears me out." I approved this plan, not without a touch of pity for poor Umberto who wasn't expecting it. And at about seven o'clock I left home, crossed Via Candia and entered the main door of Clara's block of flats.

On the third floor of staircase D, Signora Dolores' door was ajar; I pushed it open and went in. I found myself in a tiny waiting-room, full of people. There were two or three bareheaded women, fellow-inhabitants of Via Candia; there was a good-looking dark girl, who lived in the same quarter and whom I knew by sight; there was a middle-aged lady, rather worn-looking and heavily made up, wrapped in a brown fur coat. Business, evidently, was good, I thought as I sat down and took an illustrated magazine from the table, and Signora Dolores was doing well, making plenty of money, in fact. I waited for some time and then the door opened and a smart young woman came out, who kissed Signora Dolores effusively on both cheeks, saying: "Thank you, thank you, my dear." Clara's mother, in black silk Japanese pyjamas with a coloured dragon embroidered on the corner of the jacket and a cigarette-holder as long as your arm between her teeth, threw me a glance and said: "Rinaldi, just one moment and then you can come in." She ushered in the middle-aged lady with the fur coat, and disappeared; and it occurred to me, for some reason—possibly from the tone of her voice—that she did not know of the proposal I was going to make to her. Then I had a bright idea: I would make her tell my fortune, to see whether my marriage to Clara was indicated in my hand; and immediately afterwards I would make my declaration. I smiled at this thought and awaited my turn with impatience. After a quarter of an hour the lady with the fur coat slipped out in a mysterious, discreet, hurried manner and went away. And Signora Dolores beckoned me in.

I knew that, for lack of space, she worked in her bedroom; all the same I was surprised. It was a long room, in half-shadow, containing a big double bed covered with a piece of yellow material; and I could not help reflecting that Clara slept in that big bed with her mother. At the window there was a curtain with openwork embroidery of birds and baskets of flowers; near the window, a small table on which lay a pack of cards and a magnifying glass; the whole room was full of little pieces of furniture, knick-knacks, photographs with the signatures of important clients, testimonials, souvenirs. Signora Dolores, without a word, sat down at the table and made me sit opposite her. The first thing she did was to take a match, light it and set fire to a small piece of black paper, from which there quickly rose a white, scented smoke. "It's *carta d'Armenia*," she said in her refined, tired voice; "d'you smell the scent of it? Well, Rinaldi, what can I do for you?" I replied that I had come to have my fortune told; and she, having put down her cigarette-holder on the ash-tray, took my hand, held the magnifying glass over it and examined it at length.

Some moments passed and then, in an almost horrified tone of voice, she asked: "What sort of a man am I speaking to?" Disconcerted, I asked. "Why?" "Well," she said, "because this is the hand of a man who is very fond—altogether too fond—of women." "After all," I said, "I'm a young man." "Yes," she answered, "but there's a limit to these things. And you don't seem to have that limit. Your heart is like an artichoke." "If you say so. . . ." "It's your hand that says so: you're a Don Juan." "Oh well, don't let's exaggerate." "I'm not exaggerating at all; look at your heart line: it's like a chain—every link a woman." "And otherwise?" "Otherwise—nothing. Little luck in business, little will to work, little seriousness of character, little sense of responsibility." Beginning to be annoyed, I said: "You find nothing but faults in me." "They're not faults," she said, "they're characteristics. Certainly if I were a mother, I wouldn't let my daughter marry you." This made me angry, and I told her: "Well, have a look and see whether there's a marriage line." Scrupulously she took up the magnifying glass again, turned my hand in every direction and then said: "Adventures, as many as you like, but no marriage." "Signora Dolores," I said, "let's understand each other; I didn't come to you to have my hand read but to tell you that your daughter and I love one another and that we decided to-day to become engaged."

At these words she very calmly put down the magnifying glass and replied: "But, my poor boy. . . ." "What?" "My poor boy, the hand, as always, tells the truth: you're not getting married—not at present, anyhow." "And why, seeing that Clara and I are in agreement?" "You're not in agreement. . . . You think you're in agreement with Clara, but Clara is not in agreement with you." "Who says so?" "*I* say so: Clara is already engaged." "But when . . . ?" "She's been engaged for a week, to Umberto Pompei. Clara hadn't the courage to tell you because she's a shy girl, and besides, she's kind-hearted and hates to hurt anybody. But she was worrying; you don't know how worried she's been. And I must say that on this occasion Umberto has shown himself to be a real gentleman: Clara asked his leave to go on seeing you for a few days longer, until there had been a full explanation between you; and he agreed at once. I don't know how many engaged couples, in such a situation, would have acted in this way."

I was dumbfounded. And when she said to me, hypocritically: "Well, now let's have a look at the cards: I bet some more women will turn up," mechanically I took the thousand-lire fee from my pocket, placed it on the table and went out without a word. I felt stunned, as though Signora Dolores, instead of reading my hand, had hit me over the head with a hammer; and into the midst of this stunned feeling there began to creep a number of suspicions, like so many snakes which gradually awake inside a heap of straw, in the warmth of the sun. So, then, while I had thought I was acting generously towards Umberto in letting him see Clara, in reality it had been *he* who acted generously towards *me* in allowing Clara to see me; so, while I had enjoyed hearing Clara abuse Umberto, *he,* perhaps, on his side, had enjoyed hearing Clara abuse *me*; so Clara had, in short, been playing a double game the whole time; only, in the end, it was I who had been fooled. While these thoughts were going through my head I must have looked thoroughly upset, for all at once the good-looking dark girl who was waiting in the ante-room gave me a "pss pss", as one does to a cat, at the same time beckoning me with a glance. I stooped down and she asked me: "What is it? Does she say nasty things?" "Very nasty," I replied, "for me, anyhow." Promptly she rose to her feet. "Then I shan't go in," she said; "I'm so afraid she might give me some bad news." Mechanically I went out of the door and she followed me.

On the landing, I looked at her sideways. She was very dark, and her hair, cut short almost like a man's, seemed as it were to caress, to encircle her round face, continuing, as it did, in a faint down like a shadow, round her cheeks and chin. I thought her very pretty, and she, as though guessing my thought, turned towards me and said, smiling: "You don't know me, but I know you! We live in the same building."

Suddenly, from the staircase below, there came the sound of a silvery laugh, childish and limpid, Clara's laugh; and at the same time, the rather shrill sound of Umberto's voice. Without hesitating, I put my arm round the girl's waist. "What's your name?" I asked.

"My name's Angela", she said, giving me a bold glance. At that same moment Clara and Umberto passed close to us and I saw that Clara had seen us thus entwined, and that she modestly lowered her eyes. "Well, take that, then!" I thought to myself bitterly. They went on up the stairs and we went down. I took my arm from Angela's waist and said to her: "Angela dear, let's go and have a drink to celebrate our meeting." She took my arm and we went out together into the street.

THE CHINESE VASE

AS long as there's life there's hope, so they say; but I, during that horrible black winter of rain and misery, had let myself go all to pieces, partly from tiredness and partly from the job I was doing; and in spite of not having yet reached the age of twenty-five, I had no hope left. I'm not ugly; on the contrary I'm strong and dark and tall, I'm a good-looking chap; but owing to my neglect of myself I could be considered, by this time, to be really ugly. I shaved and had my hair cut perhaps once a month, perhaps not, so that I looked like a savage; I wore an overcoat that was green with age and all darns and patches, a high-necked black sweater, torn, frayed trousers, and cheap shoes that had lost all colour and shape. And so, when I trundled my handcart round the streets, crying out in an ogreish kind of voice: "Any bottles . . . Any bottles to sell . . . ?" it always happened that some woman sitting outside the door of her house would catch hold of her naughty child and say: "Now behave yourself—or I'll call the bottle-man and sell you to him and he'll take you away with his bottles." I frightened people, in fact; but I enjoyed frightening them because I had become degraded and I wanted to reach the lowest depths of degradation. And meanwhile the winter seemed to go on for ever, and the sky never cleared and it never stopped raining, and I seemed to be dragging myself, with all my rags and my hand-barrow, along a tunnel with no openings and no light, somewhere under the ground.

However, going round like this with a barrow and collecting bottles and old crockery and other rubbish, I had managed, in spite of being so down at heel, to get myself a girl friend. But since I was utterly degraded and had no hope left, I had taken up with the ugliest girl in the whole of Rome or indeed in the whole of Italy. She was called Marietta and was servant to an old gentleman who lived all alone in an old house in Via Giulia. Marietta had a face like the muzzle of a Pekinese dog: round, black eyes with an anxious expression in them, a little squashed nose, a mouth as big as a baker's oven. Though ugly in the face Marietta, to make up for it, had a very good figure: she was tall, with a well-developed bust, a waist so slim you could take it between your two hands, rounded hips, long straight legs with slender ankles, so that I used to say to her jokingly: "You ought to go about with a mask on . . . you'd be a great success." Marietta, albeit she was so ugly, took life seriously—very seriously, in fact—and wanted to get married. For some reason or other, perhaps just because she was so ugly and I, as I have said, wanted to degrade myself, I asked her, only the second time we met, to be my wife. And, since I was now on the downward path, I would truly have got married at once if it hadn't been for the question of money. Getting married isn't enough, you have to set up house. Just try setting up house on nothing but bottles and old crockery and rubbish, and then you'll see what I mean.

Everyone knows how these things go. She started getting me to come to the house when the master of the house was not there. The apartment, big and dark, was on the first floor of the building. I don't know where the owner slept; the place was like a museum, with lots and lots of rooms leading out of one another. In these rooms, apart from ordinary furniture, there were, in particular, numbers of glass cases, and in these glass cases quantities of vases, for the master of the house had a passion for vases. He did, in fact, more or less what I myself did; except that I collected vases, crocks and bottles in order to re-sell them, whereas he placed his vases and crocks and bottles in glass cases.

Marietta, then, first brought me into the house so as to talk to me. Later, one day when I was hungry, she gave me a piece of bread and a glass of wine. Finally she plucked up courage and prepared complete suppers for me—suppers to make your mouth water, for she was a splendid cook. She was the only one in the house, and she did everything; and so, when the master was out, there was no danger of being caught. I used to leave my barrow in the courtyard and go upstairs; she would open the door and then lead me into the kitchen. Whilst I was eating, with the appetite of a wolf, still wearing my overcoat, she would gaze at me with her ugly, anxious eyes, like a dog watching its master as he eats, ready to snatch at the scrap he flings it. And she too, like the dog, was expecting something from me—a caress, a kind word, an affectionate glance. She was hungry for love, poor Marietta, and was grateful to me if I so much as called her "dear". Secretly, however, I often said to myself: "How ugly she is! Is it possible I have to marry such an ugly woman?"

She would keep on sighing, however, as she watched me eat; and I, knowing well the meaning of these sighs, became impatient. "What d'you want me to do?" I asked. "Don't you know that bottles pay very little? We must have patience. Gradually I'll collect the money and then we'll get married." To this she made no reply, but poured me out some wine and then started watching me again. One day, however, when she was sighing as usual, I said to her coolly: "Listen, I was talking some time ago to a friend of mine, Gesualdo, who has a shop in Via di Parione . . . He says that if I bring him one of these vases out of the glass cases here, he thinks he can probably sell it to an antique-dealer and get me a good price for it. What d'you think?" I saw her gazing at me with her round eyes, just like a dog when its master asks it to do something it doesn't understand. Then she said: "But that's what's called stealing." "Oh well," I said, "don't let's exaggerate. He has such a lot of vases . . . he won't even notice. My idea is to take that vase that's all alone in the centre case and replace it with another one like it which I'd take from a crowded case. How would he ever notice?" I went on talking in this way, explaining how, with the money from the vase, we should be able to take a step forward towards setting up house; and all the time she kept her head bent and appeared to be reflecting. Finally she lifted her face and I saw it was all wet with tears: she was crying bitterly. "I've always been honest," she stammered; "if I take this vase I shall no longer be able to call myself honest . . . The master trusts me completely and I should be betraying his trust . . . I shouldn't even be able to look at myself in the glass." "That may be an advantage," I said—the words slipped out without my thinking—"for you'll never see anything beautiful in a mirror." At this she started crying even harder, and I, sorry for what I had said, gave her a kiss and went on: "We won't do anything, then . . . and don't cry: to me you're the loveliest woman in the world." Then she smiled at me; and her smile made her look even uglier, just as a sky full of big black clouds is made to look uglier by a ray of sunshine.

But during the following days I started insisting again that we ought to take the vase. I don't know why I was so set on it: at the bottom of my heart I didn't really want to marry Marietta. Perhaps it was because I had become so degraded and, as I have already said, I wanted to reach the lowest depths of degradation; perhaps it was because I took pleasure in being cruel to Marietta; perhaps there was some other reason that I myself didn't know. Anyhow, I tormented her, telling her that if she didn't steal the vase it was a sign that she didn't love me; and I went on about it so much that in the end she made up her mind to it. But how strange women are: one moment she was weeping at the mere thought of losing her honesty, a moment later she had not only agreed to do what I wanted but, having broken loose, seemed actually to be enjoying the idea. It happened to be a morning when the master of the house had gone out, having been invited out to lunch. Marietta took me by the hand, led me into the principal room and pressed a switch: all at once, in the semi-darkness, the glass case in the middle of the room that contained the solitary vase was lit up—that and nothing else. I went over and looked at the vase: it was a piece of crockery of the most ordinary kind, without any gilding or ornament, of a dull, muddy green, with a big belly and a thin neck, just like one of those pots which they use in the country for carrying water. This pot was standing on a base made of some precious wood, carved and perforated, and under the base there was fine red velvet; but the pot, in spite of the base and the velvet, remained nothing more than a pot. I said to Marietta: "It's all very well, but a pot like that, as far as I can see, isn't worth more than three hundred lire." "What are you talking about?" she replied. "That's a unique piece, Chinese, and he values it like the apple of his eye . . . and when people come to see it, they turn on the light as I did just now and they all stand looking at it with their mouths open and my master's as proud as a peacock." Well, to cut a long story short, I took my knife out of my pocket, forced open the glass case with the blade and took out the pot. Then we went to another case which contained perhaps a hundred similar pots, took one which from a distance looked just like the first and put it on the base, in the centre case. Finally Marietta wrapped up the pot for me in a newspaper, I gave her a kiss and went out.

My hand was still on the handle of the door when suddenly, on the staircase, appeared the owner of the vases. I knew him by sight—an old man with drooping moustaches and a little white beard round a mouth like a black hole; he looked like a seal. He had a pair of flashing eyes; and immediately I felt these threatening eyes fixed upon me in suspicion as I held the vase in my arms; I made a movement as if I were frightened, and it was this that undid me. "Who are you? What have you in that parcel . . . ? A vase, one of my vases," he began shouting as he came up the last few steps. He made as if to seize hold of me with his claw-like hand, but I jumped away from him and he fell full length on the stairs, hitting his nose. Without turning round I ran down the stairs four at a time, rushed into the courtyard, put the pot amongst my bottles, pulled the tarpaulin over them and fled, pushing my barrow in front of me.

It was pouring with rain, and this was a lucky chance, for Via Giulia was deserted as far as the eye could see; no one saw me come out of the house and run off pushing the barrow in the streaming rain. I turned into a side lane, reached Via Monserrato, also deserted because of the rain, went along one stretch of it, turned off again through Via del Pellegrino and finally came out into Corso Vittorio. Here I slowed down so as not to be conspicuous, and then went on by Via del Governo Vecchio towards Via di Parione, where my friend Gesualdo had his shop.

But in Via di Parione disappointment was awaiting me: it was late by now, well past one o'clock, and Gesualdo's shop was shut. It was raining a little less now, and automatically, more from force of habit than anything, I shouted in my usual way: "Any bottles . . . any bottles to sell", as I pushed my handcart over the shining cobbles of the street. I realized, however, as I shouted, that my mouth was dry and sticky, that my heart was fluttering and my legs unsteady. I passed in front of an eating-house and thought it would be a good thing to get some food to restore my strength and help me sort out my ideas. No sooner said than done: I put the handcart into a recess in the wall of a building and went inside.

There was scarcely anybody there, and I placed myself in a dark corner and ordered lamb with potatoes and a quarter of wine. Then, after the first mouthful and the first sip of wine, all of a sudden I was seized with a kind of intolerance. "Here I am," I said to myself; "I've really reached the lowest depths of degradation, as I wished to do: I'm a thief, and I was seen, and they'll be searching for me. And I'm engaged to the ugliest woman in Rome, and since I shall have to hide, I shall soon be without a job too." This thought kept me in a stupor for I don't know how long, my eyes staring into the void and my fork suspended in the air. Then I finished eating, paid the bill and left.

It had stopped raining, and a ray of sunshine fell between the dark buildings, lighting up the stonework and cobbles and gratings. I at once saw my barrow, a few steps farther on, with a troop of small boys round it doing I knew not what. But, as I approached, they scattered and fled, like so many sparrows, and then I saw that the tarpaulin had been pulled back, that the Chinese vase was no longer wrapped up and that there was a stopper in the neck of the vase. I had no time to think, for there was a sudden violent bang and something in the barrow exploded, and the thing which had exploded into a hundred pieces was the vase. Meanwhile the little boys were screaming with joy as they fled down the street, and I was standing with my arms hanging limp, looking at the shambles of the vase and the bottles. It's an old trick: you put a piece of carbide inside a bottle, spit on it, cork up the bottle, and in a short time it explodes. An old trick; but now the vase had gone.

I realized however, almost at once, that it was not only the vase that had gone but also that whole period of my life during which I had been a bottle-man and had loved Marietta and had stolen the vase. I left the handcart where it was, and it seemed strange no longer to have my arms stretched out to push it, and I went off to see my friend Gesualdo who lived not far off, in Via della Pace. When he saw me looking so upset, he asked me what had happened. "Nothing, nothing," I answered; "all I need is a wash-tub of hot water and a piece of soap and a razor. And then, if you really want to make me a present, find me a pair of trousers, a clean shirt and a tie . . . I'll repay everything as soon as I can."

When I left Gesualdo's house I was a different person; and this different person was now filled with hope instead of despair; and instead of going back to the place where I had so far lived, I went off to the other side of the town and found a lodging there with a family of my acquaintance. A few days later the weather was fine, and I, in a waiter's white jacket, clean and well shaved, fresh and brisk, was serving the customers in the garden of the Osteria di Malagrotta, twenty kilometres out of Rome. Marietta I have never seen again; but I don't want to be harshly judged on that account. It was not treacherousness, nor wickedness, nor cowardice. It was simply like turning the page of a book and discovering suddenly that the chapter is finished.

SILVANO AND ROMILDO

I AM not malicious; in fact, I am exactly the opposite, so good-natured and so foolishly credulous that it makes people try to take advantage of me even when they don't mean to; and Romildo *did* take advantage of me. His physical appearance—his red hair and freckled face and blue eyes that sparkled like a madman's—proclaimed his moral character, and every time he could he set some sort of a trap for me; and I, being an easy-going person, always fell into it. Would you like an example? Coming out of the newspaper offices, some time ago, with a bundle of the latest edition on my arm, I asked him: "Romildo, what news do we cry to-day? There's a complete blank." "You idiot," he replied promptly, "in the Roman news items there's the attempted suicide of a Countess." "Attempted suicide," I objected; "if at least she was dead . . . But they used a stomach pump on her and now she's already back at home." "Yes," he said, "but she's a Countess." Well, I allowed him to persuade me; and, as soon as I reached the Arcade, I started crying: "Attempted suicide of a Countess . . . full details!" If you could have seen Romildo! He rushed out from the other side, yelling at the top of his voice: "Crisis in the Government! Resignations! Resignations!" Naturally my Countess couldn't compete with his Government crisis, so he sold all his papers and I was left with mine. Later I took the newspaper and, by searching very carefully, discovered at the bottom of a column that such-and-such a person had written that, if certain facts were true and certain persons did certain things, then and only then the Government might possibly find itself in a state of crisis.

This is only one example among hundreds. You may say: why? There's no reason; the only reason lay in his malicious character which had to have an outlet; and, since malicious people vent their malice on those who are not malicious, Romildo vented his on me.

And yet I was not angry with him; in fact—I don't know why —I tried all the time to be friends with him, to be fond of him and make him fond of me. It must be admitted that Romildo had betwitched me: the worse he treated me, the more he repelled me with his maliciousness, the more attached I became to him. This reached a point when he said to me, one day: "Silvano, I don't understand you. I treat you like dirt, and instead of getting angry with me you're still friendly. What have you got in your veins? Water? Haven't you any dignity or pride? Really I don't understand you." I answered him frankly: "I don't know how it is . . . but I can't hate you. In fact, the worse you treat me, the more attached to you I become." "Let's see, then," he said: "even if I told you I had taken Gesuina away from you?" I turned scarlet, and then stammered: "Yes, even that." "Well," he concluded, "take note, then, that I really have taken her away from you, and let's say no more about it."

At the time I didn't believe him, thinking that it was just one of his usual pieces of malice; but soon I discovered it was true. Gesuina was one of those girls who go round restaurants and cafés selling bunches of flowers, and I considered her as being more or less engaged to me. She was no beauty, Gesuina; rather small, with a round, pale, jaded-looking face, graceful in figure but with over-robust legs, owing perhaps to the great amount of walking that she did all day long, with hair that was always unkempt, dressed always in a skin-tight, heavily-darned pullover and a shapeless skirt; she was not beautiful but she was attractive, perhaps because she looked at the same time like a child and a woman. Gesuina, among flower-girls, was rather like Romildo among newspaper-sellers: malicious, with a quick tongue, more persistent than a mosquito, capable of pursuing a young couple right up Via Veneto until the young man, in order not to look mean, bought a bunch of flowers from her. I had met and spoken to her when I was selling papers in that part of the town; I had believed her to be fond of me, and had trustingly introduced Romildo to her. As I said, I did not, at the time, believe that he had pinched her from me. But, some days later, soon after sunset, as I was looking for a quiet place in the Borghese Gardens to eat my sandwich in peace, I came right on them. They were sitting on a seat in a dark avenue. She had her half-empty basket on her knees, he the newspapers he had failed to sell; and they were locked in a close embrace, like people in love. In my astonishment, I could not help exclaiming: "Why, you're kissing, are you?" Romildo, hearing my voice, slowly disengaged himself and said: "Didn't I tell you I'd taken her away from you? Why didn't you believe it?" I said nothing; I felt as if I had been hit over the head, and I sat down, dazed, on the seat beside them. Gesuina, seeing me so limp, became irritated for some reason or other: "Well, aren't you going to say anything?" she asked. "Your friend steals your girl and you say nothing? What sort of a man are you? Why don't you stand up to him and tell him what you think of him?" I answered, and it was the truth: "I don't think anything." Then she turned fierce, and said: "Well, I'll tell you what *I* think. I think you're a coward . . . and I think Romildo's a thousand times better than you." Romildo laughed and remarked: "Gesuina's right: but I'd very much like to know what sort of stuff you're made of." "I'm made as I am," I said, "and I can't change myself. Good-bye." And I got up and went away.

After that day, strange though it may seem, we became inseparable, Gesuina, Romildo and I. I clung even more closely to Romildo and to my friendship with him, perhaps because I had paid so dearly for it, actually with my feeling for Gesuina; and besides, I am forced to believe that those two, in order to love each other better, needed to see me suffer, for they sought me out and would not leave me in peace. So the old relationship continued, except that now there were three of us and instead of only one malicious person let loose upon me I had two. But whereas, as I said, I still had the same friendly feelings towards Romildo, for Gesuina I had no feelings at all, not even hostile ones. I was indifferent to her, and she felt this; and, since women forgive everything except indifference, she was more vindictive towards me than was Romildo.

The evening papers do not come out on Sundays, so we decided, since it was March and the days were getting longer, to go somewhere out of Rome, all three of us. We took the Ostia train at San Paolo Station, got off at Ostia Scavi and then started off by a country path behind the Castle, which led down to the Tiber. We had brought sandwiches for our lunch, and I was feeling cheerful, for it was also one of the first spring days. The sky was full of grey clouds which never stopped still for a moment, so that the sun came out every now and then; the air was warm, damp and buzzing with insects; a slight wind was blowing, carrying off the white petals of the almond-trees that stood in the fields. "D'you know," I said, feeling contented, "I prefer a day like this, when it's almost raining, to a really sunny day. I don't know why, I feel happy." "I don't," replied Gesuina; "on days like this I feel nervy . . . I might do anything." "Who with?" asked Romildo provocatively; "with me or with Silvano?" "Idiot," she said, in her harsh voice, taking him by the arm and giving him a kiss.

We walked for some time along the top of a dyke below which was a ditch full of thick, grey running water. The frogs that lurked in it were croaking loudly—a sign that it was soon going to rain; all round there was nothing but fields, fields, fields, with that spring grass which makes you want to eat it, so green and fresh is it; the Tiber was not to be seen, but we could already make out the trees, shimmering with tiny green leaves, that grew on its banks. At last, still following the path, we came down to the river. It was a deserted spot, with nothing but bare fields on both sides of the Tiber, and there was a flock of big, dirty sheep intently grazing. At the point where the path came to an end, on the river bank, there was a small hut with the framework for a fishing-net, but there was no net, only the skeleton hanging over the water; and as we drew near we saw that the hut, half hidden amongst the willow-trees, was a mere ruin of rotting planks. We sat down on the bank, in the shelter of the hut, facing the Tiber which flowed right below our feet, livid and swollen and fearsomely deep; and there we unpacked our sandwiches. Beside the landing-stage belonging to the hut and tied to one of the posts supporting it, was a flat-bottomed boat with its oars lying inside it. Just in order to say something, I remarked: "I should love to go very slowly down to the sea in that boat; how wonderful it would be!"

Romildo, his mouth full, answered: "Well, go on, then; we're not stopping you."

"Oh, I was only talking," I replied.

But Gesuina broke in: "But we're talking seriously . . . Why d'you hang on to us like this? Why d'you butt in? Why on earth d'you come with us? Why don't you go away?"

Gesuina was always like that: fierce, aggressive. I don't know why, but that day, for the first time, her hostile tone wounded me and it seemed to me that I very nearly hated her. But, as usual, I said nothing. Romildo was now eating his sandwich in a characteristically wayward manner, twisting his curly red head backwards and forwards as he bit into it, as though he wanted to kiss the bread. Finally he said: "Silvano, you say you're my friend. Well, prove it to me; there's a way you can prove it."

"What's that?" I enquired hopefully.

"Kill somebody. Commit a really good crime. Then you'll give me the chance to shout some interesting news."

This made me feel seriously angry, if for no other reason than that they wanted to torment me even at this moment, when all I asked was to eat in peace and enjoy the country. I said furiously: "If I had to kill anybody, I'd kill you; *then* you wouldn't have the satisfaction of shouting the news."

"Bah!"

Gesuina said maliciously: "His bark's worse than his bite."

Raising my voice, I cried: "I don't bark . . . But take notice, if I bite, I bite in earnest."

She looked at me sideways, contemptuously: "Clear off, then. No one believes you—you're just a coward."

This made my blood boil. "You be quiet," I warned her. "Or the first person I bite will be you."

Then she made a gesture of calculated offensiveness. She stretched out her leg towards me, with its muscular calf, saying: "Come on then, bite me."

It was a bad moment. "Here's my bite," I said; and I slapped her in the face. She jumped up at once, her whole face contorted with hatred, and rushed off into the field, amongst the sheep. I was dumbfounded at seeing her run like that, like a lunatic; but then I understood. In a moment she stooped down, picked up a stone and hurled it at me, while the sheep fled in all directions. I dodged it, and the stone hit Romildo, just at the moment when, laughing, he was biting his sandwich. It hit him on the head, the sandwich fell on the ground, he gave a roar and, instead of going for Gesuina, he seized the stone and rushed at me, his arm raised. I was frightened; I ran off towards the hut, up the little ladder, and on to the landing-stage. Gesuina, some way away, was shouting: "Kill him, kill him!" Romildo was now coming straight at me, but I calculated the speed of his attack and jumped aside. He ran against the hand-rail of the landing-stage which was all broken and decayed; the hand-rail gave way and he fell into the river.

Gesuina had stopped shouting "Kill him!", but had started running away along the river bank, frightened, without looking back. Romildo had fallen into the water in front of the landing-stage and was now clinging to one of the supporting posts, but he was a long way from the bank and the strong current was flowing over his shoulders and striking against his head. I leant over, putting out my hand and saying "Hang on", but the landing-stage was too high; and so, resolutely, calculating the distance, I jumped down off the landing-stage into the flat-bottomed boat underneath. The boat rocked under my weight and for a moment I thought I was going to fall into the water too; but I recovered myself, took up one of the oars and held it out to Romildo. He seized hold of it, then, puffing and struggling, succeeded in getting close to the boat and holding on to the side. I pulled him up, gradually; and finally he sat down in the stern, streaming with water, and looked at me.

The croaking of the frogs was no longer audible, and in the silence a fine rain had started falling on the branches of the willow-tree above us, and this rain did my soul good and I felt a new man, seeing that after all Romildo was safe. Soaked and panting, he was looking at me, and I looked at him, and Gesuina had run away and was no longer there. All at once I asked: "Will you tell me why you've such a grudge against me?"

I saw him hesitate, and it gave me hope. After all, I had returned good for evil, I had saved him. Then he gave an unpleasant smile and said: "It's understood then, isn't it?"

"What d'you mean?"

"It's understood that you'll commit a really good crime; and then I'll be able to shout the news."

You see? He was dripping wet, he had been on the point of

drowning, I had saved his life; yet he still persisted in his malice. I was struck not so much by what he said as by his obstinacy. Suddenly I was on my feet again: somehow or other I had unhitched an oar and was threatening him with it. "Go away," I said; "otherwise I really *will* kill you. Go away."

It was he who was frightened now. He got up in the boat, without a word seized hold of a bough of the willow-tree, and leapt on to the bank. I shouted after him: "Take care we don't meet again. It's all over." But he, running along the river bank, had already disappeared.

I waited until he was a long way away, in the rain which had now become heavier and in the profound silence. I was soaked to the skin but it did not matter; I wanted to calm down, to feel cheerful again, as I had an hour earlier, when we had got out of the train, the three of us, at Ostia Scavi. But there was something that was too displeasing to me and I did not understand what it was and, thinking about it all the time, almost without realizing it I unfastened the boat from the landing-stage, took up the oars and began rowing. A short time before, I had said how wonderful it would be to go in a boat down the Tiber to the sea; but now I realized that I was rowing against the current, as I pulled the boat with difficulty through the swollen stream, all riddled with little holes by the falling rain. And suddenly I understood that I was rowing against the current because I had seen both Romildo and Gesuina fleeing along the river, upstream; and secretly I hoped I might catch sight of them at some point on the bank; and then I should call out to them to come and get into the boat too; and then we should go for a trip on the river, all three of us, in a friendly way, as if nothing had happened.

OPERATION PASQUALINO

WE youngsters of up to eighteen years old go about, as everyone knows, in gangs. But we do in fact begin to form gangs before the age of ten; and when, in some suburban streets, you see seven or eight small boys running about and exchanging blows, you may be sure it's a gang and that in that gang there is one who is the strongest who leads the others and is in command, and there are those who act as his servants and those who, either because they are smaller or weaker, are at everyone's mercy and do everyone's bidding. And what do they do, these gangs of boys under ten? Why, they play those games, of course, for which the only things needed are a few flagstones of the pavement and a small piece of chalk; sometimes they are daring enough to smoke a cigarette between ten of them, each taking one pull; they even go so far as to pool their money to buy a ball: all these are things that cost very little. But as they grow, vices grow too: cards, the cinema, football matches, not to mention girls. And for vices you need money. And as there isn't any money, you've got to get hold of it. That's where troubles begin.

Our gang used to meet, that summer, in the direction of the Via Appia Antica, out along that road which is full of ruins and cypresses and which, instead of asphalt, has big round stones like loaves of bread. At the twentieth kilometre, a little way back from the road, there is a big room built of red brick, with a vaulted ceiling and an entrance blocked with brambles. They say it's a Roman ruin; but there doesn't seem to me to be much sense in calling a ruin Roman when it's at Rome anyhow. Of course it's Roman; and there's no need to say so; if it was, say, at Frascati, it would be a Frascati ruin instead. In any case, in this ruin or room or whatever it was, our gang used to meet to play cards or discuss our adventures. We would thrust aside a bush, go in, and put the bush back in place again; nobody could have guessed that we were inside. It was, in fact, an ideal place to hide, and we went and hid there every day, although we had no reason whatever to do so. But everyone knows that when you're a boy hiding is the greatest fun there is.

We were comfortable in this room, cool and in the shade, well hidden, and it was like being inside a fortress; and since we were all boys who were full of life, hot-blooded and with lively imaginations, when we were not playing cards we used to give free play to our fancies, each one of us relating what he would do in given circumstances. We were all, to tell the truth, more or less conceited and boastful. One of us would jump up and describe in detail how he would lie in wait with a machine-gun, bump off the driver of a bank van and then escape with a load of gold bars; another had made up his mind to go to America and discover a uranium or diamond mine; someone else would talk of a raid on a jeweller's shop, to be carried out scientifically with an oxy-hydrogen flame, a mask, a pair of pliers and all sorts of other instruments. The best of it was that we discussed these things quite seriously, as if they were really going to happen; and more than once it came about that we quarrelled and started punching each other, on account of someone having raised doubts about someone else's courage or expressed the opinion that a plan was not practicable. In short, we forgot that we were all inexperienced, ignorant young boys, the sons of poor people; and we deceived ourselves into thinking that we were mysterious, ruthless, terrible men, just like the ones you see in the films or in the strip cartoons.

One day, when as usual we were seeing who could boast the

loudest, suddenly the bush at the door was pushed aside and a face appeared, the face of an old man but with rumpled hair that was still yellow, a wooden-looking face but with lively, wide open, blue eyes. He looked at us and said: "Hullo, boys, and what are you doing here?" Pasqualino, who was our chief, answered for all of us: "And what's that got to do with you?" "This is my property," replied the old man; "you're in my vegetable-garden." "If you like, we'll pay you rent." We saw him shake his head. "No, you can stay . . . It doesn't matter . . . Have you got a cigarette?" To tell the truth, we all burst out laughing at this bare-faced request. Pasqualino got up and went and placed a cigarette in his mouth. "Here's a cigarette," he said. "Have you got matches? And have you the breath to smoke it? Or would you like us to smoke it for you?" The moment he had the cigarette the old man disappeared, and we heard him muttering as he went off: "Thank you, thank you, it doesn't matter." We stared at each other in turn and Pasqualino concluded: "He must be a bit dotty." For the rest of the day we thought no more about him.

But Felicetto—that was the old man's name—was not in the least dotty, in fact he was as cunning as could be. I couldn't say how it happened, but by the end of a few days he had acquired an extraordinary authority over us all. It was either because he was so very old, over sixty, and age commands respect; or because he was always giving us presents—a packet of figs, a little basket of grapes, a glass of wine—and we all know that presents are disarming and misleading; or, more than anything, because we were all inexperienced young boys while he was an old serpent: the fact remains that we became attached to him, I don't say with affection but positively with passion. Early in the morning we all escaped from our homes in order to go and see Felicetto; after our midday meal we rushed off to join him again; in the evening we were never content unless we had seen him.

As before, we met inside the ruin; only now Felicetto was there too. And what did we do? We played cards, and he taught us some new games that we did not know. Or else we went on telling our boastful stories, each one in turn, describing what we felt we should like to do in order to get rich quickly and without effort. Felicetto would sit listening, his pipe between his teeth, his blue eyes half closed, quiet and gentle; and then he too would tell a story. But the ones he told were true stories, about highway robbers, brigands and outlaws in the part of the country where he was born, the province of Viterbo. They were stories of bygone days, but they were terrifying, breath-taking, full of murders and armed robberies. Felicetto remembered all these brigands, whether it was that he had known them personally, when he was a boy, or that he had heard about them from his father or grandfather. And he maintained that men of that kind were not born nowadays. His tone was both disconsolate and contemptuous, as much as to say: as for you, you're not men at all.

Felicetto was like a sugar-plum, always sweet; he was, in fact, seraphic, exactly like those painted wooden saints on church altars, with their hands joined and their eyes raised to heaven. But at moments he was also capable of turning nasty. As on that day when he said to Maurizio, who was the smallest of us but also the nimblest—merely because he had contradicted him: "If I was your father, I'd bash your head in, that I would." Ugly words; but the voice—hard, pitiless and violent—was uglier still. Felicetto, when he heard us talking about machine-guns and other modern weapons, said nothing; *his* weapon was the knife; and he had one, a very long one with a horn handle. And, just to amuse us, he showed us what he could do with his knife: among other things he hit a target at four metres' distance, throwing the knife over his shoulder. The result of all this was that in a short time each of us had a fine knife of his own and was trying to do the same tricks as Felicetto.

Well, one thing led to another; and one day when, as usual, we were talking to Felicetto about our lack of money, he said in a casual sort of fashion: "Ah, I daresay I might be able to tell you a way to get hold of the money you need. . . . I might be able to tell you a way. . . ." He dropped this remark and then went off. Next day, naturally, two or three of us went to Felicetto's house at the far end of the vegetable-garden and asked him for an explanation. This time, however, he drew back. "No, it's nothing," he said; "I shouldn't have said anything. . . . These things aren't for boys; these things are for grown-up men." Just imagine what we thought: "Why, aren't *we* men?" Anyhow, what with one thing and another, in the end we prevailed upon Felicetto to come out with his plan for getting money. In a lonely part of the Appian Way, he told us, there was an isolated house, very old and shabby, where they sold tobacco and cigarettes. The ground floor windows had no bars to them but only shutters. The plan was that we should force our way into the shop at night and carry off all the cigarettes we could find. Then Felicetto would pay us so much for them, and he himself would see about their disposal.

To tell the truth, at first we were taken aback by this idea: a small theft from a tobacco-shop seemed a great come-down after our uranium mines and machine-gun attacks on bank vans. Besides, we all knew this shop, and its owner, who was an innkeeper and was called Morganti, was a big kind man who let us have cigarettes on credit; and we knew his wife, Rosa, too, who was also very kind to us and was, into the bargain, a friend of all our mothers; and we were all of us, in greater or lesser degrees, friends of their daughter Giulia, a girl of our own age. We discussed the matter, inside our ruin, but without Felicetto. And possibly the majority would have been in favour of doing nothing about it if it had not been that Pasqualino, the strongest of all of us but also the most ignorant, had not suddenly taken it into his head to say that we were all cowards, that we must of course carry out the raid and that he was going to christen the undertaking "Operation Pasqualino". Where he had unearthed this expression I don't know, possibly from the newspapers; but it had its effect: Operation Pasqualino sounded much better than a cigarette robbery. Maurizio, it is true, tried to object. "Operation Pasqualino, stuff and nonsense," he cried; "it's just plain robbery." But he got a couple of good clouts for his pains; while Felicetto, who in the meantime had appeared through the bushes at the entrance, kept shouting to us as we held him down: "Hit him, the dirty little beast, go on, hit him, hit him!"

Maurizio went away in tears, repeating that he had no intention of stealing; and the rest of us, infatuated by now with the idea of Operation Pasqualino, went on to discuss preparations. We decided upon the time, the day, the method, the placing of a watch and all that was necessary. Felicetto, who was sitting amongst us now, his eyes half closed behind the smoke of his pipe, gave his approval; and his approval gave us courage because he, old as he was and full of experience, was, when all was said and done, our real chief. Finally, before we separated, he gave us some last pieces of advice: "Take any bills of exchange you can find . . . but leave the salt; it's heavy to carry and not worth much. . . . Take the tins of food that he keeps in the back shop: it's good stuff and sells well. And, besides the cigarettes, mind you take the cigars too."

A few days later, at two o'clock in the morning, we met as arranged on the Appian Way, a short distance from the shop. There was no moon, but the sky was full of bright stars, and the black cypresses, so tall and still and mysterious, like the ones in cemeteries, had a frightening look. Somebody whispered, trembling, that a mist was rising, and so indeed it was, and it wrapped the cypresses round in a kind of white smoke; but I have an impression that many of us were trembling from fear. Pasqualino, vain and infatuated, kept us waiting and then arrived all of a sudden with a low whistle, jumping into the middle of us and showing us a face covered up to the eyes with a dark handkerchief, in the Wild West manner. In a hushed voice and with a broad gesture, he said: "Now, boys, get to work. . . . This is the moment when Operation Pasqualino begins." Then, without further ado, he walked off towards the house where the shop was.

I myself was posted as sentry on a piece of rising ground at the edge of the Appian Way, close to some ruins, and from there I was able to watch the house, in which no lights were to be seen, and a good stretch of road as well. From that high ground I had a very good view of what happened that night. Pasqualino and the others circled round the shop, moving in behind it towards the windows of the back room. As much as half an hour, perhaps, went by, and then I heard a loud ringing sound that went on and on without stopping, like the ringing of twenty alarm clocks put together, and this ringing came from inside the house. A moment later a light appeared in a window on the first floor, and then in a window on the ground floor, followed by a sound of cries and curses and blows and tramplings. Finally I saw two or three of our gang running off along the Appian Way in the direction of Rome; then I realized that the raid had failed, and I rushed down from the high ground towards the fields, making for Felicetto's vegetable-garden.

I ran and ran and ran without stopping to take breath over the dry stubble in the darkness, stumbling in the furrows, my feet sinking in the soft earth, jumping over ditches. I arrived panting at Felicetto's cottage and knocked on the door, at first gently, then loudly, finally with my fist and foot. At last the door was opened, just as much as the padlock-chain permitted, and, in the dim light, I saw the face of our friend, very wide awake, with staring eyes, looking at me. "Open the door, Felicetto," I whispered frantically. "There's been a disaster . . . they've all been arrested."

He remained silent for a moment and then said: "And who are *you*?"

"Why, Felicetto, don't you recognize me? It's Ruggero."

"Well, I don't know you. Never seen you. Go away."

"It's Ruggero . . . Operation Pasqualino. . . . They've been arrested."

"Go away, or I'll shoot." As he said this, he levelled his double-barrelled gun at me through the crack. I recognized the unpleasant voice of the time when he said to Maurizio: "I'd bash your head in, that I would." Disheartened, I went away.

I did not go home, however. I walked the whole way along the Via Appia, trembling like a leaf whenever a policeman passed near me, and when morning came I went to an uncle of mine who had a joinery business in the neighbourhood of Via Giulia and told him the whole story. He, poor man, was very fond of me, and he left his work there and then and went off to the Via Appia to find out what had happened. I spent some uncomfortable hours, sitting amongst the shavings, and then he came back with the news. Nobody had been arrested; Morganti, awakened by the alarm bell, had done nothing beyond bestowing a number of good hard slaps and had then accompanied Pasqualino and Italo, the two on whom he had been able to lay hands, to their homes. He had told their families that he did not intend to report anyone, in consideration of our age and of the fact that we were all acquaintances. Their families had thanked him, Pasqualino and Italo had been given a further ration of slaps, and that was the end of it.

Nevertheless I did not stir out of Rome again. I stayed with my uncle, and in the end he took me on as a workman in his shop, and there I still am. When next I went to the Appian Way it was autumn, and I did not see any of the gang except Maurizio, who acquainted me with what our friends were doing. Most of them were staying at home, as good as gold; Pasqualino, on the contrary, had gone to Rome and was continuing the operation that bore his name, selling smuggled cigarettes in Via del Gambero; Italo had resumed his attendance at the technical school. And Felicetto? Maurizio told me that, one day when he was passing along in front of the vegetable-garden, Felicetto had called to him and, blinking his blue eyes, had said: "Listen, you can tell those friends of yours that, if they want to, they can come back here again, as they used to. . . . I've got something good to propose to them . . . better than last time." In short, he had understood nothing. He had not understood that hitherto we had been boys; that Operation Pasqualino had opened our eyes; and that now we had come to our senses and grown into men.

REPARATION

WHICH is the better friend, the man who, as soon as he hears bad news, hastens to let his friend know it, under the pretext, it may be, of putting him on his guard and assuring him that he has taken his side? Or the one who keeps the bad news to himself and does not go and tell his friend? The second, I say. The first is a friend only in a manner of speaking, a friend who secretly rejoices to see you in trouble, a friend who wishes to amuse himself behind your back without, on that account, losing the advantages of your friendship. Prospero is a false friend of that kind; and I have always come to know of all my troubles from his lips; and in fact, every time he says to me: "Listen, I've got to talk to you", I tremble because I know for certain that nothing good can come to me from him.

And so when, on that winter morning, I heard him on the telephone saying to me: "Hullo, Gigi, Prospero here; there's something I must tell you," I immediately thought: "Now we're in for it." Then he went on, cheerful, inquisitive, lively: "D'you know what they're saying about you? That you've got Mirella into trouble." There and then, I didn't know what to say; I couldn't deny it outright, and the blow caught me unprepared. However, in the end, seeing that he was silent and was awaiting a comment of some sort, I hazarded: "What Mirella d'you mean?" He burst out laughing and replied: "What Mirella indeed! There's only one Mirella, the daughter of the petrol-pump attendant in Via Ostiense." "I don't know anything about her." "All right, then," he said, "don't take any notice, consider it as unsaid . . . Good-bye." "Wait a moment," I cried, feeling uneasy, "you must tell me everything, if only so that I can know who's been speaking ill of me." "Never mind," he said, "I've told you what was said but I shan't tell you who said it. . . . Anyhow I telephoned just to let you know that, while everyone in the bar was accusing you, I stood up for you." "And what were they saying?" "Well, they were saying that Mirella's going to have a baby, and her father knows about it and you'll see what happens to you one of these days . . . They were saying that you were a thorough bad lot—that's what they were saying." At this point I had had enough of it and, while he still went on shouting into the telephone, I rang off.

For a moment I stood motionless in the dark passage, in front of the telephone, thinking: "There's the day ruined." The house was in darkness and silence, the light of dawn just beginning to penetrate the grey windows of the kitchen; from the floor, upon which my bare feet rested, the cold rose up through my legs; I had an uncomfortable feeling, a kind of nausea, in my stomach. And meanwhile I was saying to myself that it was still very early and that I shouldn't be able to see Mirella before nine. And what should I do until nine o'clock?

I no longer had any desire to sleep. I dressed, therefore, as best I could, in the dark, between the two beds, my own and my brother's. He stirred in his sleep and asked: "Where are you going?" I answered in a low voice: "I'm going to the workshop." "At this hour?" he murmured. I shrugged my shoulders and went out on tiptoe. It was really early; and as I came out of the house I saw four or five vegetable lorries go past, one after the other, on their way to the markets. The sky, behind the black spider's web of the gasometers, was pink, elsewhere of a vague white, but there were no clouds and certainly it would be a magnificent day—for everybody, I thought, except myself. Instinctively I went to Mirella's father's petrol-pump, but I did not find him there: it was still too early. Through one street after another, along deserted pavements littered with cabbage-stalks and dirty pieces of paper, past houses with barred windows, I arrived at the bridge that spans the river port and looked down through the girders of riveted iron. The Tiber, which at this point looks like a canal, was motionless as a stretch of stagnant water; the barges laden with bags of cement were motionless; motionless, too, were the cranes, their hooks and chains dangling over the barges: everything seemed dead. In contrast, as I looked at these motionless things, it seemed to me that I had a whirlwind inside my head: Prospero, with that obliging telephone-call, had put me into an indescribable state of restlessness; I had the same feeling as when, on one occasion, I had received a summons to go to the police-station and, although I had done nothing wrong and it turned out to be only a question of giving evidence, I had imagined goodness knows what. Only, this time, the wrong did exist; and I was more afraid of Mirella's father than I had been of the police-inspector.

As I was looking down at the river, all at once I heard a voice say: "What are you doing, son?" I turned and saw a little man wrapped up in a windcheater, bald and with a face as black as a rotten chestnut; sitting on his bicycle, he had put one foot to the ground, and was looking at me with a displeased expression in his deep-sunk eyes. It was Magliocchetti, Mirella's father. Ready to faint, I stammered: "Nothing; I was on my way to work."

"Well," he said, "you and I have got to have a talk. But not now . . . later. . . . I'll expect you at the pump, at twelve. You know what it's about."

I answered, haphazardly: "I don't know anything."

"Don't worry, of course you know. See you at twelve, then." He got on to his bicycle again and pedalled slowly away.

It was clear that he knew, I thought at once, and Prospero had told me the truth, and at twelve o'clock I should have to confront a furious father. I felt really unwell and thought, almost, that it was now not even worth while seeing Mirella. I had never before found myself in such a position; and I imagined that a woman, faced with certain things, would start lamenting: "What shall we do now? I'll kill myself, I'll throw myself into the Tiber"; and laments were precisely the thing I did not want. But you see what a man is like. In the end I reflected that there was still a long time to go before twelve o'clock; and that, after all, I preferred Mirella's laments to my own. It was rather early, it is true, to go and look for her, but I counted on the distance to make the time pass: the Magliocchettis lived in Vicolo della Serpe, a side street off Via Portuense; from the river port to their house, on foot, was a good long way. So I crossed the bridge and started in the direction of Via Portuense. But now I was filled with impatience, and first I walked too fast and then too slow. Finally, at a bus stop, I got on to the Fregene bus, telling myself that, if necessary, I would wait outside the house.

I reached the Vicolo della Serpe, almost in the country, a lot of little houses in a row along a ridge between deep hollows full of cabbages and lettuces; and then the Magliocchettis' house, strawberry pink with green window-frames, all on one floor. I hoped to find Mirella alone in the house; her mother, who was a fruit-seller, went to market in the mornings. But—bad luck again! When I rang and the door was opened, instead of the pretty face and slim-waisted figure of Mirella, there in front of me were the enormous bosom and rubicund face of the fruit-seller. "Is Mirella there?" I asked.

"Mirella's not well," she said.

"What's the matter with her?" said I.

"She's got a fever," said she.

Then, like an idiot, I said: "Fever, on a lovely day like this?"

"Does health depend on fine weather?"

In the end I left her and went back to Via Portuense, even

more uneasy than before. There could no longer be any doubt now; both her father and her mother knew; she was expecting a baby; and in the meantime, while awaiting my meeting with her father, they had put her under lock and key. I was conscious that, in my place, some of my many friends, more nimble than I, would have shrugged their shoulders, failed to keep the appointment with the petrol-pump man and, in short, disappeared from the scene. But I, alas, belong to a different breed. I am one of those who don't contrive to get meals for nothing; who, if they run up a bill at a restaurant, come back punctually next day and settle it. It is a question of conscience: some people have one and some haven't. I have.

In a frenzy of restlessness and not knowing what to do, I took the bus again and went back into town, and there, after wandering through street after street, I found myself in front of San Paolo, not very far from Magliocchetti's petrol-pump. Some tourists were going into the church and mechanically I followed on behind them. It was some time since I had been into that church; I had forgotten how big it was, and, faced with its vast size, I felt terrified. Luckily the guide distracted me with his chatter: "Look, gentlemen, all those medallions up there are portraits of all the Popes there have been in Rome." I looked up and all of a sudden it seemed to me that all those Popes were giving me an ugly look, as much as to say: "Hey, Gigi, you've put her in a family way and now you've got to make reparation." Then, as if a hand were pushing me, I went to one of the confessionals that are as big as monuments, knelt down and quickly said I wanted to make my confession.

The priest behind the grating, after the usual formalities, told me to carry on; and so I told him the whole story: my first meeting with Mirella, our trips to Ostia on my motor-scooter, the afternoons in the pine-forest at Castelfusano, the nights in the valley below her house, among the cabbages and the lettuces.

And then I told him also that her family knew about it; that she was going to have a child; and what ought I to do? Without hesitating he answered me, as curt as can be: "My son, you've done wrong, you must make reparation."

"In what way?"

"You must marry her."

"But I'm too young, Father, I haven't a penny, how am I to support her? We can't live on air."

"Anyhow you must marry her. The Lord will provide."

I began to be upset at so complete a lack of understanding. "But this isn't a thing that can be done in a minute," I said. "Do you know, Father, what it means to get married nowadays? Do you realize?"

"Well," he said, slightly annoyed perhaps, "that is your duty."

He was, in short, immovable. Finally I asked him for absolution and he gave it to me—but only on condition that I got married; and I said I would do so and went away, feeling gloomy. I dislike impositions; and now that so many people had combined to try and impose marriage upon me, I felt almost like rebelling and doing nothing about it. I went and sat down outside the church, under the trees, and started to think things over. Then, passing from one thing to another, I began to recollect how much I loved Mirella, to remember all the times we had actually spoken of getting married, and how much she loved me too, and how we understood one another and got on well together. And I felt that, if I forgot the impositions and looked at things from Mirella's point of view, the idea of marrying her was not, after all, unpleasant. That is how I am made: if I approach things of my own accord, with my heart, I do them; if not, there is no priest or family in the world that will make me do them. In conclusion, I said to myself: "What does it matter? I should have done as much in any case . . . a year sooner or a year later." And all at once I felt better, as though I had released myself with my own hands; as though, by accepting instead of refusing, I had lightened my burden instead of adding to it. I rose to my feet and walked off boldly towards the petrol-pump.

Magliocchetti was sitting on a straw-bottomed chair beside the pump, reading the newspaper, his spectacles on his nose. I clapped my hand on his shoulder and said: "Signor Magliocchetti, you wanted to speak to me. I've got something to say to you, too, and I'll say it at once: Mirella and I want to get engaged."

He looked up in surprise and contemplated me with a certain mistrust. "Mirella's not well," he said, "and I don't know anything about it. Come to the house and we'll talk about it."

"Mirella's already agreed."

"Well, we'll see; there's no great hurry . . . But look here, this doesn't mean you don't have to pay me for the petrol you had last Sunday, on credit. Understand that, my boy; petrol costs money, and I'm not here to give it away for nothing."

I felt like fainting. "Is that what you wanted to say to me?" I stammered.

"Certainly it is. You've got into the habit of making Mirella serve you, and then you don't pay. It comes to fifteen hundred lire."

So it had all been a misapprehension: Mirella was really unwell, and he wanted to speak to me about the petrol, and Prospero, with his pretence of friendship, had put me on a false track. For a moment I had a desire to go back on the engagement, with some excuse or other. But then I reflected that it had perhaps been the will of fate and that what fate wills is always right. I said jokingly: "Soon we shall be relations, so won't you give me credit?"

"Relations, indeed! At the pump I don't recognize any relations."

I paid him and went away, feeling light-hearted and content. That same day I went to see Mirella and it turned out that she was not with child at all, as I really knew, and I spoke to her of the engagement and she was happy that I had finally made up my mind and I was happy that she was happy. Next morning, however, I set my alarm-clock for six, and telephoned Prospero. Sleepy and out of breath, he asked me what I wanted. I replied that I was getting engaged to Mirella.

"And you wake me up at this hour to tell me a thing like that?"

"Didn't you wake me up yesterday at the same hour to tell me I was a bad lot?"

"I telephoned because I'm your friend."

"And I, as a friend, want to tell you what people say about you: that under the pretext of friendship, you're always the first to give bad news. Good-bye."

GOOD-FOR-NOTHING

THE number of jobs I've done! From the end of the war until the present day I must have changed my job at least twice a year, not counting my periods of unemployment —which, if it isn't actually a job, comes very near it. My foster-brother, an electrical engineer and a mean, narrow-minded sort of man, to whom I used to go from time to time to ask him to help me, said to me bluntly one day: "Serafino, what you don't realize is that to-day, in order to find work, you've got to specialize." "Specialize?" I said; "and what does that mean?" "Specializing," he answered, "means knowing how to do only one job, but to do it well. . . . You, on the other hand, know how to do everything and yet don't know how to do anything. You've got nothing but a pair of arms, like everyone else, and you come along with your arms and say: give me work. And you're over thirty already. Is it possible that in all that time you've never had the idea of specializing?" "It's bad luck that's prevented me from specializing," I answered. "Bad luck or no bad luck," he said, showing me to the door, "don't show your face here again until you've learned how to specialize. What's more, don't go on calling me brother. It's true that we were nursed by the same mother, but that doesn't give you the right to call me brother and, still less, to come and bore me with your misfortunes."

So, since I had never specialized, my own speciality consisted in continually changing my job. And what is there I haven't done? I have been a picker-up of cigar-ends, a collector of empty bottles, a rag-and-bone man, a film extra, a pavement-layer, a bill-poster, a waiter, an ice-cream man, a gardener and I don't know what else. And all this changing of jobs has led me to see that this specialization about which my foster-brother used to talk to me is nothing more, when all is said and done, than a fixation of the brain as a result of which a man neither proposes, nor desires, nor hopes to do anything except what he is doing; and the fixation accompanies him all his life, so that anyone who, so to speak, is born a road-sweeper lives and dies a road-sweeper, and all his life he does nothing except handle brooms and think about brooms. On the other hand, anyone who does not have this fixation becomes aware, sooner or later, of the disadvantages of the job he is doing and changes it; and for him that is the end of specialization.

Of all the many jobs I have done, the one in which I very nearly felt inclined to specialize was perhaps the post of messenger in the service of Captain Guidobaldi. I daresay he wasn't really a Captain; nor—if you looked closely—was his name Guidobaldi; however, it was under that title and name that I knew him. This Captain lived in a flat full of small children and broken furniture, in the direction of the Macao Barracks; and he had a wife who was possibly not his wife, whom he sometimes called, goodness knows why, "Countess", and sometimes "Iella", which in Roman dialect means "evil eye" but which in reality was short for Mariella. He was small, dressed always in a double-breasted blue suit with two or three ribbons on the lapel, and with a military bearing; his face was pale, drawn, shrunken, his eyes staring, his mouth full of black teeth; he smoked like a chimney. She was a great horse of a woman, bulky and worn-out, all bosom and hips, with long, untidy hair and a lustreless eye, always in a dressing-gown. What with the children roaming about everywhere, shouting and squabbling, the Countess who spent her time smoking and playing patience, and a servant called Agnesina, a peasant and a dunce who didn't know how to do anything, the flat was like a dog-kennel. Except, however, for a small study at the end of a passage: *that* was clean and tidy, as bright as a mirror. Not that much was needed to keep it in order, for there was nothing in it but a desk and a chair, and, on the desk, a telephone and some directories. It was in this study that the Captain worked.

Guidobaldi, or whatever he was called, had certainly specialized; and his speciality was good works. Actually, according to his own account, he was also a journalist, a pilot, a poet, a film-producer and a horse-trainer; but all this was what he *said*; charity, on the other hand, he *practised*. Charity to whom, you may ask. Why, to himself, of course, and to Iella and the children.

With regard to his charitable activities, Guidobaldi conducted himself in the following way. Every morning, heedless of the screams of the children and of Iella's scenes, he went into his study, sat down at the desk, lit a cigarette, and, after inspecting the directory, made his skilful telephone calls. These went always in the same way. Someone would answer and then he, in a resounding, martial voice, would shout: "This is Captain Guidobaldi, President of the Widows and Orphans Association of . . ."; here he would give the name of some deserving class of people. "The Association is organizing a charity tea. . . . We know how good-hearted, how high-minded, how patriotic you are. . . . May we send you a few tickets?" The person at the other end of the line would answer yes or no; less often he would start an argument and would even, if he smelt a rat, give Guidobaldi a piece of his mind; but the latter, cunning devil that he was, would immediately transfer the disagreement to the political level, with the remark: "You look upon such things in a different way from ours, that's all there is to it . . . I quite understand, for you certain ideals do not exist." Then Guidobaldi would take a piece of paper and write down the name and address of anyone who had agreed to buy tickets; and later I would go there, hand over the tickets and collect the money. Needless to say, the tea did not exist. But who's going to go to the police and make a charge for the sake of a thousand lire? Guidobaldi organized one of these teas, and sometimes a lottery too, every month, on an average; and every two months he changed the name of the association of which he was president, always, however, maintaining the exalted character of his undertakings. In this way he managed to rub along somehow, though Iella shouted all day long that she had nothing to wear and that the children were growing up like savages.

I spent about six months going round like this from one house to another with Guidobaldi's tea and lottery tickets. When I was not going round, I remained at the Captain's orders, keeping the maid Agnesina company in the kitchen. This girl was an unfortunate creature of the same kind as myself; in the six years that she had been working as a servant and doing the cooking, she had still not learnt to cook a couple of eggs or sweep a room properly. A maid-of-all-work, as they are called; not a specialist, my foster-brother would have said. Nevertheless, countrified as she was, with a round, red face and bulging cheeks and two little eyes like pin-points and frizzy hair standing straight up on her head, Agnesina attracted me. Perhaps it was because she was like me, non-specialized, a poor woman and nothing more; perhaps because she had kept her abrupt country ways—ways which at first seem disagreeable but which in the end are comforting, so warm and genuine are they, like the smell that comes from the village baker's oven in the morning. One thing leads to another. First we became fond of one another; then, in discussing the Captain and Iella, we agreed that they were exploiting us both, paying us badly, sending us around dressed like a couple of ragamuffins and making us eat food that wasn't fit for dogs; that, in short, now that we understood how the game was played, we might as well set about it on our own account. "You're a clever person," Agnesina said to me; "why shouldn't *we* have some tickets printed and go round selling them? The only difference would be that at present it's he who takes the money whereas in the future it would all be yours." And so, one morning, without saying a word, we left the Captain's house; and Agnesina insisted on taking away with her—to make up for the exploitation we had suffered—a bundle of sheets: there was no danger of their reporting us, she said, because they were at our mercy. I restricted myself to keeping the last lot of ticket-money I had collected, seven thousand lire in all. We took a room, with a telephone, of course, and I at once saw to getting the tickets printed. This time I put "Railway Signalmen's Widows and Orphans". The idea came to me because I myself am a signalman's orphan and I spent my childhood looking at the trains on the Abruzzi railway, in the neighbourhood of Tagliacozzo. We agreed that Agnesina should remain at home, near the telephone, to answer enquiries, as secretary of the Association; I myself, meanwhile, would be going round from house to house.

Now you can see, however, where specialization comes in. Guidobaldi certainly had specialized: he knew how to speak with authority on the telephone, he knew how to command respect, above all he knew the right sort of people to approach. But I—I didn't know how to speak, still less was I able to command respect, and besides, I was quite lost amongst the millions of names in the telephone directory and could never find the right one. I always hit upon people who were rude, or too poor, or too clever. They refused the tickets, saying bluntly that the whole thing was a swindle; sometimes they actually threatened to go to the police. In the meantime, all this tramping around had reduced me to a shocking state of shabbiness; my shoes were worn through and my waterproof was grimy, and, in the pockets of my waterproof, the tickets that nobody wanted had become grimy too, worse than the waterproof. So, in the end, I became demoralized and started wandering round without conviction, feeling disheartened and wretched, actually incapable, sometimes, of uttering a word when I presented myself at somebody's door and was asked what I wanted. As for Agnesina's assistance, better not to mention it; among other things, she couldn't speak the language correctly; and once, when a client telephoned to check up on us, she answered: "Why, what's the idea? Thought we was swindlers, did you?" The result of all this was that by the end of a month I had sold about a dozen tickets.

It was, needless to say, my foster-brother, the engineer, who dealt me the final blow. I had gone to him in desperation; and he, after a lengthy examination of the tickets, remarked that this Association was new to him and that he had never heard it mentioned. Without much conviction, I replied: "Of course, the signalmen's class is always the one that gets forgotten." He looked at me in a curious way and then said: "Serafino, I warned you that you ought to specialize. You haven't done so. I am sorry, but this is a swindle and I shall be compelled to report you." I went deathly pale and looked round me at that office of his, so cold and so bare, with all those tables of numbers and desks covered with papers and compasses and Chinese inks; and I reflected that he was a specialist, and Guidobaldi was a specialist, and that all those people who did a precise job like him or organized a precise swindle like Guidobaldi got on well in the world just because they were specialists; I, on the other hand, was not, I had only my two arms, like Agnesina, also, who didn't know how to do anything, not even how to cook spaghetti or sweep a room; and I said to myself that it was all up with me, and being hungry and feeling very weak I fainted, there and then and just as I was, and fell down on the floor. When I came to again, my foster-brother said: "We'll let it pass this time, and here's a thousand lire for you. . . . But I don't want to see you again." I went away and, as soon as I was outside, I threw all the tickets into the Tiber, which was not far off.

Now I'm married to Agnesina and she, naturally, is going to have a baby, and we live in a hut outside the Porta Portese. Agnesina goes out by the day to do washing; I do my best to sell bunches of faded flowers outside the doors of restaurants. I run after people with a bunch of flowers in my hand, I even take hold of them by the arm and say: "Come on, take it, I'm hungry", in a threatening tone of voice. Some people are annoyed by this hand on their arm; they shake it off and say to me: "Go and find some work to do, you vagabond." That's when I should like to be able to answer: "I've never specialized, this is the only job I can do." And d'you know what happened recently? A lady whom I asked for charity the other day, holding my little bunch of violets under her nose, said to me: "Certainly not. . . . But don't imagine that I don't think of the poor; I bought these only this morning;" and she waved some tickets in front of my face, adding: "I'm very willing to help widows and orphans, but not a big, tall young man like you." For some reason I seemed to recognize these tickets and I begged the lady to show me one of them; and indeed, just as I had imagined when I heard her speak of widows and orphans, Guidobaldi's name stood out clearly in the centre of the ticket; and underneath it was written, as usual, that some Association or other was holding a lottery for charity on such and such a date, in such and such a place. "Congratulations," I said to the lady; "I know him well, that swindler Guidobaldi." "You worthless wretch," she answered, "how dare you speak ill of a man like that? Be off with you, or I'll call a policeman."

THE BITE

HAVE you ever lived in a hut? No; and so you know nothing at all about huts, like the gentleman at Monte Mario that I'm going to tell you about. Living in a hut means that, if it rains, you have to be careful where you put your feet when you get out of bed in the morning, because there is mud all over the floor. It means cooking in a petrol tin, out of doors, and sitting on the bed to eat. It means using a carbide lamp or a candle for lighting. It means hanging up your clothes on nails or cords, so that they seem like a lot of rags when you come to put them on. It means huddling together like beasts to keep warm, and fighting with draughts and dampness all through the winter. And then you can never find anything, in a hut. You look for a fork, you look for a piece of soap, you look for the frying-pan, and out pops some other thing that you haven't any need of—a shoe, a cap or quite possibly a black, shaggy rat as big as a cat. For rats, of course, have a special affection for huts, as worms have for cherries. One night I heard a strange chirping sound coming from a box full of rags which I kept under the bed; I went and looked, and there amongst the rags I found eight little pink rats which looked like so many tiny little pigs. Well, I killed them; but what fault was it of theirs? Huts are places for rats, not for human beings.

Until this last October I used to take my accordion—my only possession, a relic of the good times after the war when I was working the black market—and go with Giovanna and Clementina to one of the old quarters of Rome where there are still so many kind-hearted women who don't mind listening to a song while they do their housework. Giovanna, like the accordion, was a legacy of the post-war period; she was a peasant girl with a white face, a hare lip and curly fair hair, countrified beyond words, an ignorant good-for-nothing. She had attached herself to me, and I was half thinking of marrying her and half of pushing her out. Clementina, on the other hand, was a child of about twelve, thin and brown, with a round face and a mouth the size of an oven stretching from ear to ear. About her I knew nothing, not even where she lived nor whom she lived with, and she had never been willing to tell me: I had chosen her out of a group of children playing under the walls, because I had heard her sing and had liked the way she sang. We used to go off, then, the three of us, to the neighbourhood of Piazza Navona or the Campo di Fiori, and I would take up my position at the edge of the pavement with one foot in the roadway and my head and shoulders thrown back and then strike up on my accordion. Meanwhile Giovanna would hand out leaflets to the passers-by with lucky numbers for the lottery printed on them, and Clementina would sing. You may perhaps be thinking that Clementina had a fine, sweet, harmonious voice. Not at all. When Clementina opened her enormous mouth, in which the small, meagre teeth seemed lost, she gave vent to a sound which could not have been harsher or more tuneless. It was a sound that made you shudder; but it was assured, arrogant, insolent. And it was here that her whole success lay—I should say *our* success. For Clementina's voice, tuneless as it was, said all the things that I myself wanted to say, and said them, for the most part, better than my accordion: it told of life in a hut, of bleak poverty, of the black market, of gaiety and of sadness, and of sleeping huddled together for warmth and of hunting for the frying-pan and seeing a rat jump out. At the sound of that voice, indeed, as it rose up and up, harsh and sharp and strident, to the topmost floors of the houses, people would appear at their windows, stop to listen and then throw down money.

I decided, one day, to try a different neighbourhood, and we started off along the Via Flaminia with the intention of going up to the Parioli quarter. It was early in the afternoon, on a Sunday, and as we passed the Stadium I saw the usual crowd of sporting enthusiasts and thought I would turn them to account. I took up my position a little to one side and struck up on the accordion, while Clementina started yelling the words of her song at the top of her voice and Giovanna went round trying forcibly to thrust leaflets into the hands of the waiting crowd. But it was no good, our efforts were wasted: these sportsmen, gathered in numbers of small groups, their heads together, were in close discussion of their own affairs, and did not even notice us: sport, as we all know, is the enemy of art. Then, all of a sudden, a car, with a second car following it, stopped in front of us. At the wheel sat a man of about sixty, with a face that seemed to be made in two different parts: the upper part fresh and lively in colouring, with hair that was still black, a smooth forehead and bright eyes, the lower part of a corpse-like yellow, with a purple, twisted mouth and a chin entirely submerged in a swollen, hanging dewlap like the bag of loose skin that pelicans have underneath their beaks. This man was looking at us and seemed to be listening, and then, when I had finished, he beckoned to me. So I went over to him and he told me he would very much like to listen to some good songs in his own villa, which was not very far off; he told us to get into the car and said he would arrange to send us back afterwards into the town. I reflected that rich people have all kinds of caprices, that there was perhaps something to be gained from his proposal, so I accepted it. We all three got into the car, which started off again, followed at a distance by the other car which had also stopped.

We crossed the Ponte Milvio, started out along the Via Cassia, then circled round by Via Camilluccia, up Monte Mario. We three were sitting at the back; in front was the old gentleman who had given the invitation and a younger friend of his, a fat, bald man who seemed to be in awe of him. The old man treated him very badly, and at one moment even said to him: "Don't be such a fool"; and he smiled as though this had been a compliment. Then the old man, as he drove, asked me without turning round: "Tell me, where d'you live?"

"In a hut," I answered, "near the Felice aqueduct."

"A hut?" His voice was metallic and disagreeable. "And this little girl, is she your sister?"

"No, she's not my sister, she's nothing: she sings."

"And the other one, is she nothing too?"

"She and I are engaged to be married."

"Engaged, are you. . . ? And you, why aren't you working?"

"I did have a job; I was a painter. Now I'm unemployed."

By this time we had arrived at a pair of iron gates, at the bottom of a slope which appeared to be entirely laid out as a garden. The gates opened at once as though by magic, and he turned into an avenue of cypresses leading towards the top of the hill, where a big villa became visible. As we drove up, I caught glimpses of terraced fountains with cascades of water leaping down from one basin to another, of seats and temples and marble statues; then the car stopped on a gravelled open space in front of the entrance to the house, and a white-jacketed manservant came hurrying out, bowing as he approached. The old man jumped out of the car, together with his companion; from the other car which had been following us three other men got out, all of them younger than he, between forty and fifty. They too appeared to be in awe of the old gentleman, who in fact treated them like dirt; I imagined they must be his employees or dependents. The old man led the way into a big room on the ground floor, hurling his blue coat, as he passed, at the manservant, who caught it in mid-air; and there came forward to meet him, wriggling like an eel, a pretty little fair woman, young and well-made, wearing red trousers so tight that they seemed on the point of bursting and a blue-and-white striped top like a sailor's jersey. She embraced him, saying: "Good morning, Papa", although it was obvious from a mile off that she was not his daughter; and Papa, after giving her a slap on the bottom, went off towards the far end of the room, shouting: "Now, come on boys, let's get down to work."

The work, I noticed, consisted in a game of poker. The five of them sat down at a table and began, without more ado, distributing the chips and shuffling the cards; the pretty young woman pushed a trolley laden with bottles and glasses up to them and, still wriggling and making grimaces, served them with drinks. We three, on the other hand, when we entered this vast room, full of fine furniture and with a shining marble floor, felt embarrassed by our rags and remained near the door. But the old man, after looking at his cards, turned suddenly round. "Come on, cheer up!" he cried, "get on with your playing and singing! Isn't that what you came here for?"

So I went forward and struck up on my accordion, and Clementina opened her mouth wide and began singing. The accordion sounded very loud in that low room, and Clementina's voice, harsher and more out of tune than ever, was excruciating; but the others went on playing and did not even seem to hear us. When the first song was finished, I started off on a second and then a third, still with the same result. Giovanna went up and presented a leaflet to each of the gamblers; only one of them looked at it and said: "Let's hope it'll bring me luck." I embarked on a fourth song and then a fifth; every now and then I stopped, and then the old man, without raising his eyes from his cards, shouted: "What, finished already? Go on, go on!" The little fair woman had now squatted down close beside him and was looking at his cards and from time to time giving him a kiss on the cheek; but he turned away his cheek irritably, as one does with a fly. In the end I got fed up. I slowly closed my accordion with a long, sobbing note, went over and said: "Well, we've finished. . . ."

The old man was very slowly examining his cards and paid no attention to me. Then he let forth a cry of joy: "Four aces!" and threw down his cards on the table. The other four were upset because they had lost a good sum of money. The old man collected the chips, got up and said to the young woman: "You go on, I'm going to get a breath of air"; then he walked off towards a door leading into the garden, beckoning to us to follow him. We went out on to the gravel.

"And so," he said, as he walked along a path in front of us, "and so you live in a hut?"

I thought I might arouse his pity. "Yes," I said, "I have no home, and in the hut it's terribly damp . . . especially when it rains."

"A real hut, with a mud floor and a corrugated iron roof and walls made of planks?"

"Yes, Sir, a real hut."

He was silent for a moment and then said, slowly: "Well, I would give this villa and everything inside it, and the whole garden too, for your hut, and to be unemployed and go round playing the accordion."

I gave a faint smile, and suggested: "Well then, if you like, we'll make an exchange."

I ought never to have said it. He jumped at me like a fury and seized hold of me by my sweater, high up on my chest. "All right, we'll exchange, then . . . but on condition that, besides the villa, you take over my sixty years, you miserable scum . . . and you also take over the tumour I've got here in my neck, and plenty of other nice things too . . . you miserable scum."

"Be careful what you say."

"You give me your twenty years and your health and your hopes, and you can take the villa and everything inside it . . . eh, you miserable scum, d'you want to make the exchange, d'you still want to?"

He was shaking me like a madman, and now he had difficulty in breathing and his swollen neck was throbbing, like the neck of a pelican that has just swallowed a live fish. "Here, take your hands off me!" I said, frightened.

"Yes, yes, go away now, go away," he said, calming down all of a sudden. And he pushed me violently away from him. More out of politeness than anything, I said: "Would you like us to sing you another song?"

"No, no more songs," he said, with a movement of irritation. "Here, Pietro, take these three back to where we found them . . . And take this," he said to Clementina; "this is for you all. You can divide it between you." And he put something into her hand that looked like some ten-thousand-lire notes folded in four.

Without a word we jumped into the car. The chauffeur asked us: "Where d'you want to be taken to?" Realizing that it was already late, I replied: "To Viale Castrense, outside the Porta Maggiore."

During the whole drive we did not speak. All three of us were certainly thinking about the ten-thousand-lire notes that the old gentleman had given to Clementina; and I was saying to myself that we must divide them as soon as possible, but that it would not be seemly to do so in front of the chauffeur. When we reached the Porta Maggiore it was already dark; I asked the chauffeur to stop and we got out. Immediately, right there under the walls, I told Clementina: "Come on, now let's divide that money . . . give it here."

But she said, in an impudent sort of way: "He gave the money to me."

"Yes, but he also said: divide it."

"I didn't hear anything like that."

"Well, anyhow, no nonsense; fork out that money."

I made as though to seize her by the wrist, but she, all of a sudden, bent down and bit my hand hard, with all the teeth in that enormous mouth. I felt an intolerable pain and let go of her, at the same time letting forth a yell and raising my hand to my lips. Clementina, in a flash, ran off into some fields near by and in a moment vanished into the darkness.

I went back to the hut dejected, tired and in a bad temper. My hand was hurting me from Clementina's bite, which had penetrated right to the bone. When I had closed the door and lit the candle, I let myself fall in a heap on the bed, without even unbuckling my accordion. Then I saw that Giovanna was looking at me from behind the flame of the candle, her blue eyes wide open, her hare lip raised so that it showed her teeth. "How much d'you suppose it was?" she asked; "I should say it was at least thirty thousand lire." I was almost inclined to laugh: thirty thousand lire, indeed! The truth was that that old man had ruined me: his money had made Clementina lose her head; and now we should never see Clementina again; and I should have to make Giovanna sing, and Giovanna had a sweet voice and sang in tune, but without any expression, so that it meant nothing. Clementina's harsh, tuneless voice, on the other hand, had plenty of meaning; and the old gentleman had given her all that money because her voice had given him a longing to be young again and in good health, even though he were starving and a vagabond and without a home.

A TOUGH NUT

SUMMER came, and I took to lurking in the more frequented places such as Piazza San Silvestro in front of the central Post Office, in the arcade off Piazza Colonna, in Via del Gambero. I had a very light suit of brown cloth, and I had deliberately made a tear in it, in the shape of the number 7, below the jacket pocket, and the loose piece flapped up and down like a little door; in addition I wore my shirt unbuttoned at the neck, without a tie; and on my feet a pair of canvas shoes, all out of shape: for what I had to do, in fact, my appearance was natural, convincing, characteristic. I lay in wait, therefore, and when I saw the type of man I was after, I attacked him—that's the word: "Fancy meeting you! Don't you remember? We were in the army together . . . Don't you remember? At Bressanone . . . You were with me in the officers' mess. Don't you remember?"

In order to understand these words you must know that what I had to do was to get myself recognized in one minute, or two at most, or anyhow to arouse a suspicion of having known me in someone who actually did not know me at all. Now if I had said: "You remember that café?" or again: "You remember that family?" it would have been easy to reply: "No, we've never met, I don't remember anything." But everyone goes into the army; and, as we all know, the years go by and it's easy to forget one among a thousand. And in fact, nine times out of ten, the person would look at me and remain in doubt; and then I would press my advantage: "They were good times, those . . . but alas, since then everything's gone wrong for me. If you knew what I've been through . . . And now, here I am, as you see me, unemployed, jobless." At this juncture—either because he feared he must have a bad memory, or because he was sorry for me, or perhaps, more simply, because he was in a hurry and did not want to make the effort of recollection—he would put his hand in his pocket and give me the three hundred or five hundred lire which were the whole object of the encounter. Oh yes, men are kind-hearted; out of a hundred, there wasn't a single one who answered me: "Get out, I've never met you or even seen you." And again, with regard to my story, it was lucky that it never occurred to anyone to check it, for I had never been in any officers' mess or indeed in the army at all, being the son of a widowed mother. It was precisely for this reason that I used to mention Bressanone, which is a distant town where few people go; so that no one, even if he wanted to, would be likely to catch me out.

By employing this system and various other expedients I managed to scrape along; and when I say "scrape along" I mean that I managed to get enough to eat and to pay for a bed in a hole under a staircase. But talk of bad luck! One morning, towards midday, while as usual I was hanging about in Via del Gambero, I saw a man walking along very slowly, stopping at every shop-window and closely considering each object displayed for sale. I at once made up my mind to accost him, possibly because he was the only person in that busy thoroughfare who did not appear to be in a hurry. No sooner said than done; I went up and stopped him with my usual rigmarole: "Fancy meeting you! . . . the officers' mess . . . Bressanone." Meanwhile, as I was speaking, I was able to observe him more closely and I realized my mistake; but now it was too late. He could have been of any age between thirty and fifty; he had a face like a weasel, narrow and pointed, all nose and cheek-bones, of an ugly yellow colour, with small, screwed-up eyes beneath a receding forehead and a big mouth with purplish lips. His ears stuck out like fans, and his close-cropped hair made his round head look like a young chicken that hasn't yet grown any feathers. He was thin, very thin, but he was wearing an enormous coat, double-breasted and with padded shoulders, of a bristling, hairy winter tweed with big green checks.

Have you ever seen a lizard watching a fly, without moving, and then, in a flash, darting out its tongue and swallowing it? In the same way, and with the same briskness, did he turn at the sound of my voice. He let me recite my story and then exclaimed jovially: "But of course, of course I remember you. And how are you? How are you? Splendid, splendid!"

What it means to have presence of mind! If I had had any presence of mind, I ought at that precise moment to have drawn back with some excuse or other and melted away. It was the only thing to do. But, accustomed as I was to seeing other people perplexed, the last thing I had expected was that I in my turn should be beset by the same kind of perplexity. And so, like a fool, I mumbled: "Oh well, I'm not too bad." And then, more from habit than anything else, I added: "But if you knew what I've been through . . ."

Jovial and brisk as a young cockerel, he answered quickly: "Let's hear all about it, then . . . I'm really curious to hear the whole story. But let's go into a bar; then we can celebrate our return home." Meanwhile he had grasped my arm with a claw-like hand that seemed to be made of steel, and, almost lifting me off the ground, propelled me towards a near-by bar, in Via della Vite.

As he dragged me along, he kept saying: "What a lucky coincidence! How pleased I am to see you!" He spoke in a cold, hurried, hissing voice: if a snake spoke, it would have a voice like that. I looked at him more closely: I have already mentioned his winter coat, on a day of full summer. Below this coat he had a pair of brown trousers, very carefully pressed and with a few darns here and there. His shoes were black, polished to perfection, but worn—not in the soles which were extremely thick, but in the uppers, which were rubbed thin like threadbare velvet. And then I saw something that made me turn cold: as he moved, the coat with the green checks fell open and I noticed that he wore no shirt, merely a false front or dickey tied round his body by two laces. On each side of the dickey you could catch a glimpse of his bare flesh, yellowish, grub-like. He was, in fact, a pauper actually more degraded than myself, but of a different type: I am cheerful and winning, and I have a kind face; he, on the other hand, was positively sinister.

We went into the bar, and he went straight over to the counter and ordered two vermouths; then, all in one breath, went on: "The officer's mess at Bressanone—how well I remember it. A fine town, Bressanone, with that fine river flowing through it and those fine streets with arcades. And moreover, only a short distance from Bolzano, another fine town. Bressanone—d'you remember the Cavallino Bianco Hotel, where there was that big café, and all the officers used to go there, and several little ladies in search of company used to turn up there too? Bressanone—with all those hills round it full of vineyards, and that good wine. What was it called, that wine? As yes, I remember—Terlano."

At this point the barman gave us our vermouths. He took his glass and raised it, saying: "To celebrate our return home." And I could not refrain from drinking, though I had little idea of what this "return home" might be. He emptied his glass and then, without a moment's pause, went off towards the door, saying: "Look, it's lunch-time, let's have lunch together. It's not every day that one has the luck to meet a friend like you."

"But I . . ." I began, as I followed him. The barman, who had his eye on us, said: "Here, Sir—the two vermouths." I wanted to call him back and make him pay, but he was already outside the door. So I took out the money, paid, and went out. Immediately he popped out from somewhere or other and grasped me by the arm again. "Come on, come on," he said; "there's a really good restaurant just close by . . . Come along."

In the restaurant, while I, in a dazed sort of way, sought to extricate myself by saying: "I'm not hungry . . . and besides, I have an appointment", he lolled back in his chair and, in an authoritative voice, ordered a substantial lunch with *tagliatelle* and roast lamb as the main dishes. Then he turned towards me. "The officers' mess," he said, "how well I recall it! Captain Moschitto—d'you remember him? And his habit, at any sort of party, of throwing himself at any sort of girl, pretty or ugly, and making love to her? That was what he called 'drawing a bow at a venture'. Well, well, Captain Moschitto was a real Don Juan; but love-making wasn't exactly a joking matter with you either, was it, my dear chap?"

I was dumbfounded. Not only, of all the towns in Italy, did he know Bressanone, with its hotels and cafés, its streets, its river, its women and its wine, but he also remembered Captain Moschitto and even that I was a Don Juan. I was very near, now, to a feeling of admiration for him: he was tough, extremely tough, far tougher than I would have imagined.

They brought our *tagliatelle*. He swallowed a first, enormous forkful and then resumed his jovial, glib, hypocritical chatter, so that you might have thought he had a little machine inside his mouth: "Bressanone—those were good times . . . But you, my dear chap, you did behave really badly to Nella—allow me to say so—like a real Roman tough, which is what you are . . . Really very badly indeed."

My mouth full of *tagliatelle,* I mumbled: "Nella? And who in the world is she?"

He guffawed. "No, my dear good man, no, don't pretend to

be modest; that doesn't go down, with me . . . Anyhow you got off scot-free. But that girl was a dream—fair, with blue eyes and a magnificent figure. But you, my dear chap, after drawing your bow at a venture, as Moschitto used to say, and hitting her in the heart, you left her in the lurch. . . . Even Modugno said you'd behaved like a blackguard."

"Who's Modugno? . . . And be careful what you say, too," I interrupted, hoping to start a quarrel. But there were no flies on him. "Oh yes, a great blackguard, that's what you are." He laughed, filled a glass to the brim, emptied it at one gulp and then attacked the roast lamb which the waiter, zealous as ever, had placed under his nose. "Of course you had Pina," he went on, "another splendid girl—she was dark—and goodness knows how many others as well . . . but really Nella didn't deserve to be insulted like that. She was so unhappy about it that she wanted actually to die, and she took sleeping pills . . . but she recovered, and then later she took up with—what was his name—you know—what was he called? . . . Oh yes, Lieutenant Tessitore."

"Tessitore? Never heard of him."

"Yes, Tessitore; a strange sort of fellow, very strange indeed. You two, you and Tessitore, very nearly came to blows over Nella. . . . One evening, along the river, there was a mist and it was drizzling . . . and I had to separate you. Yes indeed, Nella was pulling from one side and I from the other . . . and then in the end she went back home with you. Yes, you scoundrel, you were utterly in the wrong; you got jealous of Nella as soon as you saw she was going with someone else, and in spite of that you managed to take her away from Tessitore. You were a proper Don Juan, in fact. D'you know what Major Paternostro said when you left? 'It's a good thing he's gone; otherwise he'd have taken all the women here for himself.'" His roast lamb was finished, and he laughed again, boisterously, and, slapping me on the back, went on: "I should very much like to know what it was you did to women, eh?"

I too had finished my lamb. And perhaps because, after having had something to eat, I now felt more valiant, I decided to tell him the truth. I drew back, in such a way as to thrust aside the arm which he kept round my shoulders, and, looking him straight in the eye, I began: "Now let's stop this nonsense. . . . All good things come to an end. Anyhow I've never been to Bressanone."

"You've never been to Bressanone?"

"No, and I've never met either Moschitto or Modugno or Tessitore or Paternostro."

"But what do you mean?"

"It's the truth. And I'm not a Don Juan, though I like women as much as anyone. And I've never had a Nella or a Pina. And, what's more, I was never in the Army because I'm the son of a widowed mother, and so I got exemption."

He looked at me with his snake-like eyes. And I thought again: "He's tough, extremely tough, let's see what he'll invent now. . . . He's like a cat: he'll manage to fall on his feet." And so, indeed, he did. Nor did he take a second to think it over. All at once, in a hard, resentful, outraged voice, he cried: "Then you lied to me."

I was embarrassed. "No," I stammered, "I made a mistake, I thought . . ."

"What d'you mean—made a mistake? The first thing you said was that you'd been to Bressanone, and now it turns out you've never been there. You lied to me; you're a humbug and a vagabond and a swindler."

"Steady now, take care what you say!"

"You're a swindler and you certainly intended to cheat me. Get out!"

"But I . . ."

"That's enough. . . . And to think that I allowed myself to

associate with a swindler, a cheat, a vagabond!" Still throwing insults at me, he rose to his feet and buttoned up his coat over his dickey. Finally he said: "Don't attempt to follow me, or I'll call the police." Then, swift as a deer, he slipped through the door of the restaurant and vanished.

To tell the truth, although I had been all the time expecting a trick to make me pay for the lunch, I had not expected it to be like this, so simple and so sudden. He had been tough, very tough indeed, much too tough for me. Sadly I took out what little change I had left and paid the bill. As I came out of the restaurant, someone stopped me: "Please, could you tell me . . ." Perhaps he wanted to know the time or to ask the way. But immediately I shouted: "I don't know you, I don't know anybody." He stood there, stupefied. I ran away.

NATURALLY

VIA DELLA LUNGARA, at three in the afternoon, is a street along which no one passes, not even the relations of those who are shut up in the Regina Coeli Prison. And in springtime, at that hour of the day, with its long line of buildings, as far as the eye can reach, and its trees jutting out over garden walls, and the sun shining soft and clear on the pavements, it is a street so beautiful that it makes you want to walk along it with eyes closed, like a blind man. And it was in Via della Lungara, as I was walking in the sunshine about three in the afternoon, that I noticed a couple in front of me. He was evidently no beauty, judging, at least, by his back—a small, black head greasy with brilliantine, a very short windcheater with a hood, and two little thin legs in very tight trousers, and crooked at that. Why is a man with crooked legs such a melancholy object? You shall know in a moment. But I was seeing these crooked legs for the first time; whereas *her* back was not new to me.

Imagine a statue of a woman, one of those antique ones, nude, with marble hips, marble shoulders, marble legs; slip a little black dress on to this statue, but in a rough sort of way, without pulling it down by the hem, so that it sits all crookedly on those bulging, rounded marble forms, and then you will have an impression of what she was like.

Her head was like the head of a statue, too, but of a different and much smaller statue. The head, in fact, of a young girl, stuck on to the neck of a fully-formed woman. I remembered this disparity and realized, all at once, that it was Pupa, called by this nickname of "Baby" because, though in her figure she looked more than her eighteen years, by her intelligence you might think she was about four. A native of Rieti, she had been in Rome only a short time and was a typist; having no fiancé or other male friend, she was considered a virtuous girl. I had noticed her, I had even been introduced to her; but her simplicity had discouraged me from pursuing the acquaintance: I like a woman to be knowing and even a bit coquettish; Pupa, on the other hand, was what we Romans call "a piece of bread".

But you know how these things happen. You see a woman every day and she means nothing to you; unexpectedly you meet her and, for some unknown reason, you fall in love with her. So it was that day in Via della Lungara. I said to myself: "Just look at her; she's really very, very beautiful"; and all of a sudden I could have cursed myself for not having realized it before, especially since—judging anyhow by their behaviour—the two people in front of me were on intimate terms and the position, by now, was already occupied. Then something happened that I could never have hoped for: the young man seized Pupa by the arm and raised his other hand as if to strike her; Pupa drew back and, as she did so, saw me. She immediately called out: "Signor Paolino, Signor Paolino!"

I am not a bully; in fact I have a mild sort of character, and this can be seen even from my physical appearance, for I am small and, alas, although I am young, I have a paunch. But a paunch is always less ridiculous than crooked legs. Anyhow this appeal, just at the moment when I was discovering Pupa's beauty, electrified me. I ran promptly to help her: "Signorina Pupa!" I exclaimed. I was face to face now with the crooked-legged young man, whose face was long and cross-looking, with a red nose that drooped down over his mouth. "Signor Paolino," said Pupa, "please tell this man here to leave me alone. He keeps chasing me. And now he's started attacking me."

Violently—in consideration also of the fact that the other man was no Hercules—I confronted him: "What d'you want?" "But I . . ." "Will you kindly tell me what you want?" "Really, I . . ." "Go away; otherwise . . ." "All right, all right." He threw me a look which at the moment I did not understand, and sidled off along the wall.

Now we were alone. I felt bold as a lion, for it was the first time in my life that anybody had run away from me. And I felt even more so when Pupa, turning her big, black eyes upon me, said to me in her gentle, childish voice: "Signor Paolino, you were grand; if it hadn't been for you I really don't know what I could have done."

Well, we went off, chatting together, towards Porta Settimiana; after we had passed the Gate, I offered her some coffee and she accepted. Now please note that everything had happened in a very natural way, without any premeditation—the meeting, Pupa's cry, the altercation, my offer of coffee, everything had come about as though by chance. The bar, at that time of day, was deserted; the cat was licking itself in the sun, on the threshold; the radio was humming away quietly. In a ringing voice I ordered two *espressi*; and then, still very naturally, I made another suggestion—the cinema. She put on a mortified expression: "Oh, I'm so dreadfully sorry, but I must go home. I'm expecting a trunk call from my mother at Rieti."

Disconcerted, I stammered something or other to the effect that we might see each other next day. But she, in a perfectly natural way, said: "You know what we can do? You can come home with me and keep me company while I wait for the telephone call."

And so, I thought again as I walked off with her, through one street after another, towards San Cosimato, everything was continuing in a natural way: she liked my company, she disliked leaving me, she invited me to come home with her. And what more natural, once we were on the staircase, than that I should take her hand and raise it to my lips? "Why, Signor Paolino, I didn't know you were so gallant", she murmured; however, she let me keep hold of her hand; and so we went up four floors hand in hand, she in front and I behind, since the staircase was narrow. When we reached the fourth landing, Pupa rang the bell and—even more natural than Pupa herself—the landlady appeared in the doorway: an elderly woman in black, her face besprinkled with hairy moles and on her bosom a locket containing a grey photograph of some dead person. "Signorina," she said, "you know you ought not to bring men into the house."

"But this is my cousin. We'll sit in the hall. Only for a moment, while I wait for a telephone call."

"Well, just this once, then."

So we sat down in the hall, I on an ottoman, she in a small wicker armchair. There was little light in the room, which had two closed doors and a dark passage leading away into the depths of the house. We sat for some time in silence, looking at each other. I smiled at her, she smiled at me. Then I plucked up courage, leant forward and took her hand again. She did not withdraw it; all she did was to sigh. I asked her: "Why do you sigh?" "Signor Paolino," she replied, "I too should like to think only of love. But how can one think of love when one has so many worries?"

I could only describe the tone in which she made this remark with one word: natural. Yes indeed, with her charming ingenuousness, the ingenuousness of a simple, sincere girl, Pupa was natural. She liked me, she did nothing to conceal it; but alas, there was something that prevented her from giving me her full attention. In a low voice, I pressed her to tell me what it was; but she took a lot of persuading. She sat with her head bowed down on her chest and, although I tried to take her by the chin and make her speak, she replied obstinately that it was not a matter that could interest me. Finally she made up her mind and, still in a natural sort of way, in the reluctant voice of a little girl who has some great trouble or other, she said: "The landlady made a terrible scene again to-day because I'm behindhand with my rent. You see why I'm expecting a trunk call from my mother? So as to come to an agreement with her. To-morrow I leave Rome and go back to Rieti."

"But I don't want you to leave Rome," I said gallantly. Flattered, full of gratitude, almost incredulous, she replied: "Really, Signor Paolino, you really don't want me to leave Rome?"

Now I'm not a rich man, I keep a little bookbinder's shop; but I always carry with me the five or ten thousand lire that one needs for everyday expenses. Her hand was lying in mine, passive, trustful, asking for protection. "Look here, Pupa," I said, "I'm not rich, but if it's a question of a small amount, I could lend it to you."

I thought she must have felt ill all of a sudden, for she jumped up and, without a word, disappeared down the passage. Disconcerted, wondering whether possibly I had offended her, I sat waiting on the ottoman which was too high for me, my legs dangling in the air. Meanwhile, at the far end of the passage, a very animated but subdued discussion was going on. Someone was speaking very fast, someone else was answering equally fast; the whole apartment seemed to be full of murmuring sounds. At last Pupa came back again: dignified, stately, stiff, she went and sat down a long way from me. I noticed the distance but said nothing. To justify her behaviour, she said: "I'm sorry, Signor Paolino, but that telephone call hasn't come through yet"; and I interpreted the words as a tacit refusal of my offer of a loan.

But then the landlady arrived. She appeared in the doorway, her black bust thrust forward, the locket with the dead person's photograph dangling from her neck. Without looking at me, she said to Pupa: "Signorina, here is your bill. You must settle it before you leave, I can't wait any longer."

The bill was hanging in the air, from the landlady's hand. I felt that now, according to the logic of the naturalness which had led me from one thing to another to the room in which we now were, I ought to take the bill, pull out the money and pay it. That was what I ought to do; and that was what I did. It was a little more than ten thousand lire. I took the note out of my pocket-book, folded it into the bill and thrust it into the landlady's hand in a haughty, authoritative way, saying: "All right, all right, here it is, and now you can go away." Pupa exclaimed gratefully: "Oh, Signor Paolino, you shouldn't . . ." The landlady said dryly to Pupa: "You can pay me the rest at your convenience", and vanished. I felt bolder than ever now, with that response of the blood, as though from the sting of a shower-bath, which every man feels after he has made a generous gesture. "But what a hag, that landlady of yours!" I said indignantly. Pupa rose and disappeared down the passage.

So there I was, alone again, again left high and dry in the same silent, sudden, inexplicable manner. Half an hour, perhaps, went by, during which I heard, several times, from the far end of the passage, the quick, subdued chattering of two people consulting together in low voices; then another half-hour went by in the deepest silence, as though I were the only person left in the flat. I ached all over as a result of being stuck on top of that high, hard ottoman; so I got up and started walking about the room. Then, as if urged on by the very naturalness of the situation, I ventured on tiptoe into the passage. A little light came from a half-closed door; cautiously I pushed it open and looked in. It was a very bare, poor-looking room, a real "furnished room", with the usual pieces of old, dark furniture such as you might see in a junk-shop; through the curtainless window fell a quiet, melancholy light. And, lying on the iron bed, flat on her back, reading a cheap illustrated paper, I saw Pupa. She was reading like the illiterate she was, completely absorbed, frowning, spelling it out word by word, perhaps. For a moment, to tell the truth, I was speechless with astonishment: I had been waiting in the hall while she, calmly, amused herself with the comic strips! Finally I managed to speak: "Well really! Here have I been waiting in the hall, while you . . ."

She gave a start, and said hurriedly: "Please, Signor Paolino, please go away; if the landlady sees us, I'll get into trouble . . ."

"But the telephone call . . ."

"Go back to the hall, I'll come in a moment."

I wish I had asked her: "Are you mad, or am I?"; but I hadn't the presence of mind. So I went back into the hall and started waiting again. First the usual ten minutes went by which everyone expects when waiting for a woman, then ten more supplementary minutes, then ten quite unnecessary minutes, and then ten minutes which were entirely unwarranted. I was sweating and I was cold; I felt too big for my clothes; my shoelaces seemed to be untying themselves; I no longer understood anything. Then back came the same surly landlady: "Why, who are you waiting for?"

"Signorina Pupa."

"She's gone out."

"But wasn't she expecting a trunk call?"

"She had it and she's gone out."

"But how did she go? I've been here all the time."

"There's the back door; she must have gone that way."

I found myself once more outside that house of bewitchment, feeling stunned and dazed, as one does at Luna Park on coming out of the chamber of horrors with all its ghosts and skeletons and screams and groans. Everything continued to be natural and unforced, smooth as oil; but I saw now that this fine naturalness was not that of a love adventure but rather that of an intrigue. Feeling positively unsteady on my legs, I dragged myself as far as Piazza Mastai, went into a bar and ordered coffee.

I saw someone leaning against the counter and staring at me; I looked again and recognized the young man with the crooked legs. Embarrassed, I said to him: "I'm sorry if . . . I ought to have understood." "Understood what?" "That you had good reasons of your own for hitting that girl." "What, you too?" Well, we told each other our stories and they fitted together perfectly: the trunk call, the lack of money, the landlady with the bill, the long waiting, the disappearance. The only difference was that he had taken up his position in the street and, when Pupa came out, had confronted her. In conclusion he said, almost sadly: "I wanted to warn you, but you didn't give me time. Of course, you wanted to show up well in front of Pupa. But if you'd listened to me you would have saved ten thousand lire." I answered indignantly: "A girl calls me and asks for my help. Anyone would have done as I did—isn't that so?" Meekly he answered: "Naturally."

NOT ONE BUT FIVE

THE owner of a black six-seater saloon, for use at weddings, christenings, funerals, public ceremonies and such like, naturally wants to know whether the customer who presents himself, money in hand, and asks to hire the vehicle for an occasion of this kind is . . . But let's take things in order.

Well, the customer presented himself at about ten in the morning at my garage in Via Ofanto. A big ugly man with a big spherical head covered with dishevelled white hair, a round, red face, and prominent eyes of a washed-out blue half-hidden between eyelids and cheeks. He was stuffed out with pullovers and sweaters underneath a heavy overcoat, and with a scarf round his neck: a real polar bear. He said at once: "Signor Pescetti, I come to you in sad circumstances: I have lost a brother who was, so to speak, my second self. Suddenly, yesterday evening, the first of January 1956, my poor brother breathed his last. Well, a good beginning to the year." He spoke these words in a meditative tone of voice, rather strange, it is true, but I did not attach any importance to it: we all know that sorrow shows itself in many different ways. So I assumed a sympathetic expression, for participation in the sorrows of one's customers is, after all, a requisite for the smooth running of a business. He pulled a check handkerchief out of his pocket, blew his nose and then went on to say that the funeral would be taking place next morning and that he required two cars, for himself and for the dead man's family. I replied that I was very sorry but I had only one car; I added, however, that my saloon could, if necessary, take as many as eight people; and that in any case, at a funeral, people don't mind being piled one on top of another: close proximity provides a little comfort in sorrow. He nodded his head and said: "Yes, you're quite right: close proximity provides a little comfort in sorrow. That's understood, then, I'll hire the saloon. To-morrow morning at nine o'clock in Piazza Campitelli—punctually, I beg you. But in the meantime I want to hire the car for this morning. I have a quantity of things I have to do for the funeral and a taxi would cost me twice as much." I replied that as it so happened the car was free that morning and I would drive him myself. No sooner said than done: I brought the car out, closed the garage, then he got in beside me and, having first consulted a sheet of paper, gave me the first address, which was that of a florist in Via Pompeo Magno, in the Prati quarter.

We drove for a short time without speaking. Suddenly, as if answering a question which I had not asked him, he said: "Yes, it's true, he was my second self. We were quite inseparable, or rather, he would never leave me, so much so that I was often forced to tell him to let me alone for a little. As you know, even brothers can get on one's nerves when they're too clinging. And he, into the bargain, had certain really ugly defects, and his proximity—let me say it here between us two, now that he is dead—was very often far from agreeable." I was astonished and, almost in spite of myself, I asked: "But what were these defects?" He sighed and answered: "Ah, there were many of them. My poor brother was a publican, and his *osteria* was in the neighbourhood of Piazza Campitelli. In his case, anyhow, the things that people say about publicans were all true."

By this time I was almost enjoying myself. "Here at last," I said to myself, "is someone who is sincere: generally the dead are all good, all honest, all saints. This man, anyhow, tells the truth." Cautiously I enquired: "And what are the defects of publicans?" With another sigh, he answered: "Oh well, the usual ones: watering the wine, giving one thing in place of another, by which I mean, for instance, giving young donkey in place of veal, making the bill into a round figure when the customer has a girl friend with him and therefore pays without a word, for fear of losing face. . . . I wouldn't swear that he hasn't cooked and served up a few cats now and then. . . . All the little tricks of the trade, in fact, unless of course the publican is an honest man . . . and my brother, alas, wasn't honest; on the contrary, he was sharp, very sharp indeed. Mind you, I used to give him good advice, but he didn't listen to me; all he thought about was hoarding money. What's the point of hoarding money, I said to him many, many times, you hoard and hoard and soon Death comes along with his sickle, and then who have you been hoarding for? For your heirs." "That's to say, for you," I said. He replied calmly: "That's right, for me." In order to egg him on, I persisted: "These are merely the defects of his trade, such as anyone might have. But I daresay he was a decent chap in ordinary life." He cast up his eyes to heaven, in derision: "A decent chap? Don't you believe it! His defects as a publican were minor ones. The worst were his defects as a man." "What ever d'you mean?" "Just what I say. For instance, women. Believe it or not, there wasn't a skivvy or a scullery-maid that he didn't give annoyance to, so that he had to be continually changing them because they wouldn't stay with him. His wife, poor woman, knows all about that; many's the time she's cried her eyes out. I used to say to him: 'How can you, the father of a family and a middle-aged man, go running after little sluts of twenty, going down to the basement on purpose to be alone with them, or taking advantage of the moment when your wife is serving customers to rush into the kitchen and get your hands on them? Aren't you ashamed of yourself?' But it was a waste of effort, like talking to a blank wall. These, however, are big defects, and perhaps for that very reason still pardonable. His worst defects were the small ones." "And what were they?" He wrinkled up his face in an expression of disgust and boredom. "Oh, I don't know," he said, "all those mean little nastinesses —lies and calculations, disloyalties and jealousies, the little pieces of egotism that lurk at the bottom of a man's heart like grubs at the bottom of a stagnant pool. And he had so many of these mean little nastinesses, so many of them, my poor brother."

We had now arrived in Via Pompeo Magno, in front of the flower-shop. He said he was going to order the wreaths; he got out and disappeared into the shop. I waited for about a quarter of an hour, reading an illustrated magazine. Finally, out he came again, with a strange laugh that shook him all over, silently. "He didn't want to make the wreath for me," he said. "Why?" "Because I said to him: 'I want this written on the ribbon: *From his brother, with no ill-feeling.*'" "Why *with no ill-feeling*?" "Because he made so much trouble for me, and after all that, I might well have retained some ill-feeling, but I have not." "And how about the florist?" "The florist absolutely refused to accept those words. Even though I'd ordered the finest and most expensive wreath. Never mind. I had to give in, and we wrote down the customary lie: *From his inconsolable brother.*" This time I said nothing, because I was beginning to be rather less amused: I felt he was going too far. "And now where do we go?" I asked. He took the same sheet of paper from his pocket and gave me the address of an undertaker, in the neighbourhood of the Pantheon.

This time I did not say a word, perhaps because I was slightly vexed. He noticed this, and asked: "Tell me the truth, Signor Pescetti; does my behaviour seem to you strange?" "Well, yes, a little strange." He sighed. "Yes, I know," he said. "And yet it isn't so very strange. My brother and I—the moment has come to tell you—were enemies, truly enemies. What I am, he disliked, and what he was, *I* disliked. Ought I to pretend—why should

I?" "Well, for the eyes of the world." He paused in uncertainty for a moment and then cried: "But the world ought to know that I've struggled against him all my life, that I've never been willing to come to terms with his infamous conduct, that I've always shown him he was in the wrong, always. The world ought to know this, Signor Pescetti." Once again I did not answer, but drove on in silence to the Pantheon, while he sat sighing beside me and, from time to time, with an odd gesture of the hand like a cat doing its whiskers, smoothing back his dishevelled white hair.

In a narrow street near the Pantheon we stopped in front of a dusty shop-window through which could be dimly seen some bronze wreaths and other funeral ornaments: this was the undertaker's. He got out of the car, went into the shop and remained there for another quarter of an hour. At last he came back, with a satisfied air. "Now we'll go to the mason, about the tombstone—in Via Labicana. And d'you know what I say? The idea that to-morrow a real hearse with two real horses is going to carry him off for good and all, makes me draw a deep breath of relief. I can breathe freely—yes, that's the truth—I can breathe freely. Latterly I just couldn't bear to be with him any longer. Ah yes, death makes a clean sweep. From to-morrow, without *him*, a new year, a new life; we're at the beginning of January —a new year, a new life." He kept on saying to himself: "A new year, a new life"; then he looked again at the sheet of paper with the addresses and said: "That's all now: the flowers, the car, the hearse, and he himself, well and truly dead. That's all." "The church?" I suggested. He twisted his mouth. "That's the most difficult thing of all. I went to see the parish priest this morning. But the priest is obstinate and refuses to believe that he's dead. He says it's not enough for me merely to assert that my brother is dead. He must have the proofs." "What proofs?" "Why, the documents." I thought to myself once again that grief was giving him a distorted view of things, and I said nothing. After a moment he resumed: "It's a pity, however, that one can't die and still remain alive. To tell the truth, I should like to die and at the same time to follow my own funeral, to see who's there and who isn't there, and what people are saying, and how they're behaving. And—d'you know?—in my opinion many people kill themselves simply with the idea of getting themselves talked about." He was, in fact, obsessed with the idea of the great pleasure a dead man would take in following his own funeral. Then, all of a sudden, emphasizing the words, he cried: "O my brother, you won't be at your funeral but *I* shall be there and it will be just as if you were there yourself."

We had passed the Colosseum now and were in Via Labicana. I stopped in front of the mason's workshop and he, as usual, stepped briskly out of the car and went in at the door. By this time I had read my illustrated paper twice over, so I started walking up and down on the pavement, smoking a cigarette. Through the opaque glass door of the mason's workshop I heard shouting, as though people were quarrelling. Finally he came out, breathing heavily. "The same old story again," he muttered as he settled down in his seat. "I wanted them to write on the tombstone: *Ottavio Macelloni, born so-and-so, died so-and-so. May God forgive him all the evil he did.* That sounds well, doesn't it? But no, they absolutely refused to carry out this inscription. Never mind, I just had to give in. While he was alive, he would never let me tell him the truth; and they won't let me tell it him now, after he's dead." "Well," I said to him at this juncture, growing impatient, "you've done your round of visits. D'you want me to take you home?" "Yes," he replied, "I've done my round of visits . . . my poor brother—" and suddenly he covered his face with his handkerchief. "Mr—," I said; "excuse me, what is your name?" "Ottavio Macelloni," he answered through the folds of his handkerchief. Flabbergasted,

I stammered: "But have you the same name as your brother?" This time he made no reply: he was sobbing violently and his sobs shook his shoulders and head. My suspicions were aroused, and I tried to see his face; and all at once I had the confirmation of what I had already been thinking for some moments: instead of crying, he was laughing, in fact he was fit to burst with derisive, silent guffaws behind his handkerchief.

I was uneasy, indeed extremely uneasy. I had wasted my whole morning and my petrol. And moreover, with a madman—for there could now be no doubt that he was mad—there was no knowing: he might perhaps be dangerous. We were at the moment in a deserted spot, in a street flanked by convent walls. I stopped the car and looked round. Then, emerging from behind his handkerchief, he said: "Are you surprised that my brother and I should have the same name?" I was frightened now and, thinking it better not to contradict him, replied hurriedly: "No, I'm not at all surprised. It happens every day. Someone has a son and calls him, let us say, Giuseppe. Another son is born—again Giuseppe. I know a family in which there are five sons and all five of them are called Alfredo." I should never have said this. He looked at me, his face darkening, and then, with a roar, leapt upon me, seizing me by the collar of my coat, like a raving lunatic. "Five!" he shouted. "Repeat that if you dare. Five! This is the last straw: I, who've suffered so much with this Ottavio here, am forced to have three more Ottavios to fight against. Say it again! Five! But you're mad." He was clasping me tightly and I was trying to free myself, and almost involuntarily I cried: "No, my dear boy, it's you that's mad." "Say it again if you dare," he said. "Five! Why, you're crazy, you ought to be shut up." Well, to make a long story short, while we two were struggling and he was trying to strangle me—neither more nor less—with his two hands round my neck, and I was trying to disengage myself, some people came along, and two policemen, and they freed me and pulled him out of the car. Like a great mad clown he went on shouting and raving: "New year, new life! To-morrow there's the funeral and there'll be no more talk of Ottavio Macelloni. New year, new life!" They carried him off bodily to a taxi, four of them dragging him; and meanwhile he had covered his face again with his handkerchief and was sobbing, that is, laughing to himself, like a real madman. And how about the flowers, the hearse, the tombstone? Ah well, just for once they must have been left without a customer.

THE LOVELIEST THING OF ALL

I WENT to visit Massimina and Peppe at their home for the first time since they got married. They had invited me in the street, stopping me as I was hurrying round a corner to avoid them, for I had courted Massimina for years and I didn't like seeing her with another man, even though he was a friend. But they stopped me and they both seemed intensely eager to have me to supper, though each of them had a different reason. And so I accepted, even if reluctantly. Massimina, in case you don't know her, is a short, broad young woman, with a small, round head whose retreating curves and curly hair make it look like the head of a small sheep; when you look at her, with her fine, bright, prominent eyes, her little nose, her full mouth and her very broad face, you might think that, in certain circumstances, she would be capable of charging at you, head down, or of butting you with her horns. I had fallen in love with her before she became so broad; but it must be added that her job as a qualified masseuse—she was one of the best in Rome—had developed the muscles of her chest and shoulders and arms; and she had become broad all over, though still retaining, for me at any rate, the characteristic charm of a little curly-headed sheep. Perhaps, when I saw her again, she looked to me all the broader inasmuch as her husband, beside her, looked so very, very narrow: he was a tiny little young man but well-proportioned, curly-headed, too, but fair, with an insolent expression on his face, very smart in his puffed-out check shirt and American-style trousers, tight on the hips and legs and with stitched pockets and seams. Massimina had wanted this pretty little husband by hook or by crook, it might be said. He would have nothing to do with her; but then, when she went on insisting, in the end he yielded. He was working in a small bar in Trastevere; but since he got married he had left the bar and ceased to do anything. It was Massimina, in fact, who, by dint of massage, earned a living for them both.

And so I went to visit them in the neighbourhood of Via Angelo Emo, a new neighbourhood in which houses spring up like mushrooms and where, if you look at an open field and then turn away, when you look round again, there, where the field was, there's already a huge yellow eight-storey building. They lived, indeed, in one of these blocks of flats that looked as if it was made of cardboard and had a row of shops on the ground floor, with blinding electric neon lighting, a light that made even the cabbages at the greengrocer's look bright purple. A new quarter, a new building, and, when I had rung the bell and the door was opened, a brand-new flat. I went into the little bare, echoing entrance-hall which reverberated with the sound of the radio: Peppe, in the minute sitting-room, was listening to the latest sporting news. As soon as he saw me, he said: "Go in there, into the kitchen, and you'll find Massimina . . . I want to hear the news." I noticed that he had a troubled look in his eye and an absorbed expression, and that he was biting the nail of his first finger—always, with him, a sign that he was worried. I left him and went into the kitchen.

This, too, was minute, like the sitting-room; but with everything in place, contrived and fitted in to perfection—cupboards, sink, gas-rings, table, oven. Massimina, an apron tied round her hips, was standing in front of the cooker, her sturdy arm outstretched to grasp the handle of a frying-pan in which she was shaking to and fro a *fritto misto* of brains and *courgettes*. Beside her she had a piece of yellow paper, of the kind that is used for wrapping bread, upon which she deposited the brains and *cour-*

gettes as they were cooked. She looked at me sideways, without moving, and said: "Have you seen my little house? D'you like it?" In her voice, which was soft and gentle, there was a quiver of tenderness which moved me as I reflected that she had bought this little two-roomed flat inch by inch, so to speak, putting aside the money through year after year of massage, and now she had given the whole thing to that idler Peppe who wasn't even fond of her. "It's a really charming little flat," I said. She laughed with pleasure, and went on: "Go and have a look at the bedroom and then come back here and tell me what you think of it."

To please her, I went out and looked at the bedroom which, together with the sitting-room, comprised the entire flat. There was a big double bed, low, according to the fashion, with a blue bedspread; there were two bedside tables of dark mahogany with light-coloured sycamore feet; there was a chest-of-drawers, also dark with light-coloured feet. On the chest-of-drawers stood a coloured china ornament consisting of a round plate the colour of sea-sand, with a few small crabs visible upon it, and, kneeling on its rim, a woman in a bathing-costume making frightened gestures because of the said crabs. A door was standing open and I saw the bathroom too, all white, with nickel-plated taps and fittings. Everything was new, clean, orderly, polished. I went back to the kitchen and she at once asked me, tremblingly: "Well, what d'you think of it?" Moved, again, by the thought that it was she who had created this room out of her humble savings, I answered: "I think it's a lovely room." "Yes, isn't it? I bought the furniture in Via Cola di Rienzo. Did you see the bedspread? It's pure silk." "Lovely, lovely." "And the bathroom—did you see that?" "Yes, lovely, lovely." She laughed again, gave the frying-pan a shake and then, after a moment's silence, went on: "But the loveliest thing of all, in this flat—d'you know what that is?" I replied, just to pay her a compliment: "The loveliest thing of all, is *you*." I saw her shake her head; then she said, "The loveliest thing of all, in this flat, is my husband." I was left gaping, for I wasn't expecting a declaration of such frankness as this. She continued: "Isn't he charming, my Peppe? Such fair, curly hair. . . . Tell me, isn't he charming?" Then I burst out: "But why d'you have to say this sort of thing to *me*?" She understood, at last, and answered: "I say these things to you because I wouldn't say them to anyone else. . . . Yes, I've a husband who's a perfect little jewel. . . . But go back to him now, go and keep him company because I still have things to do here in the kitchen."

I left her willingly, because to hear her speak in that way about her husband made my blood boil. I found that Peppe had turned off the radio and was sitting biting his nails, deep in thought. Then he said: "Rodolfo, can I trust you?" "Of course you can." "Well, listen," he said, "this evening, about eleven, I have an appointment . . . and I've got to get there." "An appointment? Why, who with?" Impatiently he replied: "With a girl. . . . Now you've got to help me, if you're a true friend. At a certain time, say half past ten, you must remind me that we have an appointment together, with Fabrizi—you know, the car agent—about a question of some outer covers. You mention it and I'll confirm it, and then we'll say good-night to Massimina and go off. . . . Is that understood?" To tell the truth, I felt very uneasy: to have for wife a woman like Massimina, worth her weight in gold, to have been married barely a month and already to be making appointments with girls, at night. . . . I said with sincerity: "If you really insist on it, I'll do this for you. But mind what I say, Peppe, you're doing wrong." "And why am I doing wrong?" "Because you two have been married for a month . . . and Massimina is so very fond of you." Then he twisted round like a fury: "How can I help it if I feel nothing at all for her? She wanted me at all costs, although I kept on rubbing it in, in every possible way, that I didn't love her. . . . Well, if you're willing to do this for me, that's all right. If not, it's all the same to me." "Very well, keep calm, I'll do it."

At this point Massimina, who had finished her cooking, came into the room and began laying the table. She pulled out a small table into the middle, spread a fine tablecloth over it, and laid three places, not without pointing out to me that the set of china, for six, was also very fine, with gold flowers on it and a gold border. Gaily she went backwards and forwards from one room to the other, carrying plates, glasses and knives and forks; but this gaiety on her part was entirely for the benefit of her husband who, in contrast, sat motionless in his armchair with a serious, absent-minded look on his face. And I noticed that each time she went past him she could not resist giving him a caress or addressing some little joking remark to him, or even going so far as to rub her hip lightly against his shoulder. In short, she was in love and was not ashamed of showing it; and whatever she did, she did it for Peppe and for him only.

We sat down at the table, in front of the open window which, since the flat was on the ground floor, looked out straight on to the pavement. From outside, on that stuffy August night, came the sounds of other radios: the neighbourhood was full of radios all screaming the same song, like so many cocks crowing all together when the sun rises. Massimina brought in the tureen full of spaghetti and helped us lavishly; and I, who did not know her before as a cook, reflected that she had great skill in the art and that Peppe was a fool to be unfaithful to her with some silly little slut of a girl. We ate our spaghetti in silence, and then I told Massimina what a really fine cook she was, and she replied that she was pleased I appreciated her cooking because Peppe, on the contrary, was continually complaining. Peppe protested gloomily: "I don't complain . . . but you're always trying to stuff me. Eat, eat, eat . . . I only try to defend myself."

She gazed at him broodingly, just as a mother broods over her child, and then exclaimed: "Eat up, then, don't be afraid. If you get fat, I'll give you some special massage and you'll get slim again." It made me laugh, this idea of Massimina giving her husband massage, and so our conversation moved to the subject of massage, and Peppe, with a rather mischievous look, said: "Massimina, tell us some of the confidences that your ladies come out with while you're massaging them. Now listen, Rodolfo, and see if it doesn't make you laugh." Massimina hedged for a moment, then told us some really comic tales: of old women who had massage in order to please their lovers, so they said; of young women who confided their husbands' whims; of film actresses who recounted their own goings-on. Peppe, still with that mischievous look on his face, added: "But there's one of those ladies whom I should really like to meet—the one called Nora. Every time she telephones to arrange an appointment, she tries to start a conversation: 'You're Massimina's husband, are you? And what do you do? Are you a masseur, like your wife? And why not?'" Massimina, as she listened, suddenly flew into a rage. "One of these days," she cried, "instead of massaging that woman I'll give her such a slap on her side that it'll leave a mark on her. . . . Nasty flirt, that's all she is." Peppe, who had deliberately mentioned this lady, laughed with satisfaction.

After supper we turned on the radio again and listened to a programme of songs. Massimina, meanwhile, had gone out to tidy up the kitchen. As for Peppe, he went on biting his nails, in silence, and every now and then he looked at the clock. I felt more and more embarrassed as the time passed, because I was fond of Massimina and disliked helping Peppe to deceive her. I wanted to make a last effort, and said: "Where does this girl live?" He looked at me, hesitated, and then answered: "Not so very far from here. She lives in Via Candia." "Well, tell me where she expects to meet you, and I'll go and tell her that you'll see her to-morrow, in the daytime. Don't go this evening: can't you see how happy Massimina is? She meant this supper to be a sort of house-warming . . . and you would be hurting her." But he shrugged his shoulders and replied: "You're an idiot. I promised to go and I'm going."

Well, the time came when the lie had to be told, and I glanced at the clock and said to Peppe: "Look, it'll soon be time for us to go and see Fabrizi, about that business." "Yes, of course," he said promptly; "I was forgetting. . . . To tell the truth, if you hadn't reminded me, I should have forgotten all about it. Come on, let's be going." As he said this he got up, with such brisk impatience and such clear satisfaction that even a blind man would have noticed it. Massimina, in fact, understood, and began, in an agitated tone of voice: "Fabrizi? You hadn't told me anything about it . . ." Then, all of a sudden, I intervened: "Massimina, come in here a moment; I want to speak to you."

We went into the bedroom and I closed the door and said to her: "Now look, it's best for you to let Peppe go out, without making too much of a fuss. The more you try to control him, the more you show that you're jealous, the less fond of you he'll be. . . . Pay attention to what I say, for once: let him go out without saying anything." She looked at me; her face was so contorted, so dismayed, that it was painful to see. Finally she stammered: "All right, Rodolfo, I'll do as you say."

We went back into the sitting-room, and Massimina said to Peppe, in an off-hand way: "Well then, good-night. . . . I have to go out early to-morrow morning, but I'll be careful not to wake you. See you to-morrow evening." Her voice was trembling, but she restrained herself, as she had promised me. As for Peppe, he kept his eyes lowered; he was ashamed. We went to the door, and Peppe said: "Good-bye, Massimina", and hurried out; but I myself stopped, in order to thank Massimina for the supper. And then, as I was repeating: "Thank you, thank you so much; and I hope one evening you'll come and have dinner with me, in a restaurant", I noticed that she was crying. She was standing still, leaning against the door-post, and the tears were slipping down her cheeks quickly, one after the other, from her eyes which were wide open. I was moved, and I said: "Don't cry. . . . We really are going to see Fabrizi." She answered, in her gentle voice: "Fabrizi telephoned yesterday that he was leaving for Naples. Peppe knew, but he forgot." I felt embarrassed and, not knowing what to say, replied: "Don't cry, Massimina. . . . It's quite true that you have a lovely little home . . . and in it the loveliest thing of all is your husband." She shook her head and said: "The loveliest thing of all will be when I get to sleep soon and stop thinking about him." I said good-night to her and joined Peppe in the street. We walked past under the window; Massimina was standing there looking at us. Then we turned the corner.

THE PEAR-WOOD TABLE

RICH people travel and even go to America and then come back after twenty years and, when they see the Roman skyscrapers again, are moved by the thought that they were already there when they themselves were twenty years younger. The poor, on the other hand, do not move, and it is a great thing if they get as far as Ostia for the sea-bathing or Bracciano for an outing in October. Nevertheless, in their small way, the poor have the same feelings as the rich. I myself have never moved away from Rome, but inside Rome I have certainly moved about a bit. As a child I lived outside Porta San Pancrazio, on a farm with a vegetable-garden, for my grandfather was a market gardener. Then the family was scattered and I went to live in Via Mario dei Fiori, above the cabinet-maker's shop where I worked. Still working as a cabinet-maker, as soon as I had put aside a little money I moved to Via della Pace, behind Piazza Navona, into a loggia on the top of an old palace. This loggia had eight windows and the draughts were innumerable. You went up to it first by the grand staircase, then by an ordinary staircase, and finally by an iron corkscrew staircase. But it had a fine view over the roofs and domes and towers and the sky of Rome, from all the windows. In this loggia, shortly after I went to live there, there came to live with me Giacomina, a girl who worked as a laundress, and I spent five years with her there which were the five best years of my life. At the time I did not know that those were my best years; such things, while one is experiencing them, one never does know. And, during those good years, not a single day passed, it might be said, that Giacomina and I did not have a quarrel. I don't know how it was, but under any sort of pretext we would start arguing; I would say one thing, she would answer another, and then she, running short of arguments, would begin insulting me, calling me an ignoramus, a cad, or even a blackguard; and I would pay her back in her own coin, calling her an idiot, a fishwife, yes, even a prostitute. And from words, often, we would pass on to deeds. At some insult from her, worse even than the others, concerning my family or my trade, I would lose my temper and jump on her, seizing her by her thick, curly hair, and try to slap her face. She, for her part, would try and kick me on the shins and in the belly, or scratch me. Then, out of breath, we would separate and she would start crying—if she was really incapable of going on any longer; if, on the other hand, she had a little energy left, she would rush out, banging the door and shouting that she would never come back. But she did come back; or rather I, as if by chance, would meet her somewhere in the neighbourhood and accost her and take her by the arm; and at first she would be unwilling, but later, after many words and many promises, she would agree to come and have a meal with me at the eating-house. Here the wine would warm us up and we would discover how fond we were of one another. Then we would go home and I would put my arm round her waist, and she would do the same to me, and we would climb those hundred or so stairs closely entwined, stopping at every step to give each other a kiss, and she would say she would like to devour me with kisses, and I would answer that I would like to do the same. Ah, how we loved each other then, and we didn't know it! So little did we know it that I was convinced I did not love her, in fact that I hated her, and I stayed with her as a kind of penance and tried to avoid her whenever I could. Fool that I was, I preferred anybody's company to hers—even that of friends who were not real friends but mere loutish eating-house acquaintances; or sometimes I stayed working late in the shop, simply in order to be late for her; or I preferred even solitude. I felt I was chained by the foot and did not realize that I had a need of that chain, as I was to discover later, by which time it was too late. To my fellow-workers and eating-house companions I spoke ill of her, with contempt and disgust, calling her a nuisance and a curse and saying she had the evil eye. When I was waiting in the loggia and heard her step on the stairs, I used to say to myself: "How long is this misery to go on? There she comes again . . . I just can't bear it." And I did not realize, idiot that I was, that I loved her, that I was desperately in love with her and could not live without her. She, of course, was as stupid as I was, and she treated me in just as vile a way as I treated her; she too kept saying that I was her ruin, and cursed be the day when I met her, and better to throw herself in the Tiber with a stone round her neck than stay a single day longer with me. Thus we tried more than once to be unfaithful to each other: I with the maid in the flat below, an affected little blonde; and Giacomina, meeting her on the stairs, threatened her with a long knitting-needle, saying she would kill her if she did not leave me alone, to such effect that the girl was terrified and refused to see me again. I believe that Giacomina, on her side, was unfaithful to me with a barman in Piazza Navona, and though it did not amount to much I suffered terribly, so that I could neither eat nor sleep, until one day she came upstairs, running all the way, and threw herself into my arms, saying passionately: "You're the best of all and I shall never love anyone but you." Yes, we truly loved each other, and the more we loved each other the less we knew it. However, we reached a point when we fought so violently that Giacomina had a bruised eye, all black and green, for a fortnight, and said she was ashamed to show herself out of doors; and I had three deep scratches from eye to neck, and when I told them in the shop that the cat had done it, they all laughed at me. That day we hit each other; but another day I very nearly killed her: I took her by the throat and began squeezing and she fainted; but before that she had hit me on the head with a flat-iron, at a delicate spot just above the temple, so that it drew blood and I myself nearly fainted too. I had to go to the casualty ward at San Giacomo to get myself treated and, to add to the shame, next morning there appeared a news item in the paper: "Following copious libations, the carpenter Luigi Proietti came to blows with his mistress, Giacomina Girolini. Proietti had the worst of it. Result: should be well in a week, apart from complications." In short, such a love as ours there had never been; and, as I have said, we did not know it. And now would you perhaps like to know how this violent love affair came to an end? It happened like this. One day when we had made an appointment in Piazza Navona, she kept me waiting a good half-hour. When she arrived, I said to her resentfully: "Where did you learn your manners? You've kept me waiting almost an hour." "I had things to do," she replied; "if you like it, that's that, and if you don't like it, it's all the same to me." "No," I said, "I don't like it." "You don't like it," said she; "good-bye, then. . . . You won't ever have to wait for me again"; and off she went. It was five years that we had been together and that was the last time I saw her. Out of pique, neither of us made any approaches to the other; the days went by, I was unhappy and am sure she was unhappy too, but this time neither of us would take the first step. One morning, when I thought I heard her step on the stairs, I felt first a great hope and then a great sadness when it turned out to be the postman; and afterwards it seemed to me—but I was wrong—that I no longer felt anything. Then, it so happened, the owner of the house wanted possession of the loggia again, and I left the quarter and went back to my old room in Via Mario dei Fiori. Perhaps, if I had stayed in Via della Pace, I might have chanced to meet her and we might have been reconciled. But my change of abode was fatal. I started working very hard, trying not to think of her, and then I fell into the clutches of my wife and got married, and everything was finished. I was then thirty-three.

At thirty-three a man is still young and feels he has all his life in front of him. I did not love my wife, in fact very soon I began to be unable to endure her, but I comforted myself by thinking: "I'm only thirty-three. . . . Surely I shall meet plenty more Giacominas." But I was wrong and I did not meet even one, and so, between my wife for whom I felt nothing, the two children I had to support, and my work which never left me free for a moment, the years went by one after the other without my realizing it, first at walking-pace, then at a trot and finally at a gallop. The years went by as years do go by—day by day, week by week, month by month, season by season; and there was always something to occupy my time and to make me hope or despair, whether it was a child's illness, or a debt, or an important piece of work, or a holiday, or a period of heat or cold—there was always something, I say, that made me look to the future, not very far ahead, in truth, say three months; and so those three months would pass, for good or ill; but four times three months makes a year, and so twelve years went by. With this carrot-and-donkey system I felt I was going forward and was not aware that I was, in point of fact, going back, for life is like a mountain and up to a certain moment you climb and then you begin to descend. Nevertheless I was thinking all the time of Giacomina, yet not so much of her personally as of a woman like her who would halt me in the passage of the years with a true, strong love such as Giacomina's had been; and I was always hoping that this love would come, but it did not come. Finally, unable to bear it any longer, I parted from my wife, left her the two children and went off to live by myself in the house of a marble-worker who rented me a room in the neighbourhood of the Pantheon. I was now more than forty-five, and on the day that I moved, having hung up the mirror which I use for shaving, I looked at myself and, seeing my tired, sad face, I realized that the good time was truly past and that Giacomina would never come back again. Then I sat down on a chair in a corner, took my face between my hands and wept for about ten minutes, reflecting that, after doing so many things and moving house so many times, I had come back to the point of departure.

One day, the owner of the shop told me to go and take an order, and gave me the customer's name and address on a piece of paper. I took the piece of paper, put my yard-measure and sketch-book in my pocket and went out. Not till I was in the street did I look at the note: it gave the number in Via della Pace of the building in which I had lived, and I also saw written there: "attic, i.e. loggia". At first, I confess, I felt like going back and asking the boss to send someone else; then I said to myself that this was mere weakness and resigned myself to going.

It was late in the afternoon, in May—just the time when, having finished work, I used to meet Giacomina by the central fountain in Piazza Navona. As then, there were numbers of children in the piazza chasing each other as they played tig; and their mothers and sisters were sitting on the seats taking the air; and the swallows, rather like the children in the piazza, were chasing each other in the air, from one roof-top to another and round the obelisk. As then, I noticed that as I came nearer to Via della Pace my legs began to give way and my breath to fail; but this was due only to force of habit revealing itself after so many years: this time there was no Giacomina waiting for me, and I no longer lived in the loggia on the top of the palace.

I went very slowly up the stairs, feeling as though I were, not forty-five, but eighty: so weak did I feel in my legs, and without any desire to reach the top. I went first up the grand staircase, then, for a further two floors, up the ordinary staircase, and finally I started to climb the iron corkscrew stairs. Once upon a time I used to go flying up these stairs; now I stopped at every step, knowing that I was going up not for Giacomina but for a wooden table. I stopped at the door for a moment to get my breath; and it seemed to me that I heard voices shouting inside the loggia. Then I rang the bell and waited quite a long time. I was on the point of ringing again, when the door was flung violently open and there appeared in front of me a girl in green corduroy trousers and a black sweater; she was dark with rumpled hair and a pale face and, it seemed to me, was in a state of great irritation. She asked me ungraciously who I was and what I wanted; as soon as I told her, she turned her back on me and went away, shouting: "It's the carpenter."

I went in and saw the loggia I knew so well. The windows were all wide open and I could see the domes and roofs and towers I had looked at for so many years. The furniture, however, was not the same: the loggia had been transformed into a painter's studio, a studio *de luxe*, as could be seen from the carpets, the sofa and some fine pieces of furniture. At the far end, near the bathroom door, there was an easel with a canvas on it; other canvases were stacked against the wall. The painter himself was standing in the middle of the room, looking at me with the eye of a basilisk: he too was young and dark, and dressed, like the girl, in corduroy trousers and sweater. "You've come about the table," he said hastily; "this is the table I want you to make. . . ."

He handed me a page torn from a foreign magazine: the table was of an English type, Chippendale, of the kind that has a folding flap on each side. As I was asking: "What sort of wood shall we make it of—mahogany? Or a nice light-coloured wood —pear-wood, for instance?"—I noticed that there was an open suitcase on the sofa and that the girl was going backwards and forwards from the wardrobe, putting things into it. The young man replied: "Mahogany . . . or pear-wood perhaps. . . . Anyhow, a good quality of wood"; but he was looking at her and obviously could not concentrate on the table. He spoke to her angrily: "Stop that play-acting, once and for all. Put your things back where they belong."

"It isn't play-acting . . . I'm going away."

"You know you're not going . . . so why all this drama?"

"In a moment or two you'll realize it isn't drama."

As she said this, she went on throwing things, all higgledy-piggledy, into the suitcase. Pretending to be absorbed in the design of the table, I took the sketch-book and pencil from my pocket and began sketching a section of the piece of furniture. The young man, in the meantime, was walking up and down; then he stopped, took a knife of the type that is used for scraping paints and furiously slashed the canvas on the easel. Then he gave a kick, and upset both easel and canvas. "Who's being dramatic now?" she said hypocritically. "But don't delude yourself; you haven't destroyed a masterpiece."

I noticed that, in order to hurt him, she resorted—exactly like Giacomina—to remarks about his work. I continued with my drawing of the section: the table-legs were movable from underneath and supported the flaps when the table was open. There were no metal parts: all the mortise joints were of wood. The legs were round, slightly tapering, with the feet turned outwards. "Instead of getting angry with your canvases," she said, "you'd do better to help me close my suitcase."

He went over as if to help her and then, all of a sudden, seized hold of the suitcase with both hands and hurled it into the middle of the studio, shouting: "That's the way I help you."

All her clothes were now scattered over the floor. She said, calmly: "Now pick them up."

"I shan't pick up a damned thing."

"Mr. Carpenter," she begged, in a honeyed voice, "please . . . please pick up these things for me. Please be so kind . . ."

"Don't touch anything," he roared, beside himself with rage, "unless you want me to throw you downstairs."

What would another man have done, in my place? He would have sent him flying out of the window. But I had a feeling of pity for him and, even more, of envy. It was just the same kind of scene that Giacomina and I used to have, ten years before, in that same place. And this was love; and they, like us, did not realize it; and when they realized it, it would be too late. I answered quietly: "I came here about the table. Tell me what wood you want it made of and I'll go away."

"Yes," she cried, "have your table made. . . . You'll sit at it alone, make no mistake about that"; and suddenly she threw herself on the sofa, sobbing, holding her head in her hands. Then he did what I used to do: he sat down beside her and took her in his arms, beseeching her: "Come on, Nella; be a good girl." And he turned towards me and said: "Yes, let's have it in mahogany . . . that's all right."

Before going away, I added: "The measurements would be one metre fifty, by seventy. Or do you want it larger? One fifty by seventy would mean a table for six."

"All right, one fifty by seventy," he said; meanwhile he was trying to soothe the girl, but she answered every caress and every word with a shrug of the shoulders. I was on the point of leaving the room when her voice, still tearful but imperious, came protestingly from underneath her arm: "But I don't want it made of mahogany! I want pear-wood!"

MOTHER'S BOY

THE first flat tyre was caused, not by me, but by fate, which took me by surprise and, so to speak, forced my hand. Unemployed, as usual, I was walking down Viale Parioli one afternoon towards the Acqua Acetosa, when I noticed a car standing in a side street. I noticed it because I have a passionate interest in cars: a car that is not mass-produced, a racing car, a car of foreign manufacture, can sometimes make me stand spellbound for more than an hour, just looking at them and examining their special features. This one was a sports car, long and low on the ground, of the "convertible" type, all bonnet and boot, flame-coloured, and with a muzzle full of chromium teeth that made it look like a tiger. Fascinated by this ferocious machine, I went over to it and the first thing I saw was that it had a flat tyre. "Now," I said to myself, "a flat tyre. Anyone else in my place would manage to get something out of this." Just at that moment a plump, fair young man in a windcheater and narrow, tight trousers, came out of one of the buildings near by, opened the door of the car and jumped quickly in. Feeling sympathetic, I went up and said to him: "Hi, you've got a flat tyre." He at once got out and went and looked at it, saying something to me in a foreign language as though to thank me; then he began getting to work to take off the wheel. I was still standing near the open door, and by chance my eye fell on a camera which was lying on the seat. To snatch it up and run off took me only a second; he was busy unscrewing the nuts of the wheel with a wrench, low down at the far side of that very low car, and did not see me. But as I fled I thought to myself: "So that's the flat tyre trick."

I had now to conceal my plunder. I decided to take the camera home and hide it under the pillow at the head of my bed. I lived in the neighbourhood of Via Giulia, alone with my mother who had been a widow for some time and who, in order to live, had dealings, poor dear, with the black market in cigarettes. From the doorway of the kitchen she saw me, with her sharp eye, as I came into our dark, smelly little flat and hurried off, hiding something, to shut myself in my room; but she said nothing. Later, however, while we were eating, she appeared suddenly with the camera in her hand. I prepared for a scene, and bent my head over my bowl in embarrassment. But talk about mothers! A stranger might have kicked up a hell of a fuss: "Where did you find it? And how? And why?" She, on the contrary, like a real mother, merely said to me, in a quiet voice: "It's no good your hiding things, give them to me. A hiding-place can always give you away, your mother never will." Having said this, she went off to her room, and I can see her now, just as she was then—short and massive, with her black shawl over her shoulders, her big, grey head bent to one side; and she put the camera into her chest-of-drawers and repeated: "Your mother loves you, nobody can love you as your mother does." I was upset, I confess; and not so much because of the camera as because of the reproof which I felt in her words: how could I have thought that my mother would not understand and forgive me? This, then, was the beginning; and thenceforth, whenever I played this trick, I took the things to her; and she, as well as hiding them for me, also undertook the selling of them, for she was very smart and was acquainted with a great many people and knew the value of things better than the employees at the pawnshop.

I was already closely attached to my mother, even though I

was now almost thirty years old; and this affair of the camera made me doubly attached to her. Well, people say all kinds of things about sons and mothers; and in Rome sons like me are scoffed at as *mammaroli*—"mother's boys"; but those who scoff are wrong. A mother and son are better and more closely suited to one another than a wife to a husband, a brother to a brother or a friend to a friend. The son has no need to speak: the mother who has brought him into the world and seen him grow up understands him at a single glance and in silence provides for his needs; just as the son, in silence, receives what she gives, knowing well that between him and his mother words are useless. And to a mother her son is intelligent, he is beautiful and good and strong, even if he is none of these things, even if the whole world thinks the opposite; isn't this borne out by the saying: "Even a grub is beautiful to its own mother"? In addition to this, a mother continues to see her son as a little boy, even when he is bald and has a big moustache; and this is a great comfort, because men do not easily accept the fact that they have become grown-up and, if they could, would willingly enter into an agreement to remain little boys. But above all a mother, because of the love she bears her son, will take his side against the whole world, even though, as in my own case, he is a thief; for she is the only person who understands him and knows why he has committed a theft; and who, knowing it, helps him to remain free and unrepentant. All this, and a good deal more, I would feel at the moment when I arrived home in the evening after chasing cars all day long. It was like putting one's feet into slippers when one gets out of bed: I used to hand over the stuff to her and she would go at once and shut it up in her chest-of-drawers, and I would go into the kitchen and she would put my bowl on the table in front of me, and I would eat and she would watch me. We scarcely spoke; like animals we understood each other by a glance.

What with my mother and my car-chasing, naturally I found no time for women. Women meant nothing to me, and it may be that I was even a bit frightened of them, for, being by nature affectionate, I realized that I should have to try goodness knows how many of them before I found the one who would suit me and who would give me the affection I needed. In the meantime I had my mother, who gave me affection in a direct way, without any need for experiment; why then should I encumber myself with women? But, as we all know, when a man doesn't go round looking for women, then they start looking for him. Not very far from my home, in the Corso Vittorio, there was a well-patronized draper's shop belonging to an old couple. These two old people had had a daughter, Gesuina, late in life, and possibly that was the reason why she had turned out rather ugly, and lame, and feeble in health. My mother, who had been a friend of Gesuina's mother since the time when they were girls and who often went into the shop in connection with her own little affairs, would often, naturally, start talking about me; so that the two old people looked upon me with favour, as being a very good son who, however, had no luck and was unable to find a job; Gesuina, on the other hand, always seemed to me a bit haughty. Well, one day when I was passing the shop, I went in to buy a needle and some thread: one of my buttons was loose. Gesuina was alone, and said to me: "*I'll* sew the button on for you." Then, while she was threading the needle, she said, calmly, that my mother was not the mother she ought to be if she allowed me to go about with loose buttons. Stung to the quick, I replied that there were few women like my mother, none at all, in fact, in the whole of Rome; and she answered: "In some things, perhaps, but not in the case of buttons." I realized that she knew, but I said nothing; she came close to me, took my jacket in her hands, stuck the needle into it and went on in a low voice: "Don't you see, Gigi, that what you're doing is wrong?" I snapped back at her: "Wrong? What wrong are you talking about? I don't know of any wrong except what does me harm."

But now I had let myself in for it; and I dropped into the shop again because I liked to watch her limping along behind the counter, one leg shorter than the other, and pulling things out of drawers which were too high up for her; or doing the day's accounts, gently and precisely, with downcast eyes. She certainly realized that I liked her; and she went on as she had begun, gaining influence over me by her moralizings. In the end, as it was now summer, we started meeting outside, after the shop was closed. We went for walks, chatting as we went; and I had a feeling I can't describe when I saw her beside me with her hand on my arm, dragging her short leg and, when she spoke, turning towards me her pale face shadowed by her soft black hair. It may not have been love, perhaps, but it was a clinging kind of feeling in which there was a little of everything—pity for her, a sort of shyness, a desire on my part to settle down, the novelty of a woman who showed me the same affection that I had so far imagined only my mother could have for me.

Of course I mentioned it to my mother, for I had no secrets from her: I told her that Gesuina knew everything and condemned my behaviour; that she was fond of me, nevertheless; that she had suggested my joining her in the shop, in place of her parents who were now too old; and that I myself, just possibly, might be fond of Gesuina. As I was talking, I saw on my mother's face an expression that distressed me; it was as if somebody had told her all of a sudden that she had no clothes on but was naked; and she had realized it was true, and had nothing handy with which to cover herself. Her clothes, hitherto, had been the love which I felt for her and which she felt for me; and now Gesuina, with her moralizings, had torn them off her, and she felt that Gesuina was right, and for the first time she judged herself and feared, above all, that I also should judge her. Finally, however, she said, with eyes downcast: "My precious son, you know that for me all that you do is right. . . . If you're content, so am I." But now, for some reason, I wanted her to say to me, as Gesuina did: "What you are doing is wrong, you must change your manner of life and settle down;" but I knew that this would be asking too much of her; it would have been like making her admit that she had not been a good mother because she had encouraged me instead of condemning me. And so the evening, like all our evenings, ended in silence.

I became engaged, therefore, and thought no more about motor-cars, and, somehow or other, found myself, in company with Gesuina, behind the counter of the draper's shop. I was fond of Gesuina and tried all the time to convince myself that it was far better to be selling ribbons and balls of thread than creating flat tyres on parked cars. But I was not convinced; and often I would stand doing nothing behind the counter of the little dark shop, looking out into the street and wistfully regretting the old days and my life roaming the streets, the escape and flight after the assault, the return home with the plunder and the silence of my mother, with no moralizings and no advice, nothing but affection and understanding. In short, I was bored.

The shop shut at one o'clock and re-opened at four. One day, about two o'clock, I started off, deep in thought, along the Lungotevere Flaminio, with the intention of taking a little walk and reflecting upon my position. It was October, a Roman October, all sunshine and blue sky; there was no one in the streets, for they were all at lunch; and there were cars standing in front of entrance doors. Then suddenly, in front of one of the big buildings, I noticed a car—an ordinary, mass-produced car—which nevertheless held my attention: it had a flat tyre, like the car with which I had first started. I walked up to it, just like that, without any particular intention; and at that very moment its owner came out of the building—a bald, red-faced, nondescript man with a cigarette in his mouth, looking congested and over-eaten; just the kind of man who goes out to get a breath of air before going back to his office. With a feeling of sympathy, as on that first occasion, I had a sudden impulse to warn him: "Hi, you—you've got a flat tyre!"

But at the same moment I looked inside the car, saw a handsome, solid leather bag on the seat and caught myself thinking: "I'll pinch it and take it to my mother and I'm damned if I'll go back to Gesuina, and my mother's the only person who can understand me and I'll start life with my mother again." I was so absorbed in these reflections that I did not notice that the nondescript man had in the meantime come up to me in a threatening manner: "Hand over that spike!" he said. I was flabbergasted. "What spike?" I asked. "The spike, the tool you used to flatten my tyre." "But you're crazy . . ." "No, you fathead, it's you that's crazy. You liked the look of my bag, didn't you? Come on, no nonsense, hand over that tool!" "Be careful what you say," I warned him; and then he seized hold of me by my coat-collar and hissed between his teeth, without taking the cigarette from his mouth: "You can thank heaven I'm not a nasty kind of chap. Now change that wheel if you don't want me to call a policeman." Well, I had to give in; and for once in a way, after all those other flat tyres, I had to put on a good wheel in place of a tyre which I had *not* punctured. I dirtied my hands and my clothes; and he was watching me all the time. When I had finished, he got into the car and said: "That's fine; but next time you'll go and change the wheel at the Regina Coeli prison."

It was late when I got back to the shop, and Gesuina, who was limping along behind the counter to fetch down some ribbons for a customer, threw me a single glance, a glance so intense and so uneasy that I realized she had perhaps understood. That same evening, when I went home, I told my mother that I had now made up my mind: I would get married within a month. She embraced me, genuinely pleased, poor dear, with tears in her eyes. And I, secretly, said to myself yet again that a mother is everything and there is no one in the world like a mother.

AH, WOMEN, WOMEN...

ERMINIO, a counsin of mine from Viterbo, had come to Rome for the first time and wanted to see everything and everybody; I had to show him round, and one evening I suggested we should go to the cinema. We were in Piazza Mastai, so I went over to the kiosk with the intention of buying a newspaper to see what was on. Fiammetta, the newspaper-seller, was just shutting up to go home; however, as a favour to me, she slipped a paper out of a bundle and gave it to me, telling me: "If you look at it quickly, I'll take it back without making you pay for it." So I opened the paper, saying to Erminio: "It doesn't look to me as if there was anything much"; then all at once I realized that he was paying no attention to me but gazing, instead, at Fiammetta. Have you ever seen Fiammetta? If you haven't, go to Piazza Mastai and there you'll see a big kiosk all decked out with newspapers and magazines, and amongst all these papers and magazines a little sort of proscenium formed also of papers and magazines, and, inside the proscenium, a woman's face, of a most lovely oval shape, surrounded with big fair curls, with blue eyes, a tiny little nose and charming red lips. It looks like the face of a doll, of the kind that turn up their eyes, show their little teeth and say "Papa" and "Mamma". It is Fiammetta's face, and generally it is bent over some illustrated magazine: as she spends her whole day among papers and magazines, she has acquired the habit of reading. But tell her you want such-and-such a magazine that is not within reach but hanging up outside; and then she will come out of the kiosk, rather like a puppet-showman out of his box, backwards, and you'll be astonished that all this profusion of delights can sit huddled together on the little chair amongst the bundles of printed paper. For Fiammetta has a shapely, rounded figure, just like a beautiful doll with all its parts turned to perfection, arms, shoulders, hips, legs, et cetera. A rare beauty is Fiammetta; who does not know her? And who does not know that she has been betrothed for years to Ettore, the barman at the café in Piazza Mastai, who, from his counter, can keep his eye on her through the window at all hours of the day? Everyone knows it, everyone, that is, except a person like Erminio, who does not belong to the quarter or even to Rome but to Viterbo.

Well then, seeing that he was paying no attention to me but gazing at Fiammetta with desire clearly depicted upon his face, I said, with teeth clenched: "Fiammetta, let me introduce my cousin Erminio." Fiammetta was making a pile of newspapers inside the kiosk; however she came out and shook Erminio by the hand, turning upon him a dazzling smile and at the same time throwing him a caressing look from her big blue eyes—a piece of feminine coquettishness which Fiammetta lavished on everyone and of which, for some time, nobody had taken particular notice. But Erminio did not know this and was immediately excited by it, as I saw from his troubled expression. Fiammetta now closed the kiosk and was just on the point of picking up from the ground a large bundle of magazines tied together with string. Erminio said promptly: "If you like, I'll carry it for you." Another smile from Fiammetta and another glance. "Thank you, but I live a long way off." "Never mind," he said, "it's a pleasure." Fiammetta cast a hesitant look towards the bar on the other side of the piazza, where, through the window, could be seen the sprightly figure of Ettore standing behind the counter; then she accepted: "All right, then, thank you." At this point I intervened: "What about the cinema?" I said. But Erminio said hurriedly: "We'll see each other to-morrow,

Alessandro; we can go to the cinema another day." So off they went, she tall and he short, she upright and a little stiff, just like a doll, he with his whole body turned towards her, looking as though he were dancing the tarantella. I wanted to shout after him: "Go slow, don't get so excited, Fiammetta is engaged and will soon be married"; but then I reflected that it was their affair, so I shrugged my shoulders, crossed the piazza and went into the bar. Ettore, as he worked the levers of the machine, asked me, with a gloomy expression on his heavily moustached face (he has a hare lip and this always gives him a menacing look): "Who's that little tyke who was with Fiammetta?" "Oh, it's nothing, nothing," I replied hastily; "a cousin of mine from Viterbo, who leaves to-morrow morning." He pulled down the levers with his muscular arms, and then said: "Fiammetta's always far too familiar with every Tom, Dick and Harry. . . . I don't mean your cousin, of course. Anyhow, it's high time she stopped it."

I live with my mother, alone, in Via della Lungarina; and we have two rooms and a kitchen. For Erminio we had put up a camp-bed in the kitchen; and to get to it he had to pass through my room. That night I waited quite a long time for him to come in; finally, privately cursing all cousins from Viterbo, I tried to go to sleep. I was woken up suddenly by someone shaking my arm; instinctively I looked at the alarm-clock on the bed-table and saw that it was five o'clock. Quickly I sat up in bed, saying: "What is it?" Sitting on the end of the bed, Erminio was smiling at me in a way that seemed to me positively painful. "Goodness me," I said, "are you mad, waking me up at this hour?" "I woke you up to tell you something very important," he replied. "And what is this thing that's so important?" "It really *is* important: I'm going to marry Fiammetta." I leapt up in bed and said: "Hey, you've been drinking, have you?" "No, I haven't been drinking," he said. "Fiammetta and I spent some hours together yesterday evening and in the end I realized that she's exactly the right woman for me, so I asked her to be my wife and she accepted." "She accepted?" "Yes . . . well, it's exactly as if she'd accepted." "But she's engaged to Ettore, the barman; didn't she tell you that?" "Yes, she told me, and I pointed out to her that he's not at all the right type for her, so she asked me for a little time to make up her mind and to break with him." I looked at him in astonishment and thought I must be still asleep and dreaming; he went on talking quietly, saying that it had been like a bolt from the blue, as they say; that he and Fiammetta were made for each other; that they had the same tastes, even for the country, which she loved and where he would take her to live as soon as they were married. At last he said: "Well, I'll leave you now. I've been wandering round all night; I was so happy I didn't want to sleep, but now I feel tired"; and off he went, leaving me sitting there, still unable to make out whether I was really awake.

Later that morning I went straight to Piazza Mastai. From a long way off I could catch a glimpse, inside the kiosk, of Fiammetta's big blonde head, bending forward: as usual, she was reading. I went over and, as I put down the money for a newspaper, I said to her: "Well, so we shall be eating this wedding-cake quite soon."

She lifted her head and smiled at me: "Not so very soon; in four months' time."

"Oh well, that's nothing. I'm very pleased, really very pleased. Only I'm sorry you're leaving Rome and that you'll forget us poor people in Trastevere."

She opened her eyes wide. "Leaving Rome? But why?"

"Well, he lives at Viterbo."

"*He?* Who?"

"My cousin Erminio."

"But how does Erminio come into it?"

Suddenly I saw that there was a confusion, and I explained myself. She listened to me and then said: "Your cousin's crazy. It's true that we spent yesterday evening together, and it's true that, at the end, crazy as he is, he asked me to marry him. But I told him I was engaged and that he mustn't even think of it. Even apart from that, having to live in the country . . ."

"Why, he told me you had a passion for the country."

"Don't you believe it."

So none of it was true. Finally, however, Fiammetta remarked: "Now I come to think of it, when we parted he said to me: 'I count on it, then, you'll choose between Ettore and myself'; and I, having done all I could to persuade him that such a choice did not exist, shrugged my shoulders and didn't bother to answer him. He must have taken my silence for consent."

"I daresay," I said, "you gave your consent not only by your silence, but with your mouth and your eyes too, by smiling and looking at him. Why d'you have to be so flirtatious?"

"I'm not flirtatious, I'm just good-natured."

After that morning, things still went on in the same way. Erminio saw Fiammetta and then told me that it was now an accomplished fact and that she was merely hesitating as to the best way of getting rid of Ettore; Fiammetta, on the other hand, told me that there was no truth in it and that Erminio was putting things into her mouth that she would never have dreamt of saying, and was mistaking politeness for love; Ettore, on his side, was losing patience and, from what he said, threatening bloodshed. The time came when I had to leave for Terni, with my uncle's brick-lorry. So I said to Erminio one morning: "The sooner this is settled, the better; besides, I've got to go away. Come along now to Piazza Mastai, to the bar, and get things straightened out with Ettore and Fiammetta." "I ask nothing better," he replied.

We went to Piazza Mastai and I called Fiammetta out of the

kiosk and took her by the arm; I took Erminio by the arm too, and thus made my entrance into the bar, announcing: "Ettore, here's the engaged couple."

It was early and there was no one in the bar. Ettore immediately rushed out from behind the counter, exclaiming: "Look here, is this a joke? What d'you mean, engaged couple?"

"Let's sit down," said I calmly. "And now let's do a little cross-questioning. You, Erminio, just repeat what Fiammetta said to you yesterday evening."

"She said," he replied impudently, "that she had to choose between me and Ettore, that she knew it and only wanted a little time."

"And you, Fiammetta, what have you to say?"

"That I said exactly the opposite; that he had no reason to hope."

"Yes, but you said it in a certain sort of way, as if you wanted to make me understand that I *could* have some hope after all."

"Don't you believe it."

Ettore, who had remained standing, hands on hips, intervened threateningly at this juncture, looking like a wild boar, his hare lip raised above his white teeth. He went up to Erminio and, putting his closed fist, big as a child's head, under his nose, he turned it round and round as though he wanted to make him smell it thoroughly, and then said: "Here's your choice; this fist or the journey back to Viterbo. And now get out. . . ."

"But I . . ."

"Get out, you miserable wretch; otherwise, even if you are a cousin of Alessandro, who's a friend of mine . . ."

When we were outside the bar, Erminio rubbed his hands together. "I'm staying where I am," he said. "Did you see how she looked at me? And how she smiled at me? I feel it, I feel it, all I need is to persevere and I'll bring it off. Ah, women, women: you don't know them as I do."

"Now listen," I said, "why don't you come with me to Terni? It'll be a nice trip and we'll enjoy ourselves."

"For goodness' sake, not now when she's on the point of deciding. I must stay here, I must strike while the iron is hot."

So I went off alone, that same afternoon. I was away for three days and came back on the evening of the fourth. I happened by chance to go to Piazza Mastai and saw that Fiammetta was dismantling the kiosk before shutting it up, as she was accustomed to do every day at that time. I went across to her, and she said at once: "I was sorry about Erminio. But really he asked for it."

"What's happened?"

"Why, don't you know? Ettore and he came to blows yesterday morning. Luckily some of the boys from the garage next door were there to separate them. But all the same he punched him in the face and afterwards Erminio's eye was closed up and black all round."

"Your fault, for being so flirtatious."

"His fault, for being so obstinate. But d'you know what he said to me? 'You've got my address at Viterbo. As soon as you make up your mind, let me know; you might even send me a telegram.'"

"Ah well, love prevents people from seeing straight."

"Perfectly true."

A few months later the wedding took place, at last, at the Church of San Pasquale Bailonne. After the ceremony, the wedding breakfast was to be held at a restaurant close by, in Via della Lungarina. Outside the church I slipped away, together with some other guests; it was raining and we were hurrying along, when suddenly I heard my name called: "Alessandro!"

I turned and saw Erminio beckoning to me from a narrow lane. "I was in the church and followed the whole ceremony; I was near the altar," he said.

"A nice service, wasn't it?"

"And d'you know? She saw me, although I was hiding behind a pillar. And, just a moment before saying 'Yes' to the priest, she turned and smiled at me. Ah, women, women! D'you know what I say? That she's marrying against her will and that, after some time, if I want to, I might even . . ."

"In love," I said to him, "what counts is the feeling. Let things be. Her feeling is yours. What's left to Ettore? Only the appearance."

He seemed convinced. "That's true," he said. "But it comes to the same thing, when you're speaking of women."

"Ah, indeed, women, women. . . ."

THE RED WATERPROOF

THE trades you practise when you haven't any special trade of your own are innumerable, and I can say I've tried all of them, more or less. What haven't I tried? I've been a pedlar, a caretaker, a doorkeeper, a waiter, a road-sweeper, an ice-cream seller with a tricycle, a commercial traveller and I don't know how many other things. Yes, there's nothing like unemployment for preventing you from becoming a real person, with a home and a fixed wage and a safe profession. Finding myself, as usual, without any work, I went off to the arcade in Piazza Colonna and started wandering round amongst the crowd, eyes and ears on the alert. There were people of every kind there. Someone whispered to me: "Dollars? Sterling?"; someone else was telling a friend: "So the magistrate gave him four months with conditional discharge"; someone, looking round the café tables, said: "Hey, look at that blonde over there"; someone else announced emphatically: "Mind you, Roma can't stand up to Lazio." They were all poor devils like me, in fact: there wasn't much to be cheerful about. To while away the time, I started looking at the television with a lot of other people; suddenly I felt a touch on my elbow, I turned round and who should I see? Nardone, an honest chap and one of the best, who managed, somehow or other, never to be out of work. "What are you doing?" he asked. "You can see for yourself." "I mean, what are you doing in general?" "Looking for work." "Come over here with me, I've a proposal to make to you."

So we went to the café and Nardone ordered two *espressi* and then explained to me what it was all about. He was at present employed by a private detective agency, on the job of shadowing people. That day he was due to start on the shadowing of a woman, a kept woman, on behalf of her gentleman friend, an elderly man, who suspected that she was being unfaithful to him. But alas, that very day Nardone's fiancée was arriving from Narni and he wanted to spend the afternoon with her. Nardone, in short, proposed that I should take his place for that day. He would take me to the house where the woman lived, would point her out to me as she came out, and then all I had to do was to follow her. My reward was to be three thousand lire, plus expenses. Nardone added: "She's a beautiful young woman. Her gentleman friend, on the other hand, is sixty-five. Now what's the use of having your mistress shadowed when you're sixty-five? There can be only one answer." I told him I accepted his offer, only he would have to add something to it. We agreed that he would also give me three packets of cigarettes and we parted.

Next day, punctually at two o'clock, an umbrella on my arm because the sky was black and rain was threatening, I arrived in Via Archimede. Nardone was already on the spot, and he pointed out a big front door to me, saying: "That's where she'll come out. She always lies in bed, the lazy girl, until one o'clock, and always comes out about now. She tells her friend first one thing then another, but he suspects her and, in my opinion, he has reasons for doing so." We waited thus for about half an hour, chatting about nothing in particular; and Nardone made me laugh, telling me about the detective agency which was mostly frequented by men and women who believed they were being deceived and who paid lots of money for the sole pleasure of having it confirmed. Suddenly he nudged me with his elbow and said: "There she is." Just at that moment, owing to the dampness of the air, I sneezed, and when I raised my head again all I saw was a woman in a flame-red waterproof making her way hurriedly towards the bus stop. Nardone put the three packets of cigarettes into my hand and said to me: "At midnight, if you still haven't finished your shadowing, telephone me and I'll come and relieve you." "Agreed," I replied, and ran off after the woman. But again I was unable to see her face, for suddenly the bus came rushing up and she got in and a lot of other people got in too, and I was the last of all and had only just time to jump on to the running-board. The bus was crowded and, as it went along, I calculated that it would be best for me to stay where I was: if I pushed my way into the crowd, it was quite possible that she might get off before I reached her; but like this I should be able to get off at the same time as she did. The bus went on and on from one stop to another, and I still kept my place on the running-board. It went right along Via Flaminia and arrived at Piazzale Flaminio. I put one foot to the ground and looked out. Four or five people got out, and then—there she was—the red waterproof. I jumped off at once and followed her.

Now she was walking in front of me, in the direction of the Tiber, and I was able to observe her at my leisure. I could see that, beneath the waterproof, she was strongly built: at each step the muscles of her hips were visibly moulded against the thin red material. She was tall, taller than I, and her step was firm, resolute and rapid. I caught up with her and, as I drew level, I looked at her. She was fair; golden curls escaped from beneath her flame-coloured hood; her face was beautiful but severe, almost masculine, with a large, firm mouth, a straight nose, blue, rather deep-set eyes. The waterproof swelled out over her bosom: her figure, evidently, was statuesque. A bold, spirited girl, in fact: how could she be satisfied with an old man of sixty-five? Still with the same firm, rapid step, she turned into the Lungotevere and walked along past the row of buildings facing the river. When she reached a small, modern block of flats, with a front door all surrounded with marble, she went in without hesitating; and I went in after her. She walked over to the lift, which came down a moment later—a glass box in the latest style; she got into it, and so did I. "Which floor are you going to?" she asked me. She had a voice that contrasted with her severe appearance: soft, musical, childish. I answered at random that I was going to the top floor, and she pressed the button of the third floor. We were close together now, but she kept her head bent, resolutely. She got out at the third floor, I went on up to the fourth, then got out and rushed down the stairs just in time to see her disappear behind the door of Flat 8. On the brass name-plate I read: "Innocenti". I went down to the ground floor again and, after looking in vain for the porter, took up my position against the parapet of the Tiber, right opposite the building.

It was drizzling, and I put up my umbrella and lit the first of the cigarettes. I knew I should have to wait some time; this discouraged me and I reflected that shadowing was truly a tough job: worth more than three thousand lire. I looked down at the Tiber for a bit, still keeping an eye, however, on the front door: the river was in flood, yellow and swollen to an alarming degree, with here and there a blackened branch or piece of charred wreckage twisting and turning in the shifting whirlpools. The sky was black, and against this black sky the trees along the river on the far side seemed strangely out of harmony, with their new, pale green foliage. I waited for perhaps three quarters of an hour and smoked three cigarettes; then, at last, the porter appeared—a thin, wiry man in a grey uniform with brass buttons and a peaked cap. He stood in the doorway, looking at the rainy sky.

I immediately left the parapet, went up to him and asked: "Does the lawyer Innocenti live here, a man of about sixty, bald, with glasses, and a wart on the end of his nose?" He looked at me almost with pity and then said: "There's an Innocenti here, on the third floor, Flat 8. But he's a young man of about thirty, mad about sport. He has a passion for racing cars. That's his car over there"; and he pointed out to me, not far off, a long, low car—flame-coloured, just like the waterproof of the woman I was shadowing. "Thank you," I said; "evidently I've made a mistake"; and I walked hastily away and took up my position against the parapet again, but a little farther along, so as not to be noticeable to him. "Well now," I thought, "a sporting young man of about thirty. Good girl, good girl; so that's the explanation of why you go out at two in the afternoon. Splendid." I took out my notebook, wrote down the name and address and the time; then I waited. It was still drizzling, and I kept my umbrella open and stared fixedly at the door, so fixedly that every now and then, instead of one door, I seemed to see two or even three. How long did I wait? About five hours, from half past two until almost half past seven. I smoked one cigarette after another, and since I had no newspaper and there was nothing to look at on the Lungotevere except the cars rushing quickly past, I could not help thinking of what was going on meanwhile in Flat 8, on the third floor of the building opposite. I said to myself: "Here am I standing in the rain while, all the time, up there . . . Ah, all sorts of things going on up there—caresses, kisses, soft conversations, embracings, words and gestures of affection, gossip, drinks, all sorts of things. And how delicious to make love on a day like this, when the weather's bad: you lower the shutters and lie on the bed in the dark, in one another's arms, listening to the drip of the rain and the swishing sound of the cars on the wet asphalt. How lucky they are and what a hateful job this is!" When I had finished the first packet of cigarettes, in order to relieve my boredom I started walking up and down over a space of a hundred yards or so. I kept on thinking about those two, and angrily I took out my notebook again and wrote down this comment: "No need for any more shadowing; there is proof that she spent a whole afternoon in a young man's flat. That's enough."

At last, thank goodness, at about half past seven, the red waterproof reappeared. It was with relief that I started shadowing her again, as she walked vigorously and freely along; love-making certainly had not tired her. She went to Piazzale Flaminio, jumped on a bus going towards the centre of the city; and I behind her. There was a crowd and I found myself right against her, too closely pressed together, perhaps. She turned and said to me in that childish voice, but with a touch of resentment: "Do please stand back." I drew back as best I could; but I was thinking: "You little prude: it's all right for Innocenti, but not for me. Get on with you, you can be bought by anyone." The bus continued on its way and finally she got off at Piazza Colonna; and I still behind her. She turned up a narrow street leading to Piazza Fontana di Trevi and disappeared into the front door of an old *palazzo*. I remained outside and looked at the numerous name-plates in the entrance. There was a dance school, there was a *pension*, there was a dressmaker's establishment, there was a massage clinic. There could be no doubt, in fact, that it was a house of doubtful respectability. Numbers of pretty girls, indeed, sometimes alone and sometimes in pairs, slipped through the entrance-door from time to time and vanished. I tried questioning the heavily-moustached, gouty old portress who was sitting in a pestilential cubby-hole, behind a glass door, at the far end of the entrance-hall: "Tell me, does such-and-such a blonde girl live here?" She replied, without even turning round: "My dear boy, dozens and dozens of girls come here: how can I tell?" There was nothing left, therefore, but to wait, and this I did; luckily I had bought a newspaper and, while I read it, I ate a couple of buns which I had had the forethought to slip into my pocket that morning. I waited for an hour or more, and it was less excruciating than on the Lungotevere, for at least there were plenty of people passing along this narrow street and there was always something to watch. Every now and then I thought of the woman in the red waterproof and said to myself: "There's more in this than meets the eye. She not only has Innocenti but some other intrigue as well, goodness knows what." Out she came at last, still in the same waterproof. I hurried after her.

She went back to Piazza Colonna, took the same bus as before but going in the opposite direction and, in short, in about twenty minutes we were back again on the Lungotevere, I still on her heels. When she reached the block where Innocenti lived, she went in without hesitation and I stayed outside: it was almost nine o'clock. It was raining in earnest now, and blowing into the bargain, so that the rain whipped my face. I cursed Nardone, I cursed the job I had undertaken, I cursed the woman, and naturally I could not help thinking again: "Here am I, out in the rain; and there they are, those two, in a beautiful flat, sitting at table probably, happy, in love, without a care: 'Eat this, my pet; try a little of this, my love; take a sip of this wine, my darling.' And then, after dinner, the sweetness of intimacy, the transports of love. Damn it all, there's no justice." Well, to cut a long story short, I waited for three hours on end and then, precisely at midnight, I went to a garage close by, from whence I could still keep an eye on the door, and telephoned to Nardone: "I say, there's lots of fun going on here, eating and drinking and romping with the wench. Come and relieve me or I'll chuck up everything and go away." He said he would come; and, in fact, in about twenty minutes he joined me. I gave him a brief account of my shadowing, handed him the two or three leaves out of my notebook, added a few spicy comments and went off to bed—at last.

I did not see Nardone for a couple of days; I waited discreetly for him to put in an appearance. Finally, seeing there was no sign of those three thousand lire for which I had worked so hard, I telephoned him and he made an appointment to meet me in the Arcade. As soon as he saw me he accosted me angrily: "Congratulations; you very nearly ruined me." "Why?" "That woman that you shadowed wasn't the woman I pointed out to you but someone else." "That's not possible." "It's perfectly possible. The woman you followed is, in fact, a nurse." "A nurse?" "Yes, and a certified nurse, into the bargain." "But Innocenti?" "I'll tell you about Innocenti. All she was doing yesterday was taking care of Innocenti's old mother, who was seriously ill. No little dinners, no love-making. About three o'clock the mother died, and then that poor girl, who had nursed her up to the last moment, went off to bed. And you know where she lives? In that same old *palazzo* near the Trevi Fountain, which you thought wasn't a respectable house. She has a furnished room there, with her own key. Well done, I congratulate you; you're a first-rate shadower."

I was deeply vexed; I felt as if I had been hit over the head. But I was still curious to know how I could possibly have made such a blunder. And then, all of a sudden, I understood: the "kept woman" had got on to the bus without my being able to see her face; and the nurse was already in that same bus, wearing a similar red waterproof. And I, like a bull and just as stupidly as a bull, had rushed at that red rag without thinking of anything else. Nardone was now saying: "I learned all this from the nurse herself. Seeing that she was not the woman I was supposed to be shadowing, I accosted her and told her who I was and what I was doing and she, poor girl, very kindly gave me all this information. But d'you know what she said at the end?—'That young man who followed me, I remember him. In the bus he was so impudent that I had to put him in his place.' Serafino, I really didn't expect this of you. You must remember that shadowing is a serious thing, a mission, so to speak." I protested vehemently: "I swear it's not true." "Well," said Nardone, "man is a hunter. You had got the idea into your head that she wasn't a respectable woman. That was bad. Here's a thousand lire for you and a packet of cigarettes. Honestly I can't give you more."

THE DIMPLE

WE had been engaged, Pia and I, for a couple of years; a long engagement due to the fact that, although I was working in my father's hardware shop, I hadn't a penny; and she, though she was studying to become a nurse like her mother, had acquired nothing but the overalls. Two years of being engaged to be married; I should say, rather, two years of arguments and quarrels. The great question between us was where we should live; we could, it is true, have gone to live at my own home, with my parents, who asked nothing better; but Pia would not so much as hear of it: she had hated my mother even before she came to know her. Pia's mother, too, had a home large enough to take us in; but in this case, while Pia and I would have made no objection, it was her mother who did not wish it: she was a widow, and was still young, and she wanted to lead her own life and not be bothered with her son-in-law's family. One day, in the Borghese Gardens, I thought to make a reasonable suggestion. "Listen," I said, "I know you can't bear my mother. But I'm not asking you to live with her all your life. Just for a few months, to give us time to get settled in some other way. Let's get married, then, and go and live at my home. After that—well, one thing leads to another." Pia at once jumped to her feet: "One thing leads to another—certainly it does. Your suggestion, for instance, leads to my finishing with you for good." And, slipping her hand from my arm, she started running towards the terrace of the Pincio. I ran after her, crying: "Pia, wait! What are you doing?" As I was about to catch her up she turned like a viper and stopped in front of a policeman, shouting: "Please tell that man there to leave me alone. All the morning he's been chasing me." This took my breath away; and as the policeman faced me and demanded: "Young man, your papers", and I pulled my identity card out of my pocket, I felt desperate, standing there stock still, watching Pia as she ran off.

That same day I tried to find her at home, but she was not there. I telephoned, later, but she refused to speak to me. Finally I wrote to her by express post, but three days went by and I had no answer. So I was entirely cut off from Pia; and suddenly it seemed to me that I had lost a part of myself—that very part which allowed me to breathe, to eat, to sleep, to work, in fact to live. I suffered more than I can say; and I felt this suffering not merely in my mind, as an anxiety which I could find no means of subduing; but also all over my body, where every muscle and every nerve gave me pain. From time to time, when I was alone in my room, I started sobbing, for no immediate reason, sitting at the table with my head between my arms; or again I would go out, and my sadness would make the blue sky look black, black the sun, black the yellow and white houses, black the spring trees covered with green leaves. Of eating there was no question. The first mouthful blocked my throat, like a plug. Nor could I sleep: I awoke with a start the moment I dozed off; and then I stayed awake, my eyes wide open, thinking of Pia.

One day when I was feeling more wretched than usual, with all the muscles in my body taut and vibrating like the strings of a violin, I went into a bar in the block of flats where Pia lived, in Via Ostiense. It was early in the morning and there was no one in the bar except one woman drinking her *espresso*, her back turned towards the door, her elbows on the counter. When I saw her, I immediately said to myself that it was Pia, because of her black, lustrous hair, cut short and with a few stray, pointed locks at the back of the neck: Pia wore her hair in this way. It is true to say that, as soon as I thought it was she, I felt a kind of loosening all over my body; and my breath, which until that moment had been cowering like a frightened animal at the bottom of my lungs, suddenly returned, calmly and easily, to fill my chest. "Pia!" I said; the woman turned round; and then I saw my mistake. It was not Pia, it was her mother, who wore her hair cut in the same style as her daughter. But, strange to say, the relief I had felt when I mistook her for Pia still continued: my muscles no longer ached so much, my breathing still remained light and easy. Recognizing me, she said: "No, no, my poor Giustino, it's not Pia, it's her mother"; I greeted her and then, as we talked of one thing and another, I looked at her attentively. I then noticed something I had never noticed before: she was the very image of her daughter. The same black hair, cut short; the same round eyes, bright and rather prominent, with high, thin eyebrows; the same hooked nose, small and ruthless; the same sickle-shaped mouth with turned-down corners. The only difference was that Pia was twenty and her mother at least twice that age. In short, I saw Pia's face submerged, so to speak, in that of her mother, which, owing to her age, was much broader, and with something relaxed, swollen, blurred in its shape. Nevertheless, as I looked at her I seemed to be looking at Pia, as I had so longed to do ever since she had left me; and I felt better, just as though Pia were there in front of me and as though my longing had really been satisfied.

With the sensitiveness that women have in these matters, she realized that I was looking at her and smiled; it was the same smile as Pia's, and I smiled back at her. "Giustino, what are you doing?" she asked; and I noticed another thing that had previously escaped me: she had the same voice as Pia, only a little lower. "Nothing," I replied, "I'm not doing anything." "You know," she said sympathetically, "you look very run down." She finished drinking her coffee and then, as she walked out of the bar with me: "Giustino," she said, "I say it seriously: it would be best if you gave up Pia. She wants a home and you can't give her one. Anyhow she doesn't want to go to *your* home; and honestly I don't feel like taking the two of you into *my* home. Besides, that's only one of many reasons why I advise you to give her up." "Indeed I *have* given her up," I said, and then, stuttering a little, because I realized that the suggestion might seem odd, I added: "Look here—why shouldn't we have dinner together this evening?" She looked at me in surprise and then said: "Yes, with pleasure. But I warn you, if it's in order to talk about Pia, better do nothing about it. What's the use? I'm one person and you're another and we each have our own life." I replied with sincerity: "But it's not to talk about Pia; it's just to be with you." Again she threw me a glance of surprise; then gave me an appointment for that same evening, at nine o'clock, at a restaurant right opposite to where she lived, in Via Ostiense. And so we parted.

She appeared punctually at nine o'clock that evening, and I noticed that she had made certain preparations, for, as I have said, she was still a young and coquettish woman and she liked men and liked being attractive to men. She was wearing a close-fitting red jersey, a handsome wide belt of shiny black leather with a bright metal buckle, and a very narrow black skirt in which, to tell the truth, she looked a bit cramped, with her hips almost bursting out of the tightly-stretched material. We went to the restaurant on the other side of Via Ostiense, a restaurant with an entrance on the street and a garden with a pergola at the back overlooking the Tiber. We sat down at a big table in the open air, for by now it was May and the weather was warm, facing the Tiber, invisible in the darkness, and the long row of lights on the parapets of the far side, and, behind the lights, the black shape of the gasometer and the tall chimney with its red flame of gas flaring upward into the night. I ordered devilled chicken, and in the meantime, while we were waiting, made them bring the wine and poured out a brimming glassful for her, for I knew that she had this weakness and liked drinking. In fact she drank a first glass and then a second, and finally, seeing that I was neither drinking nor speaking nor indeed doing anything except look at her, she asked me in a coquettish tone of voice: "May I know why you keep looking at me?" I replied: "I'm looking at you because I like you"—translating this, in my mind, into: "I'm looking at you because I like what I can see of Pia in you." She was flattered and asked shamelessly: "What is it in me that you like most?" And then, conscientiously, one by one, I gave her a list of all the things that I liked in her—which were, in point of fact, the things that she had in common with her daughter.

All the time I was speaking I seemed to feel better and better; my body was rested and relaxed, my breathing quiet. But she, poor dear, who could not understand what was going on in me, said, finally: "If you were not so much younger than I, and engaged to Pia into the bargain, I should tell you that I find you attractive too, and have always done so. But alas, things are as they are and there's nothing to be done." As she spoke these words, her face wore the same expression as Pia's when she put on an air of modesty and waited for a compliment; and I, almost in spite of myself, could not help putting out my hand on the table and taking hers, saying at the same time: "What does it matter? Age doesn't count; what does count is that one should like a person." I kept her hand in mine because it was just exactly like Pia's hand—white, rather hard, rather rough, with slightly curved red nails. Excited, and appearing now even to be breathing with some difficulty, she made no resistance. Luckily, at this point, the chicken arrived, and I let go of her hand and we started eating.

I ate with a good appetite, and this surprised me because it was the first time it had happened since Pia had left me. On the contrary it was she, now, who did not eat: she gazed at me with languishing eyes that were bright from the wine she had drunk, and she scarcely touched her food. At this juncture, I don't know how, a strange thing happened, which some people may not believe, even though it did actually happen. Anyhow, I said something or other, in a joking kind of way, and she smiled, and then, transported by my love for Pia and by the pleasure I found in noting the same things in her face as in Pia's, I said to her: "What I like more than anything is your smile. When you smile a dimple appears on the left side of your face which has a very special charm." We were sitting in a bright light, so I had not even the excuse of making a mistake because it was dark.

I had, in fact, barely uttered these words before I realized that on the smiling face of Pia's mother there was no dimple whatsoever. Pia had a dimple; and I, deluded by passion, had endowed her mother with a dimple too, and had even come very near to seeing it, by a kind of hallucination. For a moment I hoped she had not noticed, but I was wrong: women have a sort of sixth sense in these matters; besides, the tone of my voice, so full of passion, had betrayed me. And so I saw the smile disappear from her face, to be succeeded by an expression of steadily growing perplexity. Finally she said: "What are you talking about? I haven't any dimple when I smile—not that I've ever noticed, at least." I felt myself blushing with embarrassment, and she observed my confusion. Her expression hardened; however she reached for her bag, took out the mirror and looked at herself with a forced smile on her face which seemed to me, at that moment, positively painful. She remained like that, with that forced smile, for some time; then she became serious again and put the mirror back in her bag. Then, speaking slowly, in a dull voice, she said: "But Pia has a dimple, hasn't she?" Utterly confused now, I nodded. Still looking fixedly at me, she went on: "Then you . . . you were looking at me simply because . . . because I'm like Pia. We are indeed very like each other and we're often taken for sisters. . . . Now tell me the truth: you invited me this evening so as to look at what there is of Pia's face in *my* face. Isn't that so?" I nodded again; I saw that I could no longer deny the truth.

After that there was silence. She appeared disheartened; she sat with her elbows on the table, her face between her hands and her eyes cast down. Then she raised them and I saw that they were shining with tears, whether of humiliation, or something else, I did not understand. She sighed and then asked me: "You're very fond of Pia, aren't you?" And I answered forcibly, almost violently: "I love her more than my life." "And you can't live without her?" "No, I can't." She was ruffling her hair, now, with both hands, and she appeared undecided and deeply troubled. She sighed again and then, all of a sudden, rose to her feet and said: "Wait for me here, I'll be back in a moment." She went out almost at a run, leaving me alone and dumbfounded.

I waited for some time, sitting at the disordered table with my plate in front of me, covered with little bones, and Pia's mother's plate upon which was her chicken still untouched. Half an hour, perhaps, went by, and then I heard the sound of footsteps and saw her appear at the far end of the pergola, and behind her Pia, letting herself be dragged along by the hand. When they reached the table, the mother looked me straight in the face while Pia, filled with confusion, stood there with eyes lowered, motionless. Her mother said: "That's all right, then. I've told Pia that, until you're earning enough to set up house, you can come and live in my flat. I'm getting on in years now and it's right that you young people should have your own life after I've had mine. Pia didn't want to accept, but I've persuaded her and brought her to you here. So now you can look at her direct, without needing to look at me. Good-bye." Having said this, she walked away unhurriedly beneath the pergola, towards the street.

Pia was now sitting opposite me, in her mother's place. And I was looking at her and, seeing her in front of me in flesh and blood, I felt truly well, as one feels after spending a month in seaside sunshine or mountain air. Seaside sun and mountain air were, for me, Pia; and now she was actually in front of me and no longer did I have to go and seek the features of her face in the face of her mother. I put out my hand and took hers as it lay on the table, saying: "D'you know how pleased I am to see you?" She answered in a low voice: "So am I." The wine was finished. I turned towards the pergola and called for another litre.

YOU OLD HARPY...

I AM a manservant by profession, and being now elderly and in search of a quiet place, I believed I had found what I wanted in the home of Signora Olimpia, a middle-aged widow who lived alone with her grown-up son. I ought of course to have recollected that appearances are deceptive; in the case of Signor Olimpia they were deceptive with a vengeance. Signora Olimpia, at first sight, seemed exactly the kind of mistress I wanted: tall, with a full figure, all bosom and hips, a small head covered with stuck-on blonde curls, a plump face adorned with two or three coal-black beauty-spots, bright, smiling eyes like a couple of velvet stars, indolent in her movements and subdued in her speech, she seemed tranquillity personified; whereas, underneath, she was a first-class tyrant. An iron hand in a velvet glove, in short. She had been an opera singer, and very well-known; and indeed her flat, a penthouse on the top of a *palazzo* in Via Flaminia, was a positive museum of photographs of her in different costumes, so much so that during my first days there, not yet knowing who she was, I mistook them for souvenirs of ancient carnivals.

Having now retired, Signora Olimpia continued nevertheless to behave like a *prima donna* in her own home towards anyone she could and anyone who accepted a subordinate position under her. In the first place, towards a whole procession of lawyers, agents, rent-collectors, stockbrokers and business men: she, who had a bit of everything, from houses to securities, from shops to landed property, liked to shut herself up with them in her study and keep them there in long conversations which must have been utterly exhausting, seeing that these people, who had gone in looking as brisk as cocks came out again as limp as capons. But I should like to point out here that the management of her estate was, in fact, merely an excuse. In reality, what Signora Olimpia liked was giving orders, and giving orders meant, to her, bullying people: in other words, getting hold of a man and reducing him, patiently and by persistent deceit, to despair, making him say what he did not mean, demonstrating to him that he was wrong and then beginning all over again and continuing in the same way, until she was sure of being able to do what she wanted with him.

But where her passion for ordering people about could best be seen was with her son and with her boy friend. The son, who was called Gianmaria, was a small, slender young man with a white, crooked face and gloomy, staring blue eyes. A neurasthenic of the first order, a chain smoker, a vigorous drinker, sometimes inviting caresses like a cat, sometimes fierce as a tiger, his great problem was getting money out of his mother; and as for her, it was obvious that she was miserly with him, for scenes were the order of the day. He shouted and stormed and cursed, walking up and down the drawing-room; she sat still in her armchair, sweet, smiling, inflexible, as though this man were not her son and she were not his mother but they were a couple of actors at the front of the stage, in an operatic duet, of the kind she had once been accustomed to face every evening. He would say, in the end: "I'm going away, I'm leaving home, I'm going to work," giving to the word "work" the significance, as it were, of a threat. She would reply: "Where are you going? What are you going to do? Why, you don't know how to do anything, my poor boy." Then he would say: "That's your fault for not giving me any education." And she: "You've no need of it, you're the son of a mother who lets you lack for nothing." "Nothing? Ha, ha ha!"

Seeing her so calm and blooming, with all her curls and beauty-spots in place, I could not help thinking that she refused him money simply for the sake of provoking these scenes, which she enjoyed as though they had been serenades. And in the end she achieved her purpose: Gianmaria, exhausted, would fall on his knees in front of her and embrace her, sobbing with nervousness; and, as a final result, would get absolutely nothing.

With her boy friend she followed a different system, since she was dealing with a different character. This friend was a young tough from Trastevere called Marcello. Dark and curly-haired, well-proportioned, with a round head, perfect features and small ears, he had been an artist's model; as he went from one studio to another, he had picked up a little of the painter's trade; and, in order to hide from himself and others that he lived by a series of expedients, he passed himself off as a painter. I do not know where Signora Olimpia had picked him up; anyhow, one fine day she installed him in a room on the flat roof, a kind of attic which she fitted up for use as a studio; and she started putting it about that she was having her portrait painted by the painter Silenzi. It was a pity, however, that the painter Silenzi worked on the portrait mainly at night, when there was no light.

The attic was reached by an inside wooden staircase that was directly above my own room. She had the key of the little door at the top of these stairs; and often at night I was woken up by creaking sounds: it was Signora Olimpia going upstairs to have her portrait painted by the painter Silenzi. And how did she keep control over this Marcello, who, as to character, was the exact opposite of her son, as calm as the other was nervous, as insensitive as he was high-strung, as obtuse as he was intelligent? Why, through the personal pride of a poor wretch, son of other poor wretches, who has a regard for decorum and wants to appear something that he is not; that is, by humiliating him and reminding him at every moment of what he was and could not help being.

One day when she had called me to the attic to bring her the camomile of which she consumed such large quantities, I heard her say to him: "You're deluding yourself, you think you're something that you're not. Leaving aside the subject of painting, of which you don't know one end from the other—take a look at your manners, which reveal you for what you are." "Why, what manners?" "Your manners. D'you realize, for instance, that you don't know how to eat?" "Who said so?" "*I* say so. And your hands—have you ever looked at them?" "My hands?" "Yes, your hands. And your way of walking. Have you ever looked at yourself in a looking-glass while you were walking?" He looked at her with the fixed stare of an animal that does not understand, an infuriated, helpless animal. Then he said: "You say you're fond of me and yet you talk to me like this." "I talk to you like this," she said, "just because I'm fond of you." At that point I gave a cough and went in resolutely with my tray.

This business of the portrait, however, must in the end have seemed a thing that would not hold water—even to her, whose life was filled with such things. Especially as her son had not taken long to understand what kind of a painter Marcello was. One day at table, after she, as usual, had refused him money, he said to her bluntly: "I'm leaving. After all, considering that I'm your son, you can give *me* a room on top of a flat roof too, since you've given one to that fellow Silenzi, who is nothing to you." "Silenzi pays his rent regularly," she said serenely. And after a moment she added, sweetly: "You're angry with Silenzi, but really he's a charming young man, refined and full of talent. I want you two to become friends."

A very bright idea, you will say: in order to lose neither her son nor her boy-friend, bring them together, make them work in harmony, force them to become friends. I waited at table on the day of the great friendship luncheon. She sat in the middle, in her elegant négligé, with a rose at her opulent bosom; on one side her son, more nervous and more gloomy than ever; on the other the young tough, embarrassed and trying to give himself the airs of a gentleman. It was just like a scene on the stage, a thing to be remembered; and although I privately disapproved the immorality of bringing together the son and the boy friend, I could not help admiring the skill, the tact and the assurance with which, in the course of the meal, she led them from coldness and almost hostility to cordiality and, one might say, friendship.

In the first place she contrived to find a subject—racing cars—in which they both had a passionate interest; she cleverly brought them together, through this subject, by herself feigning an interest in it which she did not feel; and finally she withdrew tactfully when the spark of sporting enthusiasm had been thoroughly kindled and they were engaged in lively discussion. She treated them, in short, like children to whom their mother says: "Run and play together"; who don't at first want to do so because they are shy and who then, in the end, gradually, start playing in earnest. All at once, while I was in the pantry fetching the fruit plates, I heard her voice saying, softly and insinuatingly: "You're still politely addressing each other as 'lei'! Why don't you call each other 'tu'?" And I thought to myself: "You old harpy, you've done it again."

But be sure your sins will find you out. The devil, as they say, makes the pots but not the lids; Signora Olimpia's pot, lacking a lid, boiled for a little and then boiled over. She had wanted them to be friends and, as we have seen, she succeeded; but she had not foreseen that they would become really close, inseparable friends, bound together, like the envious, by a double thread. To Marcello, obviously, Signora Olimpia's son was a step above his usual associates; to Gianmaria, my impression is that Marcello came in very useful: idle and bored as he was, he came in contact through Marcello with a whole world previously unknown to him. They stuck together, in fact, all the time, always busily occupied, always hand in glove, by night as well as by day. And when I say by night! Those two young men took to going out together at night, naturally without the Signora. They trailed round the night clubs and, in the small hours, frequented a coffee bar in the neighbourhood of Via Veneto, where all kinds of people turned up—little girls half in the films and half on the streets, tipsy Americans, variety artists, chauffeurs and porters from the big hotels. They "saw life" together, as they say; and the only thing that Signora Olimpia had not achieved, in this great friendship, was that they should call each other "tu"; they continued to address one another as "lei".

All this, of course, I learned while I was waiting at table. There was no more talk of friendship there, now; but Signora Olimpia, always sweet and smiling, not a curl or a beauty-spot out of place, would enquire acidly how they had spent their evening. They answered unwillingly; but they did not ask her how she had spent hers. If they had asked, I could have answered for her: walking up and down the drawing-room like a starving lioness, every now and then going up the little staircase to the attic, coming down again and resuming her walk. In short, she was losing patience and was no longer able to bully them as unmercifully as she had in the past: they were eluding her, becoming independent. And then, all at once, one saw that to Signora Olimpia the important thing was to be in control; and if she lost her control, even love, as far as she was concerned, could go to the devil.

One night the two young men had been out as usual, and had come in again—not so very late, however. But they did not come in alone. With the practised ear of a manservant who has grown old in his profession, I heard also two female voices, clear, silvery, shrill—the voices, in fact, of young women. They started playing a gramophone, and from the sound of scraping feet I knew that they were dancing. Then I heard the slow, calm footsteps of Signora Olimpia on the stairs. They did not open the door to her at once, I do not know why; but as soon as they did open it, tumult broke out, just as though, on her entry, the studio had actually turned into the stage of an opera house, with all the performers singing, independently of each other, at the tops of their voices. There were shouts, arguments, footsteps, thuds, and then, suddenly, the shrill scream of a woman whose face has been slapped. Then the sound of a door being violently banged—the studio door opening on to the staircase. Then Signora Olimpia's footsteps coming down again and going to her own room. At last I was able to get to sleep.

Next day, the result of this scene was immediately apparent: the attic was empty, and the doors, both the inside and the outside doors, were locked; Gianmaria's room was also empty; and for the first time since I had come to the house, Signora Olimpia ate a solitary meal at a table laid for three. That day, as if in defiance, she led her ordinary life; she kept the stockbroker on the telephone longer than usual, she conferred with the lawyer for more than an hour, and as long again with the rent-collector.

What she had in her head it was impossible to make out, so well did she control herself, consummate actress as she was. But I understood later, when first Marcello and then her son telephoned her. With the former she was gentle—too much so, even—as though she wanted to make fun of him; and in conclusion she gave him to understand that it was all over and that she did not wish to see him again. With Gianmaria, a different tone: he asked her to give him an allowance of so much, because from henceforth he wanted to live away from home; she answered him firmly that he would get that allowance only if he returned.

She spent the evening watching television and then went off to bed satisfied, not without first telling me to prepare the young master's bed as on any other evening.

But Gianmaria did not return so soon. He had always told his mother that he felt able to live on his own, to earn his living and be independent of her; evidently he was trying to prove to her that he was, after all, capable of it. What he was up to during those three weeks that he stayed away from home, I couldn't say; but, from the manner in which he returned, I think it is clear that he was up to no good; and that his mother, who knew him well, had once again been right.

In a glass case in the drawing-room she kept a number of souvenirs of her career as a singer, some of them valuable, some not: statuettes, cups, solid gold plaques weighing goodness knows how much, and many other objects besides which were pretty but not of great value, such as watches, ornaments, boxes and pieces of china. The fellows who raided it one night showed that they knew this little museum well, for they took all the things made of gold and left the rest. The glass was broken, the window wide open, and there was some disorder—not so very much, however—in the room. I said at once to the Signora, as she was preparing, quite calmly, to telephone the police: "If I were you, Signora, I wouldn't do it." "Why?" "Oh well, one never knows." She must have understood, but she shrugged her shoulders and made the call. The police arrived, made an examination, interrogated the Signora, myself, the cook, the housemaid; and then the Inspector, a quick-witted young man, repeated more or less what I myself had said: "D'you really wish to take proceedings?" The Signora replied that she insisted on doing so. The result was that all the articles were recovered that same evening, partly from the furnished room in which her son was living, in Via Mario dei Fiori; partly from Marcello's parents' home in Trastevere.

Now would you believe it? She has had all sorts of dealings with lawyers and influential people and has managed to get her son back on bail, repentant and subdued, of course. As for Marcello, he has remained in prison—although the proceedings, it seems, have been dropped—on account of some other misdeed which has come to light in the meantime. But she is paying his lawyer—one more among the many whom she sees every day; she sends him parcels of food and lots of other little things that make prison life more comfortable; and recently she has even been to see him and talk to him through the grille at visiting times. Ah, you old harpy!

FURNITURE-LEGS

WHEN I came into possession of the capital that my father had left me, I resolved to invest it in something that would bring me in a little profit. Someone suggested another shop besides the shop for household electrical appliances which I already owned in Corso Vittorio; someone else a farm below Frascati; someone else a lorry with a trailer for the transport of fruit. But Matilde, unfortunately for me, had an idea: "The Americans have a passion for old Rome. Buy a small flat in that neighbourhood, do it up with a few bits and pieces and you'll find you can let it at once, at a very good rent, to some American." So I agreed to this plan and, after some searching, decided on a flat on the top floor of a house in Via dei Coronari. Price: three million; rooms: five. But old and squalid, with a shameful lavatory and a pitch-dark kitchen, without electricity or gas, where you had to cook with charcoal and a fire-fan. There was a balcony, it is true, from which you could enjoy a view over the roof-tops, with the usual cats, the usual worn-out shoes, the usual broken chamber-pots scattered over the tiles; but, as I said to Matilde: "The Americans will like this view, I don't deny it; for myself, I wouldn't live here for a single day." In the meantime, however, no sooner was the contract signed than deficiencies began to appear, as always happens with old houses. No need to mention the steep, dark, damp staircase; it was a communal staircase and I could do nothing about it; but inside the flat, following the wishes of Matilde who had now become exigent, I had to make all sorts of improvements: modern bathroom, modern kitchen, whitewashing, painting, new floors and fixtures. And so from three million the expense rose to nearly four, including taxes and the solicitor's fees. There remained the furniture. Matilde had spoken, it is true, of a "a few bits and pieces", but you know what women are: when it came to the point, the "bits and pieces" turned into a dining-room suite of sand-blasted wood, a mahogany bedroom suite, a Venetian sitting-room and lots of other necessary trifles. The expense rose again, well above the million mark.

For better or worse I had made my investment: it now remained to find the American. And, it so happened, we found one at once, and it was an American woman, whose name was Lee. This Lee was a good-looking woman of about thirty, tall and well-made, but very like a doll, partly owing to her immovable, astonished expression and her big, wide-open blue eyes that seemed incapable of looking in any but one and the same direction, as though they were made of glass; and partly owing to the way in which she got herself up—like a little girl, with a single short, black plait of hair on her neck and wide skirts hanging out over her thin legs. Lee came and looked at the flat, and, after admiring the view over the roof-tops, said she would take it. "But the furniture's ugly," she went on sorrowfully, "really ugly. I'm a painter, and d'you think this is the right furniture for a painter, Signor Alfredo?" At the moment I was upset by this, because the furniture, to my mind, was the only good thing about the flat, which otherwise was no better than a rat's nest; but all the same I went home contented, and even a little excited: Lee's soft, childish voice, like the sing-song drawl of a Sorrento musical box, had had a curious effect upon me. Matilde, when I reported her remark about the furniture, answered brusquely, already a little jealous: "I should like to know what *is* the right sort of furniture for a female painter? Let her paint, let her produce her pictures, let her work and not be a nuisance. And if she's no good at it—which she probably isn't—let her not lay the blame on our furniture."

Well, I went back several times to see Lee, either about the lease, or about handing over the flat, or about some other detail; and one day she told me she would like to paint my portrait because, she explained, I was a Roman type, with the face of a true Roman, of whom few were to be seen. So I sat to her and was able, so to speak, to see her at close quarters. She was slovenly, neglected, more untidy than words can say, and she reduced the flat, to put it briefly, to the level of a stable. Everything lying about on the floor, and a bit of everything: stockings and sheets of drawing-paper, lipsticks and books, odd shoes and magazines, brassières and boxes of pencils. She painted, not standing at an easel, like most painters, but crouching on the floor, with the canvas spread out in front of her. She always wore a long dress, made apparently of sackcloth, which looked like a nightshirt, and she had the habit of going about barefoot, so that the soles of her feet were always red on account of the red ochre on the brick floor. She smoked endlessly, leaving cigarette-butts stained with lipstick all over the place; and always, within reach, was a glass full of something strong, which she raised to her lips between one brush-stroke and another. I am no judge of painting, but I had the impression that she was not so much a painter as playing at being a painter, acting a part in much the same way that all women do, anyhow; for them—contrary to what the proverb says—it is truly the habit that makes the monk. For her, in short, the important things were the painter's smock, the bare feet, the paint-stained fingers, the untidiness, the cigarettes, the glass of liquor; not what she did or did not do on her canvas.

We went on like this for a little time, with me coming to sit to her and neglecting my shop; she painted me, then rubbed me out, then began again and the portrait was never ready. I confess that this slowness on her part did not displease me, for, to be frank, gradually and almost without realizing it I had fallen in love with Lee. Certain things must be understood: Matilde was my wife, Matilde was nearly ten years younger than Lee, Matilde was beautiful, and yet Lee was more attractive to me and had upon me, in comparison with Matilde, the same effect as a fine dish in comparison with a good home-baked loaf. I wondered often why it was that Lee was so attractive to me; and I came to the conclusion that, whereas Matilde was a normal woman—that is, as a child she had been a child, as a young girl she had been a young girl, as a woman, a woman—Lee, on the other hand, had remained a child in spite of being a woman. Thus, when I thought to speak to the woman, out jumped the child in all its innocence; and when, on the other hand, I thought to speak to the child, out jumped the woman in all her artfulness. It was a strange mixture, which aroused my interest as a curiosity against nature; a new sensation which left me in a state of uncertainty and always with the desire to repeat it.

One day I went up and entered the flat without knocking (she always kept her door open as though she were living in the Colosseum) and who should I find there? Lee herself, as usual, seated on the floor, her head bent over her canvas, in smock and bare feet; and round her, sprawling in the armchairs, three young men whom everyone in Via dei Coronari and the neighbourhood knew for what they were—idlers, bullies, jacks of all trades and masters of none, frequenters of bars and billiard-saloons: Mario, known as the Moor on account of his dark face and purple lips and coal-black eyes; Alessandro, nicknamed Mickey Mouse because he was undersized; and Remo, nicknamed the Little Wolf, I don't know why. I confess I was upset, both because I wanted to be alone with her and because I had not expected that she would bring such people into the house. "So we meet again," I said stiffly. "Hullo, Alfredo!" they answered, mockingly, for they had noticed my disappointment. Lee, without looking up from her canvas, asked in her soft voice: "You know each other, then?" "Yes, indeed," I replied emphatically. "Signorina," they said, laughing, "here in Rome we're all friends."

Thus, for me, began an unpleasant period. I continued, it is true, going to visit Lee on account of that portrait which never got finished; but now there was never an occasion on which I did not find those three there, or even, indeed, others of the same tribe. Where she picked them up, I don't know; I suspect the word went round. All these young men alternately scowled at one another or chattered about their own affairs, smoking and drinking, as though they had been in the bar at the corner of the street or at the headquarters of some sports club. Chafing with impatience and hoping all the time that they would go away, I would get up from time to time and wander round the flat, or snort and look at my watch; but there was no doubt, they purposely abstained from moving; and meanwhile Lee, who understood nothing of what was going on, continued to wield her paintbrush, squatting on the floor. The end of it all would be that I was the first to leave, being the only married man in the whole company; filled with jealousy and bitterness I would go home, where Matilde received me with harsh words, knowing very well by now where I had been and why I had been there. If only Lee had provided me with some pretext for not going there any more! But, like the scatter-brained child she was, she had an unexpected way of giving me hope just at the moment when I was in despair. But alas, she gave hope, to some extent, to all the others as well.

But it was she who, in the end, gave me the opportunity I was looking for, to break off our painful relationship. One day when the flat, as usual, was full of toughs and teddy-boys and I myself was sitting, worried and miserable, in a corner, Lee announced that she had decided to give a big party in the flat and invited everyone present to it, and, in fact, anybody who would like to come. "A studio party," she added complacently. I said nothing, but I felt that this party, for some reason, would be the finishing stroke. Then Lee rose and went into the bedroom, and I followed her. She was fumbling in one of the many drawers that were always left open, with things hanging out of them. I closed the door and took hold of her by the arm. "Lee," I said, "I'm not coming to this party. . . . In fact, thinking it over, I've decided it will be best for us not to go on seeing each other."

She looked at me in surprise. "But why? A studio party . . . we'll decorate the flat and drink wine and have a gay time. Why?"

"Because these young men that you bring into the flat—they and I don't get on together."

"Why don't you get on together?"

"Because," I said angrily, "I'm an honest man and they're nothing but a bunch of crooks."

She laughed in a childish, scatter-brained sort of way. "Ugh, how unkind you are! But why don't you stay and try to be friendly with them?"

"Because it's not possible."

She spoke as if she were annoyed. "What's the matter with you all, that you hate each other like this? The others, too—they're always quarrelling. Why can't you be friends? I want you all to be friends."

This time I didn't even answer her; I went out into the hall. In the passage she took me by the arm and, giving me a strange look, said to me all at once: "Wait a moment." I had a faint hope, I don't know why, that she was going to kiss me good-bye. Instead, she led me into the bathroom. There, above the bath, my portrait in charcoal was pinned up on the wall. She took a pencil out of her pocket and touched up the picture, looking at me repeatedly. Then she pushed me out again, saying: "All right, all right, now you can go."

So I did not see her any more; and, as it was now summer, in early August I closed my shop and went off to the country, to Palombara Sabina, to stay with Matilde's parents. There I remained for two months, prolonging the visit as much as I could, partly in order to forget Lee, partly in order to restore peace with Matilde. At the end of September I came back to Rome, and the first person I met in Corso Vittorio was the Moor.

"Hullo, Moor," I said; "well, how are things?"

He understood at once. "What," he said, "didn't you know that she went away immediately after the party?"

"Went away?"

"Well," he said rather hesitantly, "the party wasn't exactly a success. You see, she gave us all some reason to hope. Some of the boys got excited with the wine, there were arguments, somebody went too far, they started hitting and swearing at each other. Perhaps she was frightened, perhaps she was afraid she would be forced to make a choice. Anyhow, next day she packed up and went."

I remembered that she still owed me four months' rent. "She went off without paying me," I said.

"If that was the only thing . . ." he blurted out.

"What d'you mean?"

"Oh well," he said, "that's woman's crazy. Go up, and you'll see what I mean. Good-bye, Alfredo."

Disturbed, I ran off to Via dei Coronari, rushed upstairs, opened the door and went in. As soon as I was inside, I had an impression that something was changed. I am not speaking of mere disorder, for the flat had always been in a state of disorder: everything had been left as on the evening of the party—chairs overturned, glasses and bottles on the table, bits of food on plates, knives and forks all over the place. On the walls hung festoons of coloured paper, Venetian lanterns from the beams. Broken crockery was scattered over the floor, showing that the arguments of which the Moor had spoken had been serious ones. But the impression of change was caused by a strange feeling: it was as though the floor had sunk. Then I looked more carefully and saw that it was not the floor which had sunk, but rather the furniture. Chairs, table, stools, even the sideboard—all had had their legs sawn off. I rushed into the bedroom: here too all the legs had been cut down. I went into the sitting-room: no legs there, either. All the rooms, in short, had become stunted; later someone explained to me that Lee had performed this clever operation in order to give an "artistic" look to her party; but at the moment I really thought she must have gone mad. I went back into the dining-room and my eye chanced to fall on an open drawer in the sideboard: it was full to the brim with a dark liquid in which cigarette-ends were floating. I then discovered that Lee, in the haste of departure, had emptied all the bottles of liquor left over into this drawer; whether out of spite or mere idleness, I do not know.

Thus I had lost four months' rent, plus the time wasted, plus the furniture-legs—not to mention the quarrels with Matilde. I went round the rooms again and finally discovered, lying on the disordered bedcovers, a large sheet of drawing-paper on which was the portrait of a man with staring eyes, hair standing up like pins in a pin-cushion, and a crooked mouth. The man was myself. Underneath the drawing Lee had written, in charcoal: "To Alfredo, a souvenir, Lee." I went home feeling very melancholy. To Matilde, who immediately asked me: "Well, has she paid you?" I replied curtly, throwing down the rolled-up drawing: "Yes, with this."

A POLICY OF SILENCE

PASSIONS are not all alike: there are good passions that sustain you in life and, in the end, pay you back a hundred per cent, better than a bank account; and there are, on the other hand, passions that gradually undermine your life and, in the end, bring it tumbling down like a tree with a rotten trunk. At the time when I knew Tarcisio and we were both of us gardeners at the Orlandini nursery in Via Aurelia Antica, he had for his profession one of the passions I have called good, which, if he had retained it, might have made him one of the best gardeners in Rome. Tarcisio was a strange type: thin as a rake, his pate covered with fine black hair, with big dark eyes and a long nose, he reminded me of one of those brisk, hungry-looking seminarists that you sometimes meet on out-of-the-way roads, walking along two by two, chattering together.

He had big, strong hands, real gardener's hands, with earth under the nails which was always there; he was dressed in corduroy like a peasant; and in his pockets he always had some bulb or root and on his big boots always a bit of mud. Bringing, as he did, this exceptional passion to his gardening, he paid little attention to his own interests: he accepted low wages, he put in hours and hours of overtime work for nothing, he even spent his Sundays at the nursery, busy with the plants and flowers. Orlandini, who was no fool, had at once taken a liking to him and trusted him completely, sending him round on the most ticklish jobs—those, in fact, that demand real passion, such as arranging greenhouses, grafting, embellishing roof-gardens and other things of the kind.

A man of this type, when he changes from one passion to another, ought to stick to the good passions, otherwise he is lost. From gardening Tarcisio might possibly have gone over to—what shall we say?—bee-keeping. But not to women. And yet that is what he did; and it led me to think that it is better not to have any passions at all, either good or bad, for there is always the danger that they may turn and rend you, like snakes that don't know their master and bite him when he least expects it.

Near the nursery garden, behind the old walls that run along Via Aurelia, there was a farm inhabited by a family of peasants who cultivated a small piece of land at the bottom of a valley, right below the Villa Doria Pamphili. The grandparents, who had established themselves there when it was still open country, were real peasants; the father and mother had already become less like peasants; and the daughter Marsilia had ceased to be a peasant altogether. It is true that she worked in the fields like her parents, but in all other ways she might be said to be a young lady of the city. With my own eyes I have seen her haymaking dressed up as a young lady, wearing a tight skirt that impeded the movement of her legs and grasping her rake with fingers whose nails were painted red. Marsilia was one of those small but solid girls of whom young men, as they watch her go past, say: "A small cask means good wine."

She was a Roman type, not of the city itself but rather of the country round Rome where it is most rustic and untouched. Her face was oval and brown, her eyes large, round and black, her nose in a straight line with her forehead, her mouth firm, with turned-down corners and rasp-like teeth like the teeth of a trap. She had frizzy hair, a wild mass of it which she tied up with a red ribbon in a bunch on the back of her neck. One detail I was forgetting: she had been born with a hare lip and they had performed an operation on her soon after birth, with the result that she had been left with a curved scar on her upper lip which gave her mouth something of the look of a wild animal's. Her silence, too, and her way of looking had also something of the wild animal about them: she never spoke, and in her eyes was the staring, motionless, expressionless look that animals have.

How it came about that Marsilia attached herself to Tarcisio, I could not say. In the neighbourhood we all knew each other; and perhaps it happened one evening at the wine-shop behind Porta San Pancrazio, where the young men and girls of the quarter used to meet on Saturday afternoons and Sundays. However that may be, between the nursery garden and the fields belonging to Marsilia's family there was a barbed wire fence: one day I found a gap in it wide enough to let a man through; I put it back in place again, but next morning I found the gap had been made again, and, into the bargain, there was a tuft of red wool clinging to one of the spikes. This seems like a riddle, but it isn't: Marsilia had a red sweater; at the nursery there was a cottage for the watchman, a half-witted old man called Ignazio; in the cottage there were two rooms; that night Tarcisio had stayed to sleep at the cottage. Now what do you make of that? That same day I seized a moment when we were alone, Tarcisio and I, and spoke to him frankly: "Be careful with Marsilia. . . . She's not for you. Don't you know she's engaged?" I expected him to protest; but he looked at me for some time, with a special kind of look, as though he had neither heard nor seen me and were looking through my body at a tree behind me; and he never opened his mouth. "Here," I cried, "I'm speaking to you. Are you dumb?" Another look; then he turned his back on me and walked away in a leisurely fashion. Thus began what I may call the policy of silence.

Marsilia's fiancé—fiancé in a manner of speaking—was a first-class idler, an aggressive, arrogant, fair-haired young man nicknamed Vischio, or Mistletoe, possibly because he clung on to women and aimed at getting himself kept by them. He said he was a boxer; but I am of the opinion that his strength lay not in his arms but in his jaws. When I saw all three of them, Tarcisio, Marsilia and Vischio, sitting together in the open at the wine-shop behind Porta San Pancrazio, I thought to myself: "Poor Tarcisio, you've done a stupid thing." Vischio behaved affectionately towards Tarcisio—a bad sign; Marsilia, on the other hand, was aloof, sitting there motionless and without expression, exactly like an animal, in fact, a calf or a mule, between two peasants who are haggling over it. Then they got up, Tarcisio paid and they went off down the Via Aurelia. I paid too, and, without attracting attention to myself, followed them at a distance: I wanted to see how the bargain would be finally concluded. Well, at the darkest part of Via Aurelia, where there are woods on both sides, Tarcisio pulled out a little bundle of bank notes and gave them to Marsilia; Marsilia, in a free and easy way, handed them on to Vischio; and Vischio, having put them in his pocket, began to walk more slowly, so that he hung behind the other two, and finally stopped: at that same moment Tarcisio and Marsilia turned away and vanished.

Next morning I took Tarcisio aside and said to him, point-blank: "I don't know anything and I don't want to know anything . . . but I saw you give money to Marsilia and her pass it on to Vischio, and I know that you haven't any money, and so I say to you once again: be careful of what you're doing." Again he looked right through my head, so to speak, just as though it had been made of glass and there were some interesting object behind it; then he turned his back and went away. So the policy of silence continued. But the other policy—the policy of exploitation—also continued: one evening Vischio inaugurated a new motor-scooter by coming and caracoling in a brazen manner right in front of the wine-shop, where Marsilia and Tarcisio were sitting. He circled round with one foot on the ground, showing off and back-firing, then, with a grand salute, rushed off at full speed in the direction of the Janiculum.

By now the barbed wire was down on the ground and I didn't even bother to put it up again; and Tarcisio was sleeping every night at the watchman's cottage; and the latter, whose wine-cask they had evidently filled, was always drunk. Something seemed to have gone wrong at the nursery garden, but it was difficult to tell what it was. On the other hand, everything was going extremely well on the adjoining piece of land where Marsilia's farm was: it was summer-time and they had cut the hay in the valley, and I often saw Marsilia there, dressed up as a city young lady, plying her rake over the mown fields.

To cut a long story short: one day when Orlandini, a big man with a red face and a neck even redder than his face, was going over his accounts, sitting in the watchman's cottage, a gentleman came rushing in, full of indignation. "You must have gone mad," he said. "Just take a look at this bill that you've sent my wife for arranging our roof-garden."

"What bill? Who's gone mad?"

"Look; rhyncospora, ugly little plants, fifteen thousand lire each, bougainvillea the same, tulips, roses, geraniums, all three times as much as last time. And the terracotta boxes are marked here as being Tuscan, whereas they're really Roman boxes, of the poorest quality, the kind that crack with the first frost . . . and three sacks of special loam."

"Quietly, now; please don't shout. . . . And look here, this isn't one of our bills. It's written on paper from a note-book; if it was ours it would be on headed paper."

"Headed paper, indeed! What you say is unworthy of a respectable firm. . . . You'll have to pay me back the money", etc. etc. This gentleman was stout and pale, Orlandini was stout and red-faced, the gentleman had turned red, Orlandini had turned pale. I said to myself: "What's going to happen is that they'll both have an apoplectic fit"; and I slipped out of the cottage.

I don't know what the end of it was; nor do I know what happened during a whole month, for next day I went off to Albano, to work in the garden of an old villa whose new owner was putting it in order. When I came back a month later, I noticed that Tarcisio was absent and asked Ignazio the watchman, who was sitting smoking outside his cottage, to tell me what had happened. "They arrested him and he's in the Regina Coeli prison," he replied complacently, taking his pipe out of his mouth. "Shameless crook: he's been stealing, you may say, for years, and people here are saying that he's caused Orlandini a loss of millions of lire." "But how is it possible? Tarcisio? I can't believe it." "Oh well, these young men, they think of nothing but women. . . . How many times have I said to Tarcisio: mark my words, leave women alone and take to wine instead; it costs little and never lets you down. . . ."

He was still talking when I reached the boundary of the nursery and clambered over the barbed wire into the adjoining farm. Marsilia was down at the bottom of the valley, small in the distance, a basket over her arm, under a fig-tree. I ran down to her and seized her by the arm as she stretched up to pick fruit from a branch. "So Tarcisio's in prison," I said. "And I know why he's in prison; it's all your fault, you ugly slut. Tarcisio's in prison and Vischio's amusing himself with a motor-scooter bought with the stolen money. Are you content, now?"

And would you believe it? She looked at me, as Tarcisio had done, right through the head, and said nothing. She too had adopted the policy of silence, or rather she had that policy in her blood, so to speak, for she was an animal and, like all animals, she could not talk. I had been waiting for this moment, however, for some time, and now it had arrived. "So you don't say anything, eh, you hussy?" I cried; "well, let's see if this'll make you speak"; and I took careful aim at her brown face, between the nose and the ear. I raised my hand and gave her a couple of hard slaps, first on one cheek and then on the other. Her head moved slightly with the blows, like a tree when the wind strikes it. Then she turned her back and went away, very slowly, her basket over her arm, across the sun-baked valley, towards the farm.

I did not see her again for three or four months. One morning in November, very early, I was going along the Viale del Gianicolo, deserted at that hour, with its rows of marble busts and its empty seats under the damp, dejected trees, and the night mist still hanging in the air, white and motionless. When I reached the beacon, where there is a terrace commanding a view over the Regina Coeli prison below, with its long, gloomy buildings full of barred windows, I saw a woman leaning against the parapet and gazing down towards the prison. I at once recognized Marsilia by her mass of frizzy hair tied in a bunch at the back of her neck—wild hair belonging to the old days when women did not have permanent waves and peasants were still peasants and Rome was the capital of the peasants. Urged by some obscure impulse, I went over to her and said bitterly: "What are you looking at? I suppose you're looking at the prison courtyard to see Tarcisio in his striped suit? You're looking to see how well it becomes him, eh?"

She turned round and stared at me wide-eyed, like an animal; and I saw that in her eyes there was a look of anguish, but this anguish was the anguish, also, of an animal. Then she opened her mouth and said: "I'm expecting a baby."

EYE-WITNESS

THEY say that the day will come when we shall all be masters and there won't be any servants. They say that the occupation of a servant is unworthy of a man who is a man because one man ought not to serve another. They say that the day will come when we do everything for ourselves, without any servants, like savages. I'm not disputing it: man never stands still; he feels a need to make changes in everything that exists, and very likely the changes are for the worse, but he is bound to make them and then, to comfort himself, he calls them progress. But there's one thing I'm sure of: out of ten men—as far as I know, anyhow—two, perhaps, are born masters, but the others are born servants. The master who is a born master likes to give orders from the very cradle; but the others are not content until they have found a master to give orders to *them*. Well, well, men are all different; and in spite of all sorts of progress there will always be masters and servants, only they'll call them by another name; as we all know, words, to men, are everything; and the man who is offended at hearing himself called "porter" will no doubt run up eagerly if someone shouts "luggage-carrier" at him.

As for me, I was born a servant, I have lived up till now as a servant and I shall die, I daresay, as an old dotard, but still a servant. I like to serve; I like to obey; I like to submit to the will of another. To serve: there is a possibility, however, that the word may be misunderstood. For if you come to think of it, while I am serving my master, he is serving me. I mean, in fact, that if there wasn't a master I should not be able to be a servant. And what should I do then? Become a gravedigger?

And so, from one place to another, changing either because I did not like my master, or because he did not like me, or for some other reason, I finished up in a villa on the Via Cassia, where I thought I had found a good situation. In this recently built villa lived a recently married couple: she a blonde, with a long, lovely face and enormous, intense blue eyes, very thin and tall and elegant, her boyish appearance emphasized by her golden hair cut short *à la* Bonaparte; he small and dark and powerfully built, with disproportionately broad shoulders, a square face, a loud voice, his whole person full of authority and importance—one of those small men who make up for their size by a domineering, arrogant manner. He was evidently a proper rustic by origin—judging, anyhow, by his mother who turned up at the villa on one occasion and whom I very nearly mistook for one of the peasant-women who go round with baskets of new-laid eggs. His wife, on the other hand, came of a good family; I think she was the daughter of a magistrate. I said it was a good situation, but I did not say it was an ideal one: for we were isolated, twenty kilometres along the Via Cassia, and for a manservant who did not have a contemplative character like mine this would have been a serious disadvantage. Then, the villa was a large one, with a ground floor all reception-rooms and an upper floor all bedrooms, and there were only three of us servants, not counting the gardener: the cook, the housemaid and myself. Finally—and this, in my opinion, was the worst thing—neither he nor she was really and truly a "master", that is, a master born: he was a peasant, son and grandson of peasants; she was of good family but uprooted; she set herself up as mistress of the house but she hadn't the habit of it, and, as everyone knows, in these matters it's habit that counts.

Early in the morning, after breakfast, he would leave the house, get into his powerful, expensive car and drive off along the Via Cassia; generally he would stay out all day; and I have an idea that in Rome, apart from his import-export office, he also had some sort of a love-nest. She also had an expensive car which she drove herself, but she used it rarely, either because she did not like going into town or, more probably, because she did not know anybody there; so she stayed at home, wandering round, in trousers and jumper, from one room to another, from one floor to the other, and also, if the weather was fine, round the garden. She was always doing something, it is true, for in such a big house there was always something to do; otherwise, especially in the afternoon, she would curl up in an armchair, sitting on her own legs, and read; but whatever she was doing, wandering round the house or reading, you could see that she was discontented and bored. Sometimes she would stand behind me, in the garden, while I was helping the gardener to put in plants and prune trees; or again she would get on her horse—for she had a fine horse in a stable at the far end of the garden—and go galloping off round the countryside; but always, whether in the garden or on horseback, she had that discontented, bored look on her face.

At last, often after dark, he would come home again, and would begin furiously blowing his horn as soon as he reached the turning from the Via Cassia. From the sound of that horn it was clear who was master in the villa: she would jump up from the sofa where she was reading and run to the door on long legs tightly encased in very tight trousers; beside her, barking, ran two enormous Great Danes, as big as calves, which had been sleeping, curled up at her feet, all the afternoon; the maid, too, would come running, tying on her apron and adjusting her cap; the gardener, who was also the custodian, would run to open the gates of the drive; and I myself would run to open the front door. He would bring his car round the curve of the drive, enveloping us in the dazzling light of his headlamps, then get out and enter the house with the deportment of a Mussolini. His first words were always the same: "Is it ready?" Then he would go and stretch himself out on one of the many sofas in the drawing-room; and she, like an amorous cat, would nestle close up to him and, taking his hand, begin stroking the long black hairs on his wrist with her finger-tips. He abandoned his hand and arm to her, and meanwhile, with his other hand, held up the newspaper, which he read without taking any notice of her. Then I would button up my jacket, throw open the double doors of the dining-room and announce, with a slight bow: "Dinner is served."

Have you ever seen, in some humble eating-place on the outskirts of the city, a poor labourer, all dirty and sweaty and with his little hat made of newspaper still on his head, gulping down a big plateful of beans and pork crackling? Well, my master behaved just like that, for all that he had come home in an expensive car and had suits made of English cloth. At one end of the very long yellow marble table, with its lace mats and its glass, silver and porcelain that could not have been finer, *she* sat, stiff and upright and full of dignity; at the other end, sprawling crookedly at the table with his napkin tucked into his collar, sat *he*—in other words, the labourer. But why do I say the labourer? I'm slandering labourers. He, like a child that hasn't yet learned to walk and that tumbles down on all fours every other step, he, I say, tried to eat with a knife and fork but often resorted to his fingers, especially if it was a case of chicken or veal cutlets. No need to mention that he chewed with his mouth open or drank with his mouth full, that he wiped his lips with the back of his hand, that he balanced a row of peas on his knife and thrust them into his mouth: with him, one vulgar gesture succeeded another like so many pearls on a string. Naturally his wife suffered, for, as she often repeated, she set great store by good manners. I used to see her staring at him with her big blue eyes, then looking at me, and then at the flowers in the middle of the table; or again she would sigh and bend her head. But he took no notice and went on worse than before. Finally she would say to me: "Remigio, change the plates, please"; but he, as he gnawed away at some bone or other, would protest with a growl, just like a dog; and so I waited with the clean plate in my hand till he had finished.

I went on like this for about a month, and, apart from these regrettable dinners, I liked the place. I was left in peace, I had a nice room with a bath, and I was able, into the bargain, to devote myself to gardening, for which I have a passion. But one evening the storm broke which, secretly, I had always foreseen. He, as usual, had thrown himself on his plate of meat with his hands; I recall that it was grilled lamb cutlets; she was watching him and, as usual, the sight pained her. He gnawed all the cutlets, one after the other, four of them in all, covering himself with grease up to the ears, and then, when it seemed that he had finished, he started all over again. Firmly she said to him, from the other end of the table: "Valentino, couldn't you stop eating always with your hands? Apart from anything else, you wipe your fingers on the napkins and one would need a set of two dozen of them to keep up with you."

He was crushing a bone with his teeth, which were strong, close-set and white, like the teeth of a wolf. He rolled his eyes fiercely, and said nothing. She blinked her eyelids and persevered: "Valentino. . . ."

He put down the bone for a moment and said, very clearly: "Leave me alone!" Then he picked up the bone again.

"You oughtn't to eat with your fingers," she resumed, in an agitated nervous way; "it's only boors who eat with their fingers."

"I'm a boor, then, am I?"

"Yes, if you go on like that, you certainly are."

"And d'you know what *you* are?"

"I don't know and I don't want to know. . . . But do stop eating with your fingers."

"You're a pauper, a bore and an idiot."

She flinched at these insults as though someone had thrown a glass of wine in her face. Then she said, with dignity: "I may be a pauper, but in my home people didn't eat with their fingers."

"Of course not: you didn't have anything to eat."

"Valentino!"

"Shut up, you idiot!"

Then she lost patience. Leaning forward on the table, her eyes narrowing with hatred, she hissed: "I've never told you all that I think of you . . . but the moment's come to tell you now: you're a boor, you're a peasant, you're a lout. . . . You're no good for anything but making money. If you were at least good-looking—but you're not, you're just a dwarf."

To be called a dwarf was obviously the indignity that hurt him most. I drew back only just in time; otherwise he would have knocked me down as he rushed from his place to the other end of the table where his wife was sitting. She sat quite still and watched him coming with a pale, twisted smile. As her husband reached her he raised his hand; she stared straight at him. He struck her in the face, once and then again. She rose and walked slowly out of the room; her husband followed her, in a towering rage; and then I heard cries and yells but it was *he* who was shouting all the time, and there must have been blows given, but I saw nothing. Quietly I cleared the table, just as I did every evening, and then went to my own room. To tell the truth, this scene had not made any particular impression upon me: in the first place I had, as I have said, foreseen it for some time; besides, as we all know, the table is the place where scenes happen, and during my career as a manservant I had witnessed I don't know how many scenes of this kind—and even more violent ones.

Next morning I got up very early and went to the pantry. The villa was immersed in deep silence, the silence of the country. I took a pair of his shoes and started cleaning them, humming under my breath, in front of the wide-open, sun-filled window. At that moment, suddenly the door opened and she appeared on the threshold.

I looked at her and at once realized that the blows must have been many and violent. One eye had swelled up and was half-closed in the middle of a circular bruise—one of those dark bruises that go green and then yellow and take a month to disappear. This bruise gave her whole face a strange look, at the same time both comic and sad. I looked at her, and the bruise was one of those things which, the less you want to look at them, the more you do so. Then she said: "Remigio, I'm very sorry, but I'm forced to give you notice."

This, truly, I was not expecting. I stood there open-mouthed, with the shoe in my hand. Finally I stammered: "But Signora, what have I done that you should have to give me notice?"

She replied coldly: "You haven't done anything; in fact I'm very pleased with you."

"Well, then?"

"I'm giving you notice because of what happened yesterday evening."

"But what has that to do with me?"

"It has nothing to do with you, but you heard and saw, and I can't bear the idea of your staying in the house after what you heard and saw."

"But, Signora," I said, understanding at last, "these are things that happen. . . . All husbands and wives come to words and blows—in the upper as well as the lower classes. I swear to you that, as far as I am concerned, it's just as though I hadn't seen or heard anything."

"That may be so, but I can't bear to be waited on by someone who heard and saw these things. I'm sorry, but you must go."

"But, Signora, you're ruining me."

"I'll give you a very good reference," she said. And, with these words, she went away.

You see? It was they who came to words and blows; but I, who had nothing whatever to do with it, got the sack. I did not try to press this point, nor did I wish to refer the matter to her husband, who would certainly have admitted that I was right; fundamentally I liked her, and I understood her and was aware that for her it would be yet another humiliation. Furthermore, she would then have hated me and I should have had to leave just the same. So I did not breathe a word; I packed up and went away that same day, without waiting for my week's notice. But now we come back to what I said before: with one who was truly mistress in her own house this would not have happened. A real, born mistress does not even see her manservant; for her he is transparent like glass. Why, she can even take off all her clothes in his presence, or get exasperated with her husband; it's just as though the servant were not there. Well, well, it seems there are no real masters and mistresses left in the world.

THE SMALL HOURS

UNTRUSTWORTHY. Insolent. Brazen-faced. Cheap Roman scum. Rosario is the boy who, with his foot on a chair and his guitar resting on his knee, used to sing in the restaurants of Trastevere, thrusting his face forward under the noses of Communist deputies, insinuating as a snake, and whispering: "You've only to look at him and you get a crazy longing to kiss him"—alluding to Stalin's big moustaches. And then, later, he would repeat exactly the same refrain for the American tourists, in honour of their President. A time-server, I say; and a coward as well: with those stronger than himself he was meek and cringing; with those who were weaker, arrogant, tough, aggressive, truculent.

My greatest misfortune, amongst many others, is that I can never succeed in going to sleep early, in such a way as to be able to get up early and work like everybody else. After midnight, instead of feeling sleepy, I suffer from nervous irritation, and then I would do anything rather than catch the late bus and trail back to the Grottarossa neighbourhood, where I live. Luckily I always find someone to accompany me on my wanderings, either a friend or an acquaintance, or a passer-by, or a girl. Latterly, it was Clementina. This Clementina is one of those girls who sell little bunches of flowers with their stalks wrapped in tin-foil, in restaurants and at the doors of expensive cafés in Via Veneto. Clementina is not ugly, though she's a bit awkward, with her harsh voice like a man's, and her red hands; but it is mainly because of the clothes she wears that she perhaps looks ugly—a skirt all out of shape, shorter at the back than in front, a shrunken-looking jacket, shorter in front than at the back, a sweater right up to her neck and socks rolled down round her bare calves.

I grew fond of Clementina, if only because she was like myself: after midnight she liked wandering about the streets, without aim or purpose, even braving the police patrols who make no bones about arresting you, under the pretext of law and order, and putting you into a cell for the night. What did we do? Well, we just wandered. After she had finished palming off her bunches of flowers on loving couples, I used to meet her at the Borghese Gardens, on one of the first seats facing the riding-track. She would count her takings and then we would go down Via Veneto, full of large, rich American cars, towards the Tritone Fountain. From there, after reconnoitring the neighbouring streets and perhaps even making a detour by San Bernardo and the gardens near the station, we would walk along the tunnel, which at that time of night is empty—nothing but gleaming white tiles—and along Via Nazionale until we reached Piazza Venezia. At this point there was an alternative: either we went to Piazza Argentina, down to the river and across to Trastevere, or we walked home by the Corso, the Galleria, Piazza del Popolo, Via Flaminia and the Ponte Milvio. Miles and miles, you may say; but we never noticed it. On our way we would meet old acquaintances or make new ones. We went into all-night bars, and I would give Clementina a cup of coffee or a drink or she would give me one. In these bars there were all kinds of people: minor performers from variety shows or curtain-raisers, women of the streets with their clients, plain-clothes policemen, cabmen and taxi-drivers, tipsy Americans who punch you on the nose for no reason and immediately afterwards offer you a drink, and even a negro or two, as black as your hat.

It was the end of September, with an unspeakable scirocco, hot and damp; and every twenty minutes the rain came down;

and Clementina and I were wandering round Rome with muddy, worn-out shoes; and as we had no umbrella, there were nights that we spent hopping from one shelter to another, from the projecting roof at a tram-stop to that of an hotel entrance, from a balcony to an open doorway. The air of Rome, in short, was the typical air of Rome—by which I mean that heavy, enervating air that gets on your nerves so that you never want to go to bed, and although you haven't the money to go into cafés and night-clubs and the streets are almost deserted, you wander endlessly and never feel tired. Clementina and I, of course, loved one another; or rather, I loved Clementina and considered her more or less as my fiancée. In fact, I introduced her to my friends like this: "Now, mind what I'm saying, this is my fiancée"; and she would respond, with a smile which I did not understand: "If he says so, no doubt it's true."

One night later on I understood that smile, all in a flash. We had met, as usual, at the entrance to the Borghese Gardens. It was drizzling, and as we walked towards the Viale del Muro Torto Clementina said that she felt strange that evening. "How d'you mean, strange?" I asked. "Strange—don't you know what strange means?" "Well, if you feel strange, what can I do about it?" "You never understand anything: it's your fault that I feel strange." "But why?" "Don't go on introducing me as your fiancée; and let me tell you once and for all: I'm fed up with you." I felt my heart sink, but I controlled myself and asked: "Why are you fed up with me?" "What d'you do in life?" she said; "will you kindly tell me what you do? You get shabbier every day. I'm almost ashamed of going about with you. I should like to know what you do?" I told her: I sold cigarettes on the black market; in any case she knew this perfectly well, and very often she had put the packets into her bosom, as I hadn't enough pockets to hide them. "That isn't a proper job," she said. "Now look at Rosario; he goes round the restaurants playing the guitar; that's a real job." And so, in the rain which was coming aown in torrents, we started a quarrel which lasted all the way along the Muro Torto. However, when we reached the Piazzale Flaminio she calmed down at last and said: "Well, we won't say any more about it. . . . Give me some coffee and a couple of cakes instead: I'm so hungry I can hardly stand." As luck would have it, I had no money that evening, because I had not been well for a couple of days and had been out of touch with the agent. I told her this, and added: "This evening you must pay; I'll give it you back to-morrow." I realized at once that this answer had put her in a bad humour again. "Oh, all right," she said, but in a voice that foreboded no good.

We went into a bar which was all brilliant with neon lights: I at once went over to a mirror to examine myself, and saw that my face looked thoroughly ugly. But, as I looked, I saw also another thing: Rosario, his guitar under his arm, paying at the desk for our drinks, mine included, and at the same time laughing and joking with Clementina. I reflected that they must have made an appointment; and, already feeling jealous, I went over to them. Rosario pretended not to see me, so I said: "Hey, don't you recognize your friends nowadays?" "What's the matter?" he replied; "haven't I even gone so far as to pay for your coffee?" Clementina started laughing, so did the barman, and I was confused. This was how we drank our cups of coffee: I sat alone, to one side, and Clementina and Rosario two yards away, very close to each other, almost embracing. Clementina also ate a couple of cakes, smearing cream all over her face. Then we went out along Via Flaminia.

As soon as we were outside, I said: "Clementina, say good-night to Rosario and let's go. . . . We've a long way to walk before we get home." But she replied: "Serafino, I've already told you I feel strange this evening. . . . You go home; I'll go for a little walk with Rosario. We'll see each other to-morrow." Anyone else, in my place, might possibly have submitted, even though unwillingly, and gone away without making a fuss. But it was two o'clock in the morning, and I was by now full of the nervous irritation that attacks me in the small hours; I was frightened at the idea of going home alone. And so, with a certain show of bluster, I said: "Come along; you can see Rosario some other night." "Hey," she said, "leave me alone; don't pull my arm." At this point Rosario intervened. I must point out that he, although he has very broad shoulders, is small, below the normal height; but I, alas, am smaller than he is, and, in the matter of shoulders, mine are pitifully narrow. "Well, are you going away?" he said. "Go away yourself, you bloody nuisance," said I. "Clementina's coming with me," he said; "what are you waiting for?" "D'you think you frighten me?" I asked. And then—would you believe it?—without a word he raised his hand and gave me two hard slaps in the face, one on each cheek—just like that, in cold blood. Then he said: "Now go away, will you?" And, without taking any further notice of me, he took Clementina by the arm and went off towards the Corso.

Thus began the most unpleasant night of my life. I had started crying, partly from the violence of the blows I had received: and still crying, I followed Rosario and Clementina, who were about fifty paces ahead of me. They were laughing and joking, and I, through my tears, kept repeating: "You bloody swine, you bloody swine"; but I hadn't the courage to catch up with them because I was afraid he might hit me again. On the other hand, I hadn't the courage to leave them: in the first place I felt myself bound to Clementina as though by an invisible cord; and besides, there was always the fact that I was frightened of being left alone, of going home alone. So I followed them at a distance, sobbing. Rosario turned round, from time to time, and shouted at me: "What d'you want? I don't know you. Who are you? Why don't you go away?" Clementina rubbed herself up against Rosario and laughed.

We walked on, on along the Corso; they went into at least three bars and in a leisurely way consumed coffee and drinks and cakes: they were doing it on purpose. I myself, meanwhile, being without money and therefore unable to buy anything, remained outside, waiting for them to come out again, and all the time I was crying and a sort of wetness was coming out of my nose. Then they would come out and I hadn't the courage to confront them and so I waited until they were some way off and then started following them again at a distance. In this way we went all along the Corso as far as the Largo Goldoni, and then down Via Tomacelli and then over the bridge and along Via Vittoria Colonna. However, when we reached the gardens in Piazza Cavour they were swallowed up under the trees and I could no longer see them, though I continued, blindly, to follow them.

All of a sudden I ran right into Rosario, who had stopped in a determined fashion. "Will you kindly tell me what you want?" he asked. I replied: "Clementina is my fiancée . . . she's got to come with me." "Who says so?" "*I* say so." Clementina, who was standing quite close, in the darkness, called out in a nasty sort of way: "Give him a good clout, that'll get rid of him; come on, Rosario." Cruel words, which stabbed me to the heart; and the clout followed swiftly after them. I was on the point of hitting Rosario in the chest, but he was too quick for me; he tripped me up so that I fell on the ground, on the wet gravel. I heard Clementina laughing as they ran off among the trees. When I got up again, there was nobody there.

What a night! Sobbing more violently than ever, I really did go away this time, in the direction of the Ponte Margherita. I was in floods of tears, and I could not say why; in those tears there was a bit of everything—the nights without any money; the days spent in Via del Gambero whispering: "American" to passers-by; the camp bed in the room at Grottarossa; my stinking sweater; my soaking shoes; Clementina who no longer loved me; Rosario who had hit me. Above all I felt lonely; and when I thought of all I had been through up till then and of what I was going through now, I had a feeling of deep bitterness and a great longing to give vent to it by talking to someone, even a stranger. In Piazza della Libertà a person with glasses and a brief-case under his arm passed close beside me, and I, instinctively, took hold of him by the arm and said: "Please. . . ." He stopped abruptly, giving me a disagreeable look, and with an effort I went on: "Life is like a staircase, with some people going down and some going up . . . but I'm always going down." Then he said: "Yes, I know. What we need in this world is patience"; and without more ado he fumbled in his pocket, brought out a hundred-lire note, pushed it into my hand and walked away.

You see? A hundred lire. Obviously I had the face of a beggar, and I was no longer surprised, now, that Clementina should have felt strange that night. I started sobbing again, saying to myself: "A hundred lire . . . and nobody who wants to listen to me, nobody who loves me." At that moment I was crossing Via Principessa Clotilde, a street full of advertisement hoardings through which no one ever passes; goodness knows why they stick up posters there. And then, as I saw a row of these posters, all just the same, advertising some kind of soap, with a huge picture of a film actress saying she washed her face with this soap every day, I had a sudden impulse to write. There was a big blank space round the actress's head, so I took a stump of pencil out of my pocket and to begin with, inspired by hatred towards women who now seemed to me to be all of them like Clementina, I gave the actress a pair of moustaches and a goatee beard in the Victor Emanuel style. Then, still sobbing, I wrote in the blank space: "You ugly, vile slut, to betray me with a crook like Rosario. Very well, when the Russians come, we'll see about it." I wrote some more abuse of Clementina on two other posters; on a fourth I wrote: "Rosario, scum of Rome, dirty swindler"; and gradually, as I was writing, I realized I had stopped sobbing, and little by little I felt better, more and more relieved. I understood now why so many people write books: they relieve themselves in the best way they can. At the far end of Via Principessa Clotilde there was still one poster left: I gave the actress a moustache again and then turned back towards the Piazzale Flaminio, feeing as light as air and almost completely comforted.

SLAVE-DRIVER

ANYONE who thinks, at a bad moment in his life, that he could go down into the street and start holding out his hand, just as he is, would be making a mistake. You can't become a beggar in a day, nor in a year; the begging profession does not quickly disclose its secrets, but demands patience, intuition and imagination. Take me, for example: I am fifty and I have been begging for at least twenty years, but it's only during the last ten years or so that I've really understood the job. At first I used to go about without a beard; to understand that I ought to let my beard grow, because a beard is a rough sort of thing and a beggar has got to look rough with a view to arousing pity—to understand all this, how long did I take? I should say at least two years. Then let us come to the question of clothes: anyone might think that all a beggar has to do is to wear a suit with a few darns and grease-stains and patches; but how many people manage to discover, as I discovered after giving much thought to the matter, that wearing a heavy suit in summer and a light one in winter goes straight to the heart of the passer-by, who himself wears heavy clothes in winter and light ones in summer, and thus the difference between him and me produces remorse, and remorse produces alms? In summer, therefore, I wear clothes as thick as a mattress and, in winter, a suit as thin as gauze, and in the latter, into the bargain, I make an L-shaped tear in the trousers so that a little flap of the material waves in the cold wind and the skin of my leg can be seen.

Now let us consider the question of ailments. The ailments of beggars may, or may not, exist in reality, but in all cases they must be seen. Internal ailments—of the digestion, the lungs, the intestines—these are no use. They must be visible ailments that leap to the eye—obvious infirmities, deformities, disablements. And so I clamp my leg into a couple of wooden splints and then wrap it up and on top of the wrapping I put a bandage, and I keep my foot in a bedroom slipper. With a leg like this, and two sticks with rubber tips, a beggar has no need to proclaim his ailments; even a blind man could see them. No need to mention facial expression. How many expressions I tried before I found the right one! After trying and trying again, I decided in the end to copy the expression of a kneeling Saint Joseph in an altar picture in a Trastevere church: eyes raised to heaven, an air of entreaty, of hopefulness, of demureness. The painter who painted that picture knew what he was doing; even in a special field like ours, art, as we all know, is always the thing that can say the last word. You will be thinking that, by now, I was perfect. But no; it seemed to me that there was still something lacking. I fancied that, in order to complete my personality as an elderly, ailing, good-hearted beggar, I needed a child to accompany me. But alas, the best is the enemy of the good. I ought to have been content with what I had already accomplished; I tried to do too much and was punished for it.

In Via Panico, between Lungotevere Tor di Nona and Piazza Chiesanuova, where I had my garret, there were plenty of children; and of parents who would have been ready to allow one of their children to go with me, no doubt there were some. But I did not need to look far. A slovenly, cross little woman, ugly and deformed, by name Aurelia, who went to work early in the morning as a daily office-cleaner, had drawn attention to herself by the strange manner in which she treated her only daughter Clementina, a child of five. At one moment she would embrace her violently, covering her with kisses, smothering her with caresses, running off, all hot and bothered, to buy her a cake, or a doll, or a new dress; and then again she would have shameful scenes with her, shouting and tearing her hair, telling her that she was the curse of her life, that she refused to drudge for her any longer, and saying other things of the kind such as ought not to be said to children. Luckily Clementina showed that she was more sensible than her mother: placid, with a round, red, solid face and small, sleepy-looking eyes, she was strong and healthy, and she accepted kisses and screams with the same indifference, munching an apple or playing with her doll. She was, in fact, just the kind of child I needed, quiet, peaceable, with no bees in her bonnet and no nerves. One day when, as usual, her mother was shouting that she refused to sweat for her any longer, I went into their little flat, just below my own garret, and made a point-blank proposal: three hundred lire a day plus her food. I should never have done this: Aurelia poured out her anger upon me, shouting all kinds of insults at me, among others that I was a slave-driver. But next morning, by a miracle, they knocked at my door; when I opened it, there was Aurelia leading Clementina by the hand.

So I started going round with Clementina. We would go to the great flight of steps in Piazza di Spagna, where I would sit down with my back against a wall, my bandaged leg stretched out in front of me and beside it my hat for receiving alms; and there I would remain, eyes raised to heaven, hand held out, muttering the usual rigmarole. As for Clementina, most of the time I held her on my lap, her head supported on my arm and her legs lying over my knees, as though she had gone to sleep or fainted. She was an intelligent little girl, and she would flop back into my arms in a languid sort of way, playing the part of a starveling to perfection. In reality she was languishing from boredom, poor Clementina, compelled as she was for hours on end to look like a fading flower; but the passers-by mistook this boredom for weakness and did not notice that this dejected-looking creature had cheeks like red apples, bursting with health. When I grew weary of holding her in my arms—for she was as heavy as if she had been made of lead—I told her to go and play on her own, close by; and in complete silence she would start playing with her doll, only a step away from me. Finally, I would sometimes make her hold out her hand, or actually catch hold of the trousers of a passer-by who was already showing pity for us. A child's hand pulling at one's trousers, and a child's face looking up imploringly, can accomplish miracles. Clementina did all these things with precision and with her customary massive indifference. So much so, that sometimes I wondered: "She's small, it's true, but she's intelligent too. I should like to know what goes on in her head." However we got on well together; and I, who usually do not like children because they are mischievous and often follow me and make fun of me as I go through the streets, had grown as fond of Clementina, it might be said, as if she had been a daughter.

It was Aurelia, on the other hand, who would not leave me in peace; the mother was as restless as the daughter was quiet. My one consolation, after a day spent in begging, is wine. Back in Via Panico, as night was falling, I had a habit of retiring, tired and with aching bones, into a little wine-shop where they have a speciality of Cesanese wine, and there, all alone, all on my own, drinking a litre or two. But from the very day when I started going round with Clementina, even these two hours of peace and intimacy were poisoned. That harpy of a woman, knowing this habit of mine, would come plunging into the wine-shop almost before I had had time to wet my lips in my first glass, would sit down at my table without my inviting her, oblige me to offer her a drink, gulp down half a litre in a mad hurry and then, already tipsy, start railing at me. Quietly at first; but then, if I made the slightest protest, she would raise her voice and make all kinds of rude remarks; and meanwhile the other customers would be enjoying the scene and would even go so far as to provoke her by saying: "Aurelia, don't you realize he's living on your daughter's earnings? Come on, tell him he's a ponce." You can imagine that Aurelia had little need of such encouragement. She would shake her finger under my nose and shout: "Slave-driver! Three hundred lire for my daughter and thousands for you! And you drink the whole lot here, in this wine-shop. And then, into the bargain, you have the face to come and tell me you're fond of Clementina. Yes, you're fond of her in the same way that a greengrocer's fond of the donkey that pulls his cart. You're shameless, you're insolent, you're a ponce and a slave-driver. But I'll take her away from you, darling Clementina who's worth her weight in gold, I'll take her away from you and report you."

I tried to soothe her, even offering her more to drink, but she would not calm down, and in the end, to the amusement of all the customers, she seized hold of the child and dragged her away, shouting at me that I would never see her again. But this was merely the effect of the wine. Next morning she appeared punctually, all humble and repentant, begging me to take Clementina back. And so on, over and over again. I felt I could not go on like this; but, as I have already said, I had grown fond of Clementina, who was so quiet, so lovable, so different from her mother; and besides, Clementina now formed part of my personality as a beggar, and to get rid of her would have been rather like getting rid of the bandages in which my leg was wrapped: I should no longer be myself. So I put off the decision from one day to another, in the hope, always, that Aurelia would show a little understanding and calm down.

One evening, after I had been begging for ten hours on end, I went with Clementina to a quiet place to count up, as usual, the day's takings. The quiet place was one of the flights of steps which lead down to the river from the Lungotevere Tor di Nona.

Well then, I put Clementina to sit, with her doll, on one of the upper steps, and placed myself on a step lower down and turned out my pockets. They were full of small change, and as I took out the money I arranged it on the step, making a little pile of five-lire notes, one of ten-lire notes, and one of fifty-lire notes. I put aside, in two separate piles, the five- and ten-lire coins. I also found, that evening, two hundred-lire notes and one of five hundred: the latter had been given me by a youth in order to make an impression on his girl friend, who had stopped and exclaimed: "Ugo, do look what a darling little girl!" While I was counting out this money with my attention so deeply absorbed that I did not even hear the noise of the Roman traffic all round me, a voice, all of a sudden, made me jump. "A good day, eh?"

Instinctively I placed my hand over the money, as though to protect it. It was a voice I knew, it was the voice of Aurelia who was, in fact, hanging over the parapet, her hands stretched out threateningly towards me. Angrily I answered: "What d'you want? What's the matter? I was just coming to you, to bring back Clementina."

She shook her fists over my head: "Slave-driver, slave-driver. . . . Three hundred lire for my daughter and thousands for you! Slave-driver!"

Hurriedly I picked up the money, all higgledy-piggledy, and stuffed it into my pockets. Then, as best I could—for I was impeded by my leg and my two sticks—I seized Clementina by the hand, climbed the steps to the Lungotevere and confronted the old hag. "Here you are," I said, "take your daughter and take the day's money and take these two hundred lire extra, as a parting present. It's all finished. Don't let me see you again. I don't know you. Go away and God help you if you cross my path again."

I intended to escape to my own home, in Via Panico; but she, enraged, perhaps, at seeing me so determined, started following close on my heels, holding Clementina by the hand. She was like one possessed of a devil; she kept shouting at the top of her voice: "You ought to give all that money to me, every bit of it, you ponce, you thief, you swindler;" and I, like a mouse pursued by a cat, was trying to escape, hobbling along with my two sticks and my bandaged leg beside the parapet above the Tiber. We went about fifty yards in this way, with her screaming and me trying to run away; and meanwhile a regular little crowd had collected behind her and was following her; and I realized that this little crowd was angry with me because I was ugly and dirty and a man, whereas she was a poor woman leading a child by the hand. Suddenly, in desperation, I stopped and said: "I'll give you anything you like, but now leave me in peace", but this made things worse because she saw her advantage and began screaming again that I was living on the child's earnings and was a fraud and a slave-driver. Finally, as we reached the Ponte Sant'Angelo, she seized hold of me by my overcoat, and then, losing my temper, I turned round and dealt her a blow with one of my sticks, across the shins.

What happened afterwards I do not intend to describe in detail; anybody can guess. An elderly, severe, military-looking gentleman made his way through the crowd and said: "I know this man: he's a fraudulent beggar and a vagrant." Aurelia, in the meantime, was making a scene like a real madwoman, biting her hands and trying to hurl herself upon me; and Clementina, held by some good woman who had taken her up in her arms, watched her mother with her accustomed placidity. And then, needless to say, the three-cornered hats of the *carabinieri* appeared on the scene. We all went off to the police-station—I myself, Aurelia, Clementina, the military-looking gentleman, the *carabinieri*, the crowd. But they released Aurelia at once. I, on the other hand, was put into the cells: for begging, and being drunk and disorderly. Some days later they made me take the bandages off my leg, gave me a travel order and packed me off to my native village of Zagarolo.

Well, well, life is like a seesaw, all ups and downs; and the higher you go up, the lower you come down. After building up for myself, day by day, a personality as a beggar in Rome, here am I now reduced to holding out my hand at Zagarolo. And so many people who, in Rome, would have given me alms on account of my bogus leg, my rags, and poor little bored-to-death Clementina, here at Zagarolo, where I am really hungry, deny me even a crust of bread. Nevertheless I don't despair; the seesaw will go up again and I shall go back to Rome.